—— ★ ——

IT WAS A SMALL SHEET, TORN FROM A NOTEPAD

"This was found in an inside pocket on the body," McCoo said.

I pulled it toward me. Half of the paper inside was soaked with blood, but the black pencil notation was still readable. It said: "RLP Marsala n. attrib."

McCoo said, "Okay. Wanta explain this?"

"I can't."

"What's RLP?"

"I haven't the foggiest idea."

"You deciphered the calendar entries."

"Well, I can't decipher this! 'N. attrib' must mean 'not for attribution.' RLP is probably somebody's initials. But if I don't know the name, I can't guess it from the initials, damn it!"

"You sure you don't know those initials?"

"Hey! What do you think I am? I'm not trying to sabotage you, and I'm not trying to solve the case myself and spring the solution on you! I've never heard of RLP, whatever he, she, or it is! What's the matter with you anyway?"

—— ★ ——

"D'Amato's descriptions of state lottery problems and procedures are factual and fascinating, and her characters . . . are lively and believable. Odds are most readers will enjoy *Hard Luck*; it's definitely a winning number."

—*Booklist*

Hard Luck

Barbara D'Amato

W✪RLDWIDE

TORONTO • NEW YORK • LONDON
AMSTERDAM • PARIS • SYDNEY • HAMBURG
STOCKHOLM • ATHENS • TOKYO • MILAN
MADRID • WARSAW • BUDAPEST • AUCKLAND

For Joan Turchik, who loves mysteries, and to the memory of Paul Turchik, who loved Joan

My thanks to two anonymous members of Gamblers Anonymous who took the time to talk with me and share their knowledge and experiences

HARD LUCK

A Worldwide Mystery/July 1993

This edition is reprinted by arrangement with Charles Scribner's Sons, an imprint of Macmillan Publishing Company.

ISBN 0-373-26124-1

Printed in U.S.A.

ONE

ANYBODY WHO WANTS to teach survival skills for the modern age can start with how to find a parking place in the Loop. All of downtown Chicago, for that matter.

I had one hand under my mother's elbow. It was two blocks farther to the Rehab Institute, where they were going to check on how well she was doing with her new bionic knee. My car was in a garage half a block behind us. When we got done I would pay the garage approximately what I had paid for my used sofa to ransom back the car.

"Mom, the appointment's for ten-thirty."

It was ten-thirty now.

"I know, dear," she said.

"Didn't they tell you not to wear those high heels?"

"Catherine, I can't go into the Loop in *bedroom slippers*."

I started to say there were other choices of shoes in the world, but it was an argument we had had before and it availed me nothing to try.

She hobbled slightly faster. I would have been more sympathetic, but she had walked pretty smoothly this morning as she left the beauty parlor—until she saw me out in front waiting for her. Having her hair done is another thing my mother considers a necessity before going to the Loop, even if she has to get a seven A.M. appointment.

"Now, listen, Mom. I'll be leaving you at Rehab for an hour or so."

"But you said you'd stay—"

"No, I said I'd be there to take you home. I have an interview with a man in this building here at eleven." I pointed at City Hall, which we were just passing. It was a preten-

tious pile of the Monument school of architecture. At eleven
floors it was not as tall as most of the newer surrounding
buildings, but cubic foot per cubic foot it surely must out-
weigh them all, unless you count the hot air inside. It occupied an entire city block between LaSalle on the west,
Clark on the east, Washington on the south, and Randolph
on the north. Whole mountains of gray granite had died so
that City Hall could live. The gray was the color of cooked
calf's liver. Totally useless Corinthian columns, as big
around as Cadillacs, began at the third-floor level. They
didn't support anything, roof or balcony, they just rose,
shouldering their way up five floors and terminating in bul-
bous granite acanthus leaves. Mom craned her neck to look
up at the structure.

"I shouldn't be here more than an hour," I said, "and it
always takes you at least two."

"Well. You'll come *right* back?"

"Of course. We'll go to lunch."

"Birthday lunch, dear. Don't forget."

My mother is always sure that, if she's left alone in the
Loop, she will get lost or be mugged or run down by a taxi.

The streets were moderately crowded. In another hour
they'd be jammed. A bus farted its way past. Up ahead, a
policeman whistled angrily at a Toyota and a Caddy who
were having trouble deciding who got to turn first.

We passed one of the revolving doors to City Hall, and I
glanced in, wondering whether some of the people I'd met
who were involved in the lottery conference might be
standing around waiting for news cameras to turn up. I
heard a whistling sound, but with the cop whistling and all
the other noises it didn't register. Suddenly there was a moist
thwack!, like bread dough thrown against a wall.

Then dry hissing gasps and screaming. My mother's nails
sank into my forearm.

On the sidewalk four or five feet in front of my mother,
lying on its back, its head toward her and feet pointed away,
was a body in a gray glen plaid suit, skull split up across the

top and over the forehead, brain matter spewed out in a viscous fan.

The falling body had barely missed a young child, a girl maybe three or four years old, walking just ahead of us with her father. The falling man's leg must have struck an elderly woman, who stood cringing and stupefied, holding her arm as if it might be broken. My mother's mouth was a big stretched O, and a high keening sound was coming out. She didn't even have to take a breath. Everybody around was screaming, and people who had not been quite as close were rushing up behind us, gabbling questions.

But me, I was looking at the man's face. It seemed I didn't have an appointment at eleven o'clock after all.

TWO

THAT WAS Tuesday morning, the fifteenth of October. I had met Jack Sligh, the victim, Monday for the first time.

Hal Briskman at *Chicago Today* phoned at the crack of dawn on Monday and asked me to come into his office. When I got there he suggested I do a story on the lottery. I had hesitated. Until he also suggested he would pay me in advance.

Well. Ever since I went freelance it's been hand to mouth. Not that I don't sell some nice pieces now and then, nice meaning well paid. But it's so irregular. Whereas things like rent and food are distressingly predictable.

"Everybody thinks the lottery is a fact of life," Briskman said. "Once you've got one, it's there forever."

I nodded. When I don't know anything about a topic, I nod a lot.

"But this proposal to start a Central States Lottery has blown it all wide open again. All the arguments about compulsive gamblers, and TV advertising where children can see it, and all that stuff."

"I thought this Central States Lottery idea didn't include Illinois."

"It didn't at first. The idea was for several of the states with smaller populations to get together and do a lottery so they could compete with Illinois. By themselves, they just can't mount as large a jackpot as we can. But then somebody got the idea it could be even bigger if they got Illinois in too. They're talking about a large, humongously, *obscenely* large jackpot."

"The bait you can't afford to refuse," I said.

"Exactly."

"Are the Illinois State Lottery people feeling left out? Got their nose out of joint?"

"That's for you to find out."

"Some of the churches up in arms?"

"That's for you to find out, too."

"Sure. I knew that."

"I was thinking a *big* piece. Tell 'em the odds of winning, all the different games, you know. Not a piece on the conference. The news people are doing that. A think piece on how lotteries really work."

"Big, huh? What are you paying?"

Well, he named a figure that was no jackpot. But it would keep body and soul together for several weeks. Plus, the story sounded interesting. I said sure.

Then Hal said, "You'll have to start today if you want to catch everybody."

"*What? Today?* I'm finishing another project."

"Can you put it aside?"

"Well—maybe not exactly—I suppose I can work on it at night. But why the rush?"

"The conference kicks off today. There'll be a lot of people you can catch easily if you start now."

"Oh?" Well, it was obvious there was something he wasn't telling me. I could have seen it by his face, even if I hadn't had years of experience with Hal. Except for some big breaking story, he always gives me plenty of notice. He realizes freelancers have businesses to run and have to organize things.

"All right, Hal. Who did you assign to this first?" I asked.

"Oh, well. What difference does it make?"

"Why did they drop out?"

"Cat, just do the project."

"Hey, no. You need me more than I need you on this one. Who'd you give it to first?"

He gave me a stonewall look for three seconds, saw it wouldn't work, and said, "Mike."

Mike, my significant other. Semi-significant other.
"*Mike?* Well, why isn't he doing it?"

"Oh, you know."

"He can't have! I saw him night before last. Saturday. He
can't *possibly* have gone off on a bender."

"Well, maybe he can't have, but that's what he did. I saw
him at Clancy's yesterday at lunch, and he wasn't eating, I
can tell you that. Except liquefied hops. And he doesn't
answer his phone, and he hasn't gone to the lottery contact
I set him up with yesterday afternoon, and we are basically
down to the wire here."

"Oh, shit!"

"I know."

All the usual stuff went through my mind. Was Mike lying in a gutter someplace freezing to death? It had never
gone quite that far, but you never know, either. Should I go
look? Look where? In his apartment? But if he's in his
apartment he's reasonably all right.

Hal said, "Cat, if you're gonna make Mike's nine-forty-
five appointment with Dorothy Furman, you'd better rev up
your motor."

"You left the appointment on her book, knowing Mike
couldn't keep it?"

"No, I called and changed it."

"Changed it to when?"

"Not when. Who. I told her that you'd be coming instead of Mike."

"Without asking me?"

"Well, *before* asking you, anyway."

"Someday, old sock, you're going to go too far."

"But you're going to do the article?"

"Yeah."

"So—since I'm right, I'm right. Mmmm?"

HAL IS A GOOD editor. He lets his freelancers, and his staff,
too, I think, take control of their stories themselves. There
are editors who would say, "Do the lottery. Start out with

five hundred words on two happy winners. Then give me two thousand words on the problems of the compulsive gamblers. Then seven hundred and fifty on where the money from the lottery goes, and close out with a quote from a politician.''

Hal would never do this. He'll help you. He'll give you contacts. But never push them on you. He probably only set up the appointment with Dorothy Furman himself because she no doubt was extremely busy this week with the conference. And of course *Chicago Today* had clout with her that neither Mike nor I as freelancers would have.

From here on in, after Dorothy, I could follow my own leads.

The best editors know that's the way to get a story that has life. They are aware neither they nor the writer knows what will be really interesting until the writer gets out into the field.

After all, that's one of the things freelancers are for: to bring in a story that's a little different from the staff story. Something that has its own slant, not the company form.

Of course, one of the other reasons to use freelancers is that they don't have to be paid regularly.

DOROTHY FURMAN'S OFFICE on the ninth floor of the City Hall building was not large, given the size of her job and the amount of paperwork it seemed to generate. There were flow charts all over the government-issue cream walls. Printout was stacked so high in front of her that after she shook my hand and we both sat down, she had to move the stacks in order to be able to see me.

She was a slender, dark-haired woman I would guess to be in her early forties. She had black-black eyes, the kind that used to be called shoe-button eyes, back in the days when shoes had buttons and people still knew what that meant. The manager is head honcho in the lottery. Dorothy Furman had held this position, lottery manager, for six years now, and from all accounts was efficiency in motion. She could hold it another twenty as far as my information went.

She was wearing a white silk shirt with a gold Chanel chain of heavy links around her neck. Navy blue Anne Klein skirt. This signaled businesslike and expensive at the same time. After a couple of seconds I realized what she reminded me of: women who run art galleries and want to sell you half of an elephant's skull with a silver turtle in it. (I'd done an article on the smaller art galleries in Chicago recently, and I do not exaggerate. The price on the skull et cetera, by the way, was breathtaking.) These women are usually possessed of flashing dark eyes, mondo energy, and are thin enough to be called slender while skirting the edge of skinny.

"I suppose Briskman's been triggered by this conference," she was saying.

"Hal? Triggered, yes. But this isn't a news story; he wants something in-depth."

"Sure. Otherwise he'd have sent a staffer."

So she was savvy as well as energetic and capable. This made me feel slightly itchy. I said, "Assume I don't know anything about the lottery."

As if I hadn't spoken, she said, "On the other hand, Briskman may want you to do a piece on 'How the Evil Lottery Turns Nice People into Gamblers.'"

This was going too far. I waited until she could tell I was being silent, then I said in an extremely quiet voice, "I don't write other people's opinions. Being freelance is no way to get rich. In fact, it's a way to get poor. But I paddle my own canoe."

"I see." She nodded, reading me. "All right. Where do you want to start?"

"The lottery in Illinois has been around—what? Fifteen years?"

"Seventeen."

"Right." I always carry a dozen or so pencils and at least six pens. I unholstered one of them now. "When I was a kid,

I didn't know anybody who gambled. You heard about numbers runners and gambling 'rings' being broken and all that. In movies the bad guys were usually gamblers, plus whatever other nasty things they did. I remember once my Uncle Andy and Aunt Louise decided to go to Las Vegas for a vacation and everybody in the family was saying to them, 'Are you going to *gamble*?' Uncle Andy said kind of sheepishly that, sure, you went to Las Vegas to gamble, but Aunt Louise really looked embarrassed. Like they were going to do something faintly dirty. You know how kids pick up on emotions. Anyhow, I must have missed something while I was in college, because it seems like the next thing I knew, there was a state lottery in Illinois. And Louise and half of my other relatives are buying tickets.''

"And you wonder how did something dirty get to be something clean."

She was sharp all right.

"Yes."

"It wasn't always that way. Dirty. It's what we were used to as kids, but that was just one phase in American history. In colonial America lotteries were commonplace. And accepted. In fact, they were used to finance public projects. Faneuil Hall was built by lottery money.''

"Faneuil Hall? The Cradle of Liberty?''

"Right. The first buildings at Harvard, Yale, and Princeton were built by lottery money, too. It was considered perfectly respectable.''

"What kind of lotteries? You mean people contributed money on a chance of winning—''

"You'd buy a ticket and the money went into a pool. Then there was a drawing for the winner. They paid out about eighty or eighty-five percent as prizes and the rest went into the building fund. One round usually wasn't enough. Often, they'd just keep holding lotteries over and over until finally they got the building built.''

"No kidding! It was easier to get people to buy lottery tickets than pay taxes, I guess.''

"Undoubtedly." She produced one of her dry smiles. "After the early 1800s lotteries started to be outlawed, state by state. The churches thought they were evil. By 1900 they were totally prohibited just about everywhere in the country. Gambling was more strictly prohibited than tobacco or alcohol in practically every state in the union."

"Up until?"

"About 1963. The closest semilegal thing during that time in most places was church bingo. The authorities quietly averted their eyes. As a matter of fact, church bingo was illegal in Illinois until 1972. Which didn't stop it, of course."

"But they didn't go around arresting people in church basements."

"No. And of course, once the state legalized it," she said dryly, "they could tax it."

"Mmmm. So you're saying that antigambling laws were sort of a blip in U.S. history and were unequally enforced anyhow."

"No, not for attribution I'm not. I'm not saying any such thing."

"My mistake. So how was the resistance to public gambling ever overcome?"

"It started out in the East. Illinois wasn't the first state lottery, but it was one of the first."

"Which?"

"Which what?"

"Which was it?"

"It was the fourth. First New Hampshire in 1963, then New York in 1967, then New Jersey in '71 and Illinois in '74."

I was writing furiously. Hal surely does know his business. Dorothy Furman knew her lotteries.

"So by the time the idea came to Illinois," she said, "they could see it had been tried a couple of other relatively normal places and the world hadn't come to an end. At the time Illinois started to think seriously about it, there was a huge crisis in the Chicago transit system."

"Things never change."

"What? Oh, no, I suppose they don't. Anyhow, the proposal was linked to raising emergency funding for the collapsing transit system. Dan Walker was governor then, and he supported it, and Mayor Daley—Daley the First—supported it. The legislature in Springfield passed it in December of 1973 and the first tickets were sold in July of 1974."

"And you never looked back."

"Well, no. Unfortunately, it didn't exactly work that way. The first lotteries weren't instantly successful. Here or in any other state. The public was skeptical and the sales weren't spectacular. It took a while."

"What made it grow, then? Familiarity?"

"No. Changing the game structure. Inventing new games. Marketing."

"I'd like to know about that."

"I'm not the best person to talk to about marketing."

"Never mind, then. Who should I see about it?"

"You could try the people at Marks and Sales. That's the company that actually designs our ads."

"What about this notion of throwing Illinois in with several other states and making up a humongous lottery?"

She gestured at the wall behind my head. I hadn't looked there when I walked in.

There was a poster, maybe three by five feet. It was a map of the United States, and in the center of the country were five concentric circles, alternating blue and red. A target. Letters across the top, angled to radiate out as if they were exploding, said CENTRAL STATES LOTTERY.

I said, "So you're going ahead with it?"

"No. It's not settled. The whole point of this conference this week is to explore the idea. See, of all the central states, Illinois needs this the least. We're doing just fine as we are. We're big enough to generate big jackpots, so we don't really need to combine with somebody else."

"Why would anybody?"

"Combine? Well, bigger really is better in lotteries. Up to a point, at least, and nobody is sure where that point is. Missouri started its lottery in 1985, and it didn't do well at all, mainly because the Illinois lottery had bigger prizes. Missouri players would drive to Illinois and buy tickets. Still do, for that matter, especially when there've been a couple of rollovers. Some entrepreneurs drove to Illinois and bought *lots* of tickets and took them back to Missouri and sold them. The same thing happened in the Northeast. The New York State Lottery was so big it overwhelmed the nearby states, so Maine, New Hampshire, and Vermont formed the Tri-State Lottery, and after that they competed pretty well. There's another multistate lottery that includes the District of Columbia and neighbor states, called LottoAmerica. In fact, there are national companies that buy lottery tickets from all across the country and resell to subscribers through an 800 number. They had a real run when the California lottery had several rollovers and went so high. The biggies still do the best."

"If we're big and don't need it, why are we hosting this conference?"

"We may need it. If they do it without us, they might overwhelm *us*, depending on how many states they bring in. Plus, there are some economies of scale in bigger lotteries. The bigger the advertising area, for instance, the less the advertising cost per household. Plus, you would only need one computer system. And so on."

"One administration?" I thought if they combined with other states, some employees would certainly be fired.

She knew what I was asking. "We're not going to cut longtime employees, no matter what. Anyway, the goal is to attract some states that don't already have lotteries. So we'd keep approximately the same size staff and do more with it."

"Economies of scale that way, too?"

"Absolutely."

"So you're in favor of the Central States Lottery?"

"I make no political statements whatsoever."

"Well, tell me this, then. Which states don't have lotteries yet? The ones you're trying to woo."

"I'm not trying to *woo*—" she didn't like the word— "anybody. I'm not political. I'm an administrator. The decision is up to the legislature."

"Put it this way, then. Which states don't have lotteries that might be possible joiners?"

"The states that are somewhat central that don't have lotteries yet are Nebraska, Oklahoma, Tennessee, North Dakota, Wyoming, Utah, and Arkansas." She reeled these off without any reference to notes.

"The other central states have them?"

"Right. Michigan, Ohio, Iowa, Indiana, Minnesota, South Dakota, Kansas, Missouri, Kentucky—it depends on how far away you want to go. After a certain distance they're not central states anymore, of course."

"All those states have lotteries?"

"And plenty of others outside the central area. Most of the population of the United States lives in lottery-legal states now."

"How are you going to sell the others on lotteries if they haven't done it by now?"

"I'm not going to sell—" She tilted her head and started over. "If they have a lottery, they get money. Five percent of the entire revenue of the state of Illinois is lottery profits. More than taxes on alcohol and tobacco combined. Plus it helps a great many local retailers. The typical retailer here in Illinois makes over fifteen thousand dollars a year on his lottery sales."

"Why don't all the states jump at it, then?"

"Some of the churches don't like it. The Catholic Church has had bingo just about forever and Catholics by and large don't object to the lottery. But the Baptists don't like it. Most fundamentalist churches don't. So states with a lot of fundamentalists have a lot of grass-roots opposition. The Latter-day Saints don't approve of gambling, and so I think there's just about no chance that Utah will join in any lottery, regardless of the financial advantages.''

"Well, they've got snow, anyway."

"What?"

"Skiing. Never mind. Moving right along—from the player's point of view for a minute here, what percent of that is paid out in prizes?"

"In Illinois? Fifty-one percent."

"Gee, players these days don't get as good a deal as the ones who built Faneuil Hall."

"It's a more complicated world," she said calmly.

Her Teflon exterior was beginning to get to me. Professional interviewees are the worst. They know how to pause before difficult questions and get their answers straight. Worse yet, they may have given the answer before. It'll be clear, but it'll have the life ironed out of it.

"You feel these churches may be too strict—"

"Choosing by lot goes way back in human history. It's mentioned in the Bible."

"And I imagine you could quote me chapter and verse," I said, fixing her with a frustrated eye.

"Yes. Proverbs 18:18, for example, or Numbers 26—" She paused, catching a glimpse of the wry look on my face. Suddenly she smiled, an ordinary, amused smile. "I guess I sound like a salesman," she said.

"It's your job."

"Yes and no." She started to laugh. "Hell, I'm sorry. I have to be in favor of the lottery. I have to build it up, for that matter. But this is still a very public kind of job. I shouldn't be proselytizing."

Suddenly she seemed much more likable. I could imagine some of her problems. Suppose she goes to her child's grammar school picnic and somebody asks her what she does. She says she runs the lottery. The other person looks at her like she's a riverboat gambler and asks her if she really ought to be doing that kind of thing.

CENTRAL STATES LOTTERY WEEK SCHEDULE

NOTE: Your banquet ticket is included in your registration fee. Please check to be sure the ticket is enclosed in your conference packet. The other evening events are optional. Reservations for them *must* be made at least 24 hours in advance, as seating is limited. Cash or check must accompany the reservation. To make a reservation see Cheryl Weeks in the Lottery hall. All seminars and panel discussions will take place in meeting rooms at the Hotel Stratford. Room assignments will be posted daily in the Stratford lobby.

	10:00 A.M.	11:00 A.M.	LUNCHEON	2:00 P.M.	4:00 P.M.	EVENING
MON			Kickoff lunch	The Central States Proposal		Cocktails: The 95th (John Hancock Building)
TUE	Panel: Lotteries, pro and con (double session)				Satisfying special interest groups	Dinner in Greek Town
WED	Start-up costs	Running costs		How the lottery generates jobs	Typical expected state revenue	Theater: Second City (comedy)
THU	What to expect from the retailer				Treating the compulsive gambler	Free evening
FRI	Television advertising	Radio advertising			Point-of-purchase advertising	Cocktails (delegates only): City Hall, 6:00 P.M. Banquet: 8:00 P.M., Stratford

"Probably everybody you meet has an opinion about what you do. And whether you ought to be doing it."

"Oh, God. If you only knew! Tell you what," she said, loosening up. "You should get some contrary opinions. And you've certainly picked the right week for it. The five-day conference starts today. Some of the delegates are still arriving, but mostly they will have checked in by noon. There's a kickoff lunch."

"What hotel?"

"The Stratford. The meetings are either in the Boul' Mich Room there or here at City Hall. Here's a schedule."

She scrabbled two sheets out of a pile of papers under a pile of printout. One was a schedule of events for the week; the other was a list of the delegations present. I glanced at the schedule. It had all the characteristics of a government-sponsored junket week: enough panels and lectures to be real, but plenty of white spaces for sightseeing and plenty of social evenings.

"Try to find the Utah delegation," she said. "I think they're not here to learn why a lottery might be good but to dig up reasons why a lottery might be bad. They'll give you the other point of view."

"Any chance Illinois might decide the lottery it already has is bad?"

"No state has ever terminated its lottery. There's never even been a serious challenge. Ever. Anywhere."

THREE

THAT WAS WHEN I met Jack Sligh.

Dorothy Furman walked me to her door. I was thanking her as I opened it and stepped out into the corridor. Watching her, I didn't see Jack until I hit him with the door. It caught him solidly in the left shoulder.

"Oh, hell, I'm sorry."

"I'm not," he said with a courtly bow. I didn't know who he was at this point, but it was clear that he knew Dorothy. "Introduce us, Dorothy," he said, waving his eyebrows up and down like Groucho Marx.

Dorothy had a slight frown line between her own eyebrows. "Jack Sligh, Cat Marsala."

"Cat. Nice name."

Dorothy said, "Jack is my brother-in-law, Cat. Cat is a reporter." Her voice held an unmistakable tone of caution, but which of us was she cautioning? Was I supposed to read it that her brother-in-law liked women? Or was he supposed to be careful what he said because, being a reporter, I might quote him?

Jack took over. "Excellent! I love to talk to reporters. See you later, Dot."

Dorothy closed her door firmly.

"She hates to be called Dot." Jack chuckled. "Hates it. I called her Microdot once and she wouldn't speak to me for weeks. Let's go to my office. If you have just a second, though, I want to drop something off." He knocked on a door across the hall and maybe two doors down from Dorothy's. It was opened by a woman who looked a lot like Dorothy. When she saw us she said, "What do *you* want?"

For a second I thought she was speaking to me, but in fact she was talking to Jack.

"Just to have a little chat later," he said.

"I don't want to talk to you."

"I have a proposition to make."

"You have a proposition, you make it to my lawyer!" She slammed the door in his face.

He turned to me, smiling wryly. "She doesn't like me."

"No, sounds that way."

"My ex-wife, Doris. Soon to be ex-wife. It's a great life if you don't weaken." He turned a corner and came to another door. "Come on in. This is my executive suite." The "suite" was a single room, smaller than Dorothy's. There were fewer papers on the desk, but a lot more stuff stacked around the walls. There were pasteboard and foam-core sheets stacked vertically against the wall to our right. There were lottery posters on the wall flanking the door. Even some posters taped over other, earlier, lottery posters. There were boxes and gadgets against the third wall. In the fourth wall was a narrow window, with the desk sitting under it. The window was taller than it was wide, typical of those in older buildings. It was an ordinary sash type, with two moving sections. The lower one was pushed up an inch for air. The windowsill was about thirty inches from the floor, the same height as the desk surface. Outside the window I could see the thickness of the granite building stone. I noticed these details and probably would soon have forgotten them, except for what happened the next day.

While I looked around, Jack had been dragging over a chair for me, having freed it from a tangle of mailing tubes.

"Who do you write for?" he asked.

"I freelance."

"Oh. Is this a fishing expedition, then, or do you have an assignment?"

He was quite inquisitive for somebody who had invited me in, without my asking. "I'm doing an article for *Chicago Today*."

"On the conference?"

"No, on the lottery."

"The lottery in general? How it's run? How it's administered?"

"I haven't got my theme, yet. The assignment was general. But what I think right now is this—people play the lottery, but they don't know how it actually works. Nuts and bolts. How do the tickets arrive at the stores? Why some stores get to sell tickets and not others? Why certain types of games and not others?" This was enough about what I was doing. It's one thing to try to put an interviewee at ease by chatting about yourself. But the old saying was never more true than in reporting. You learn more by listening than by talking. Anyhow, Jack didn't need to be put at ease. He was thoroughly at ease already.

"You do something for the lottery?" I asked.

"Ha! Obviously my fame is pretty limited. I'm advertising director."

"You design the ads?"

"No, the ad agency designs the ads. I direct them. Different games need different ads. The games change as tastes change. Plus, people get bored. We rarely run any one ad more than a couple of months." He was scooting his chair, which was on casters, closer to mine.

"Television ads?"

"All media. The Illinois lottery ad budget runs about fifty to sixty percent television ads. Radio is fifteen percent. Print media about seven percent."

"Print isn't your best forum, then?"

"No." He smiled. "Not even print on billboards. Although we put maybe five percent of the budget into them."

"Sixty plus fifteen plus seven isn't a hundred percent."

"Quick lady. Ten percent of our budget, maybe more, goes into point-of-purchase advertising. We like to get the lottery display right near the cash register at the retail outlets. See"—he edged still closer—"it's often kind of an *impulse* buy." He put his hand on the arm of my chair.

"Impulses are a fine thing in their place," I said, leaning back. "I don't go in for them, myself."

"Mmm. Really?"

"I've heard you target your television ads on Thursday and Friday, to get people when they have money—payday."

"Not true."

"And the first Tuesday of the month, when the Social Security checks come out."

"Also not true. The statisticians have been all over that question. We peg our ads pretty evenly through the week. Except Sunday. Sunday is a bad day to advertise the lottery."

"Religious reasons?"

"Not necessarily. People just don't want to buy. Who knows why?" He was still leaning close.

I had taken out my notepad and was busily writing. Didn't faze him. He went on.

"Not that we don't try to attract players—"

"Players? Not bettors?"

He gave me a sharp glance but said, "Call them whatever. We do target marketing, not mass marketing. For instance, radio. You might as well forget about advertising on classical music stations. Country and western, Hispanic, and black stations, or easy listening. That's it."

"You target ethnic groups?"

"Well, in a way. We try to develop games everyone will like. Take instant winner games, now. They're most popular in lower-middle-income neighborhoods, especially with an older population, and especially Eastern Europeans."

"Hmm," I said, thinking of Aunt Louise.

"Numbers like Pick Four and so on—black neighborhoods and rental housing neighborhoods. Future drawing games, where you buy a ticket any day of the week but they don't draw winners until Friday night—that appeals to older people. Which is strange, isn't it? Wouldn't you think older people would want it right now? Hell, they might be dead by the weekend."

He leaned his elbow on the arm of my chair. I said, "Hey! I'm at work here."

"No problem." He didn't get any less cheerful. If anything, he became more relaxed. I'd seen this happen before. There are men who think they have to come on to you. Either they believe you'll be disappointed if they don't, or if they don't, they'll be disappointed in themselves. Then you turn them down and they're relieved.

"These ads—" I pointed to the walls. One poster showed coins raining down on a happy couple. They also were knee deep in the golden coins that had already fallen. The word BINGO! rose behind them like a glorious sunrise.

Another poster was a huge bank check. It was made out to "Your name!" and the amount was $20 million.

One was for a game no longer being offered as far as I knew, the Instant Money Game. The poster showed a fat blue genie popping out of a bottle, his hands filled with bouquets of dollar bills.

"These are pretty hard sell."

"Whattaya mean hard sell?"

"They imply that if you play you have a good chance of winning."

"No, no. They say if you play you have a *chance* of winning, and that's true."

"Well, there's nothing there that tells players what the real odds are."

"Darn right there's not."

"Shouldn't there be?"

"Why? Suppose it cut down on the enjoyment people get out of the game?"

"Well, shouldn't you tell people the drawbacks?"

"Look. The actual odds are printed on the backs of the tickets. But on the ads—no way! When Missouri started its lottery, the legislature put a restriction on the advertising. The ads were supposed to say they weren't intended 'to induce any person to participate in the lottery or purchase a lottery ticket.' Would you believe?''

"And?"

"And sales were crummy. Plus, it was stupid. You could even argue that it was hypocritical. Say I'm trying to sell Cadillacs and I stick a disclaimer in the ad that I don't actually want anybody to go out and *buy* a Cadillac. What in hell does that mean? What are ads *for*, except to induce you to buy? Missouri dropped the disclaimer pretty goddamn fast, by the way."

Hmmm. I pointed to the poster for the discontinued Instant Money Game. "How do you develop new games for the lottery? How do you know what will work?"

"You don't always know what'll work." He practically bounced in his chair with enthusiasm. "But you definitely have to keep changing them. People get bored. There are certain necessities every game has to have. Basics. We call it the four P's. Product. Place. Price. Promotion. Product: You have to have an interesting game. Place: It has to be easily available. Price: It has to be affordable. Promotion: You have to let people know about it."

"Sounds simple."

"Even obvious, huh? But when you get down to cases, it isn't. After the basics, you need variety. There's more than one kind of game. Some people like an instant winner game, like I mentioned. They usually want play value."

"Play value?"

"Play value is sense of participation on the part of the player. Simulated sense of participation. Picking your *own* lucky numbers is one way. Like we do in Grand Lotto. The instant games, like Quick Cash, don't have that. You get the ticket you get. So they need suspense. Like, you're scraping the opaque covering off the symbols on the card you just bought. There are nine covered symbols, three rows of three. You know that three matches of the same symbol in one row will win you big money."

I didn't, but I wasn't going to admit my ignorance. "And—?"

"We try to arrange it so a lot of people will get two matches in a row. We call them 'heartstoppers.'"

"I can see why."

"You have to keep changing the themes of the instant games. We're doing a football theme right now. But they'll be bored with it out there in playerland by middle of next month. Then we'll do basketball. It'll be the right time of year."

"So when you bring in a new game does everybody run and try it?"

"A lot of people try it, but oddly enough not to the detriment of existing games. As a matter of fact, every time we fly a new game, it seems to make all the existing games sell better."

"That doesn't make sense, does it?"

"Who knows? People are weird."

"That's a technical analysis for you."

"It's true, though. Like in Vegas, add more blackjack tables and more people play the slots, too. Now, with new games, when people are just learning it, we give out a lot of free tickets as prizes. It gets people used to it."

"I see. Get them hooked."

He looked at me, raised an eyebrow, and shrugged. "What's coming next in lottery games?" I asked.

"Take a look at this." He pointed at a gadget on the floor against the wall. It was about the size of R2D2. "This is a VLM, Video Lottery Machine. Also sometimes called the PALM, Player Activated Lottery Machine. It's basically an Instant Game machine, but with lights and sound."

I punched a button where he was pointing, one in a row of six buttons. A star came up, accompanied by bells and whistles. The machine asked me to punch another button. My choice. I did. Another star. Now we had bells and whistles and lights. It asked me to punch a third. I did. A lemon.

A declining whistle told me I had lost and a voice said, "Better luck next time. Would you care to play again?"

"Jeez!" I said. "How does this differ from a slot machine?"

"Not a hell of a lot. This little sucker is made by Bally. But it's an early model. We've got a potential here for pinball machine betting! On-line betting. Maybe Touch-tone phone betting from your home. Can you imagine—it's lottery night! The jackpot has rolled over three weeks in a row! A fifty-million-dollar jackpot out there waiting for somebody to win it! Everybody is watching the drawing on their television! At the last moment everybody and their uncle is phoning in bets on their Touch-tone phones. Phone lines will be tied up from here to Carbondale!"

"Yeah, it's—it's staggering."

"All that excitement! Wired right into your home!"

"Um—Mr. Sligh?"

"Call me Jack."

"Sure, Jack. How do you feel about the issue of making gamblers out of nongamblers?"

"Man oh man, I certainly try."

After Dorothy, Jack's frankness was refreshing, if a little bizarre. "But wasn't the excuse for the lottery—I mean the idea of a lottery in the first place—something like people would gamble anyway, unfortunately, so they might as well donate some money to the state while they do it?"

"Sure."

"I mean, it wasn't 'Let's go out and convert a lot more people to gambling.'"

"Hey. I'm in charge of advertising. Suppose you're the state. You appoint me ad exec. I take over and immediately the lottery revenues fall over thirty percent. Do you think I'm doing a good job?"

"Well, no."

"The *government* makes policy decisions. I'm hired to do something, I do it. Okay?"

"Yes, I have to admit it makes sense." I looked at my watch. There was some basic research I'd better do, before showing my ignorance to many more interviewees. Jack Sligh saw my glance.

"Let me buy you lunch?"

"Thanks, but I can't. I'm running flat out today. I just got this assignment, and I don't know yet how long it'll take me."

He walked me out into the hall and a little way along to a larger central area. It was filled with people coming and going and standing in clumps, talking. Delegates passed, wearing badges that identified them as from Kentucky, South Dakota, and Tennessee.

On the first floor, where the ceilings were high and arched, the architect of the building had used straight corridors running the full length of the place to bisect it, a full city block lengthwise and another crosswise. He'd apparently decided that up here a straight corridor would be too disheartening, stretching, as it would have, off into the distance to a vanishing point. However, what he came up with was possibly worse. For one thing, the building, and therefore this floor, was divided into two halves, city and county. On this floor, for instance, the county part was the Cook County Engineers and the city part was leased to the Illinois State Lottery. The elevators were in the middle, dividing the two. The architect had put space for a central pool for secretaries in the center of each half and run two snake-like corridors out of each central pool. This produced a confusing maze. The corridors were S-shaped, assuming the turns of the S to be right angles, and they fed into fire stairs at both ends. You could get lost up here.

There was no telling how many people worked on this floor, but just eyeballing, it had to be at least a hundred and fifty. I asked myself the prime philosophical question of all city dwellers: Where did they all park? Many of these poor souls had offices without windows, too, since about half faced interior parts of the building. Judging by a couple of open doors, these offices were brightly lighted—even harshly lighted—to make up for the lack of outdoor light. They were fed fresh air by an immense square snake of a* air system on the ceiling that loomed over everything, sen ing branches off to every room.

The effect was functional, not luxurious. There was car peting throughout the place, but it was industrial, low loop and easily cleaned. Without it, the noise would have mac work impossible. Footsteps and phones and printer soun⸱ s would have bounced off the walls and metal air ducts eve⸱ worse than they did now.

In the central pool for the Lottery wing, a large open are⸱ four secretaries' desks were butted together in two kissin pairs. Not that the secretaries could see each other over the computer monitors. There was a water cooler, a hot water dispenser for making instant coffee or tea, and a wall of metal shelves of the size needed for file boxes. One of the secretaries had tried to soften the effect. She had an African violet growing under a plant light on her desk and behind her loomed a large silk ficus tree, not real, but a very good try.

As we walked out, conference attendees and Lottery officials were milling through the whole area. Most of them wore stick-on delegate badges: HELLO! I'M ___ ___. There were a couple of print media reporters and a minicam from Channel 7. I saw at least two aldermen and a downstate politician. Dorothy Furman was there, talking to two men in three-piece suits who had to be from a large corporation or some large law firm. These were Hickey-Freeman custom three-piece suits that cost as much as a fairly decent used car.

"Are all these people Furmans?" I said to Jack, intending a joke.

"No. It just seems like it sometimes."

He wasn't laughing. Did he feel swamped by them? "How many of them are there?"

"In the Lottery? A couple more. Hector Junior is in charge of security. Dorothy's son, Fred Furman, is a stores inspector."

"Fred Furman? Wouldn't he have his father's last name?"

"You don't know Dorothy. She shucked the guy before the kid was born. Changed her name back. Fred was baptized Furman and Furman he will always be. I never met the guy because I came along later, but Doris says he was great looking and lazy as a rutabaga."

"Well—nice to hear that she knows what she wants."

"Not that Fred is any great shakes. Looks at a store or two, wanders off and plays poker or something with his buddies. But he'll never be fired. Not with his ma as the big boss."

Jack eyed me closely to see how I'd react. I shrugged. "Well, it's not unheard of—"

"Ah, the saint," said Jack.

I looked around. There was a thin, angular, tallish man behind me. His lips were pursed at the sight of Jack Sligh.

"I don't see anything on the schedule about set-asides for a fund."

"Not my department," Jack said.

"It's the responsibility of everybody who profits from the lottery."

"Look, tell it to the politicians."

"I'm telling you!"

Jack said to me, "This guy thinks we ought to take money out of the lottery to treat gamblers." He was laughing.

"Compulsive gamblers," the thin man said.

"These guys waste their money, then they want somebody to come in and call it a disease," Jack said. "Have their fun first and then have the rest of us cry over them."

"You're the one making the ads," the man said. "Seduce sick people into buying more tickets."

Jack's posture changed. He leaned slightly forward and went up on the balls of his feet.

"Shit. If they can't afford tickets, tell 'em not to buy any."

"You're destroying these people's lives!"

"Hey. Denny. You have a mental problem. Get help!"

With no warning, Denny punched Jack in the eye. Jack turned just a little to deflect the force of it. Then he slapped the man in the face with the palm of his right hand. As Denny straightened up, Jack cut the side of his left hand fast into the man's solar plexus. Gasping, Denny tried to hit Jack again, flailing with both arms, but Jack sidestepped, hardly even working at it, and slapped him again, this time on his ear.

It was no contest. Jack was fast, wiry, strong, and accurate. I grabbed at him to pull him off.

The room was so crowded that the people in back couldn't see what was happening, but the ones in front were already pulling at Denny. A gray-haired older gentleman helped me pull Jack away. Jack didn't resist. All he said was, "He hit me first."

The thin man was shouting curses.

Across Jack's shoulder I caught a glimpse of Dorothy Furman. She was standing directly in front of a minicam, held by one of the TV channel people. She was adroitly blocking the lens with her body.

The gray-haired man said to me, "Let go and I'll take him into the men's room. Wash the cut."

"What do you mean?"

"Let go of him."

Sure enough, I was still gripping Jack's arm. There was a small split over his eye and a little blood on his cheekbone. I released him to go with the older man, who looked exactly like a banker.

I studied Denny. He'd simmered down some, but was still sputtering, "I'll sue. He can't hit me like that!"

Two or three of the men standing around him said, "Hey, give it a rest."

"That's battery!" he said. "Assault and battery!"

One said, "You hit him first, guy."

There was a sleek, dark-haired man among those holding him. He reminded me strongly of somebody. He said, "Let it drop, Denny."

The thin man shook them all off, like a duck flapping water off its wings. "Well, he hasn't heard the end of this!" He stomped out, a path clearing ahead of him in the crowd.

I sidled over to Dorothy. "Jack's got talents I wasn't aware of," I said.

"You're not going to write about this?" She seemed seriously worried.

"Come on. It's not my kind of thing."

"Then what angle are you taking?"

"I think how the lottery actually works. But it hasn't jelled in my mind yet. A person could probably do one on the Furmans. 'The Lottery Family.'"

"Oh, God! Don't do that!"

"Just kidding." To change the subject, I said, "I didn't know Jack was trained as a fighter."

"Not trained. Hobby." She wasn't pleased with Jack, and I didn't blame her.

"You would have handled that man differently," I said.

"Certainly. I would have agreed with Denny, told him he had a valid point, told him it was a political question, and asked him to take it up with his state rep."

"Which wouldn't have satisfied him."

"No, of course not. But it wouldn't have started a fight, either."

Doris had not come out of her office to see the fight, although she wouldn't necessarily have noticed the noise. Her office, like almost all the offices, was down the corridor and around a corner, out of sight.

"I met your sister," I said to Dorothy.

"Oh?" Obviously she didn't intend to say anything more. But when I let the silence hang, she thought it was necessary to talk. People mostly do, I find. "Doris is having a difficult time right now."

"Separation from her husband? From Jack?"

"Yes."

"Who was that other man?" I asked, still thinking about the man who looked so familiar.

"Seymour Dennisovitch. He's always trouble. He's an ex-gambler. Reformed gambler. They're very intense—very polemical people."

"No, I wasn't being clear. Not the guy who started the fight. The man holding him. I thought I knew him from someplace."

"There were two or three—"

"Dark hair, slender?"

"Oh. That was Hector. My brother."

"Hector?"

"Hector Furman, Jr."

No wonder he looked familiar. He looked like a male version of Dorothy. "What does he do here?"

"Lottery security." She was still gazing around, trying to be sure that the television cameras weren't rolling. Can't say I blamed her. So often television went for personality conflicts when they could go for issues, and we'd had personality conflict galore for them today. I realized, looking at the lines of strain on her face, that Dorothy had a lot to deal with, and in a way a lot of bosses. Leaving aside the legislature and the governor and the state lottery manager, who all probably gave her orders, there was the whole body politic. Anybody and everybody could criticize her if they wanted to. They paid their taxes, didn't they?

"Well, I've got stuff to do," I said, "and I imagine you've got a meeting."

"This whole week is one long meeting," she said wearily. Then she perked up. "Speaking of your business, you ought to try to catch Dennisovitch. *He'll* certainly give you quotes!"

"You're right. Okay. I will. I'm going to talk to the Utah people when I can. The ones you recommended."

"Great!" She was back in her stride again. "See you later."

She marched away, which was okay with me, because I wanted to poke around just a little more.

Where had Jack gone?

I wanted to try to meet Hector Furman, Jr., while I was at it. Security problems with the lottery sounded like just what I needed. But I couldn't see him, either. Of course, with the crowd of people, it wasn't all that easy to tell who was nearby.

Then I saw Hector Junior just coming out of the north corridor. I hurried over and stood in front of him. "Cat Marsala," I said, holding out my hand. "I've been trying to find you."

He smiled. A public smile. You could photograph it if you were a cameraman, all those white teeth against the dark tan. People who deal with reporters a lot get an instinct. "Stopped in to see my sister," he said.

"Dorothy? She was just here—"

"Doris." Well, it made sense that he had gone to her. I bet he ran in to tell her what naughty Jack had done now. "Anyway, what can I do for you?"

"Can we set up an appointment? I'd like to know how lottery security works."

"Come to my office." We walked down the south corridor. He asked the usual questions as we went—who I worked for, who would publish what I wrote, and since I told him I was freelance, what I'd done before. He unlocked his door with a key, which surprised me.

"You keep it locked when you step out?"

"No. I've been on vacation." He grinned. "The Bahamas. Just walked in ten minutes ago. I've got to admit I hate to come back."

So that was why the tan. Sure enough, the office had a faintly stale feel. The desk was bare and a little dusty. He pulled out a drawer and found an appointment book. "You know this is a busy week."

"I'd like to do the interview as soon as possible."

"Well, maybe late afternoon tomorrow."

"At your convenience."

"Four? No, four-thirty would be better."

After I left, I got to thinking about Hector Furman, Jr. He was not as chatty as his sister. In fact, under the appropriate language, he was rather silent and ominous.

The other thing I wondered was why he felt it necessary to carry a gun.

That particular full cut in an expensive jacket on a man who wasn't trying to hide a potbelly, that particular bulge at the left upper waist was pretty obvious. Maybe I'd ask him about it tomorrow, especially if he went on being smooth and not very communicative. After all, why did he need to be armed, if he just administered lottery business?

FOUR

I COULD HAVE agreed to eat lunch with Jack; I didn't have another appointment or anything. But I didn't want to, not right today. I had too much to do and too little time. I didn't want a working lunch. I wanted to clear my head while I ate. It was the wrong choice.

On the ground floor of City Hall, I stepped out of the brass-cage elevator into a maelstrom. The lobby was swarming. It had been crowded but not like this when I went up in the elevator an hour and a half before. There were shouted greetings and arguments, blending into a background buzz, over which a loudspeaker—maybe a police loudspeaker?—was saying, "You must vacate the building. You must vacate the building. There is to be no picketing in this building. All picketers must move to the sidewalk outdoors immediately. There is daily business being transacted in this building. You must vacate the building—"

The speaker repeated himself as I pushed through the crowd. The revolving doors to the street could only disgorge one person per second or so, so I had to wait in a disorganized pack of people all trying to push through at once. The ones who could get to the revolving doors did seem to be moving out of the lobby to the street. But from here it looked like there was a dense crowd on the sidewalk already. After a couple of minutes I was spun through the door.

The LaSalle Street sidewalk was mobbed. I tried to get some perspective on what groups were coalescing where. Usually at demonstrations the various factions form clumps, clustering around a spokesperson or a group of signs.

There seemed to be three or four loose bunches, excluding the cops, who were also caucusing near a squad car. Just when it looked pretty clear, Channel 2 drove up in a white van with the cam on top that looks like a harpoon gun. It was only a matter of time before Channel 5, Channel 7, Channel 9, Channel 32, and a variety of radio reporters arrived. I'd best get cracking.

There was a big knot of people just outside the City Hall doors. In fact, they were making it difficult for other people to exit the revolving door. They carried white signs with black lettering. All the signs were the same size, about thirty inches square, and all had the same kind of printing. The group either had money, or it had a member who was a printer. In the maybe ten or a dozen signs I could read from where I was, there were only three messages: GOD HATES GAMBLING, WAGERING IS SIN AND THE WAGES OF SIN IS DEATH, and GET RID OF THE MONEY-CHANGERS.

Their leader, a tall man with white hair, gestured to them to spread out. He pointed and shooed and shepherded them into a line, apparently feeling with good reason that the signs all lined up would have more impact than clumped together.

"Good morning." I approached him with my pad and pen out. It was almost noon, but not quite.

"Good morning. Are you a reporter?"

"Yes. And you are—"

"Reverend Meinke."

"You are from—"

"Carbondale, Illinois. The Sixth Baptist Church."

"Can you tell me why you're here, Reverend?"

"We think there's a chance of overturning this sinful gambling. Now that the eyes of other states are on us."

"But couldn't it equally well bring other states in?"

"Well, in that case we're here to warn them. It's a sad thing to have our own government encouraging people to wager their earnings."

"Doesn't the Bible say—"

''The Bible mentions choosing by lot. That's like drawing straws to see who undertakes a difficult job. There's nothing in the Bible that approves lotteries for money and dice and gambling on horse races and so on. Nothing at all.''

''I see, sir. You're three hundred miles from home. It's a long way to come just to march in front of City Hall. What else do you plan to do while you're here?''

''We're going to be on this spot testifying to our beliefs every single day of this conference—'' Even while he spoke, his eyes wandered away from my face. I turned around to see why I was losing him.

A minicam on the shoulder of a strong young man poked up next to my neck. Near it was a carefully made up young woman in a suit chosen for the camera—medium blue with white edging on the lapels. ''Channel Two,'' she said to the minister.

''Yes. I'm Reverend Meinke from Carbondale, Illinois.'' His eyes sparkled. His vivacity quotient rose two hundred percent.

I backed away. It was hopeless. The last thing I heard as I turned was ''The eyes of other states are on us. It's a sad thing to have our own government encourage young people to take up wagering.''

Some thirty feet away was another group. These people had hand-printed signs, and all the signs were different: WEST CHICAGO OPPOSES THE LOTTERY, THE LOTTERY IS A TAX ON POOR PEOPLE, ROB THE POOR!

Most of this group was black. The leader was a woman of about forty-five. She had formed her soldiers into a loose oval, and they were walking around and around. She was absolutely correct, strategically. A team that moved would attract more attention than one that stood still. And look better on television.

''I'm Cat Marsala,'' I said, holding my notebook like a badge. ''Would you tell me why you're here?''

''This lottery,'' she said. ''It's a tax on people who can't afford it.''

"What do you mean?"

"How many rich people do you see buying lottery tickets? I'm a teacher and I can tell you, the people who buy this stuff don't know the first thing about probability."

"Tell me."

"Listen, let's say you could buy a lottery ticket every week. You know how long it would take you to win?"

"No, how long?"

"Twenty thousand years! But folks don't know that. There's people out there spending fifty, a hundred dollars a week they can't afford. Taking milk out of the mouths of their own babies."

"I see."

"I could tell you some *sad* cases—"

Her eyes went away from me, like Reverend Meinke's had. I turned around. Channel 5.

"Take the lottery advertising out of the West Side!" the woman shouted at the minicam. Channel 5 stopped, and a photogenic young man eased over next to the woman. Staffers flanked both of them to keep stray people from stepping in front of the camera.

I left. What the hell. It was time for lunch. Past time. As I turned away, I heard, "Live at City Hall, Theresa Mowrey, Channel Two News."

Before I had gone three feet, I felt a touch on my sleeve. It was a small gray man. In fact, he was not much bigger than I am, and I'm five feet one or two—two if I've had a lot of rest.

He had grayish wispy hair, a grayish complexion, and he wore a three-piece suit in a gray-and-brown heather mix. He whispered, "You're a reporter. May I talk with you?"

"Sure." The State of Illinois Building across the street had a variety of restaurants and stores inside. The hot dog stand was calling softly to me. But I contented myself with edging away from the other groups while the little gray man talked.

"You see," he said, "I know those people get distracted by television. It's a terribly powerful medium, and some of them aren't readers anyway, so they don't know any better even though their hearts may be in the right place. But television isn't going to do justice to our opposition views. It's these fifteen-second sound bites, you know. They can't say anything pithy in fifteen seconds."

"You're right about that."

"They'll do a fifteen-second sound bite of her," he pointed at the black woman, "and fifteen seconds of him," he pointed at the white man, "and fifteen seconds of a couple of people who are in favor of the lottery, and then they'll start talking about the weather. What do you write for?" He talked so quickly, it was hard to hear him above the crowd noises.

"Different papers. I'm freelance."

"See? You're your own boss. You can get into the issues."

He was so right that I considered asking him to come and get a hot dog with me. I was getting hungrier every second. "What are the issues, in your opinion?"

"The most basic issue is what should the state approve of. If the state is doing something, the implication to the people is that the state thinks it's right. Therefore, if the state is approving of gambling, children will grow up thinking gambling is a perfectly good use of their money."

I stared longingly across the street at the restaurants. The crowd around us was swelling in numbers and getting denser. And oh, hell—here came Channel 7, Channel 32, and Doug Cummings for WMAQ. Suddenly a drift of breeze came toward us from the State of Illinois Building; the smell of hot dogs was stronger. Mmm—and onions. Mustard. Relish.

I said, "People say that gambling will go on whatever you do."

"Of course it will. That's why I say the issue is what example the state sets. I mean, if you're going to say that whatever bad thing the people may do, the state should take it over and make money out of it, well, then, we might as well set up state houses of prostitution and tax them.''

"I hadn't thought of it that way. But logically, you've got a point.''

"Will you write that?''

"Sure I will. I think most people like to read something that they can really *think* about. So much that's printed condescends to the reader. Television more so, as you were saying. You're *so* right.'' We were into heavy mutual admiration here.

"Besides,'' he said, "the money they take in from the lottery—you know how it was supposed to go to schools and improve them?''

"Public transit and schools. Yes.''

"All they do is cut down on appropriations from other sources. I know it for a fact—the lottery hasn't helped the schools at all, if you originally thought in terms of the schools getting extra money.''

"Say, would you like a hot dog? I'm going to get one.''

"Oh, no, thank you. You shouldn't either. If you eat meat it makes you angry.''

"It does?''

"You take in all the anger of the animal at being killed and you develop the biochemistry of the predator in yourself.''

"Oh. Well, the thing is, I'm in that kind of a business.''

"What? Oh, I see. You're making a joke.''

"Yes. Actually, I don't eat hot dogs all that often.'' It seemed to me best if we finished our discussion right here on the street after all. "Do I understand that you think gambling is intrinsically a bad thing?''

He leaned closer to me. "Yes. It's evil. God has commanded us to husband our resources. Throwing money away is as bad as throwing away health on drugs and drink.''

"I can understand that point of view.''

"Thank you for saying that.''

"Well, let me get lunch now." I held out my hand. "I'll remember what you said about the hot dogs. Nice to meet you, Mr.—"

"Nice to meet you too." He shook my hand, but he did not let it go. "It's very important to recognize evil when you see it."

"Yes?"

"Otherwise it can lurk around you. It's very hard to see. You can't be sure when evil is right behind your back."

I didn't like this. We were surrounded by people. Surely I was in no danger? Then again, when the mob guns down people on the street, who ever admits to witnessing anything? If this man stuck a knife in my ribs, would anybody in this packed crowd even notice?

No, I was being silly. He was a harmless eccentric. I pulled my hand. He held on.

"I have to get to an interview now."

"You said you were going to lunch," he whispered.

"That's why I was going to get a hot—lunch. I'm in a hurry."

His other hand clutched my wrist. "No, you can't leave yet. I haven't explained about evil."

Don't argue with people like this. "Could we talk later?"

"No. We have to talk now. Before it's too late."

Suddenly a hand came down on both my shoulder and his. "Say! Do you want to interview this man, Cat? We could get a photographer to take his picture—"

It was Jack Sligh. The little gray man wiped all expression from his face. His fingers let go of my wrist. I glanced at Jack. When I looked back at the little gray man, he was gone. He must have slipped between some bodies in the crowd and faded away.

"Where did you come from?" I asked Jack.

"I was looking for you. Just dumb luck that I found you, really."

"Lucky for me."

"Yeah, he's a very strange man."

"You know him?"

"How the hell else do you think I knew how to scare him away? He hangs around the Lottery corridors and talks about evil. Doesn't *do* anything, so it's hard to get the cops to turn him away. But he refuses to give anybody his name, ever, so I figured the idea of being photographed would really throw him into fits."

"Apparently. Thanks. I owe you."

"*De nada.*"

"Why were you looking for me?"

"I've asked around a little bit about you. You have a reputation of writing what you want. They say you don't take orders well."

"If I can find out who 'they' are, I'll strangle them."

"It was a compliment. What I'm asking is, do you do exposés?"

"Depends on what you mean. I don't do that stuff where you interview somebody and then sneer at him in print. Like, um, 'Alderman Grigson stated, "I consider myself the representative of the little man," as he patted his Sulka tie and stole a surreptitious glance at his Rolex.' Stuff like that. But if you mean—"

"Misappropriation of public funds."

"Theft?"

"No, well, maybe yes. Depends on how you look at it. I don't want to pin it down without having the time to—well, frankly, to ask *you* some hard questions. I'd want to know how you'd use it."

"Can't you be more specific?"

"Not now. I could, maybe, if we sat down for an hour or so. How about tomorrow?"

"Sure. I have to take my mother to the Rehab Institute at ten-thirty."

"Nine? Or if you like to start the day late—"

"No, no. I'm starting my days early right now. But I have to go pick her up."

He pulled out an appointment book. "Oh. Nine won't work for me either. I have a breakfast meeting. Eleven?"

"Sure. I'll drop her off and come right over." We started to walk apart. "I'll be here as early as I can," I called.

"Eleven," he yelled back. "I'll be waiting for you."

SOMEHOW THAT NICE hot dog didn't seem so appealing now. I bought a bag of popcorn in the lower level of the State of Illinois Building and wandered around eating it for a few minutes.

I put in a call to the retail inspector to ask whether Fred Furman, Dorothy's son, could show me how they inspect stores. He gave me Fred's phone number and also a list of stores with the times he was supposed to go there. I'd catch him when I could find time.

The State of Illinois Building, designed by Helmut Jahn, is a real weirdo. You take a huge stepped and rounded Mayan pyramid, made out of reflective glass. Cut through it vertically into quarters, set one quarter down so that the ninety-degree-angle point is at the corner of Lake Street and LaSalle, the rounded side toward the Clark and Randolph corner, and you've got your basic State Illinois Center. Then inside you leave all the heat ducts, wiring, and plumbing showing and paint them purple and rose. You leave the glass rounded side without floors, so you have an atrium going all the way up. Then you have the most hellacious heating and cooling problem architecture can imagine.

But, gee, it can certainly get your attention.

Regretfully, I finished my popcorn and threw the bag in a wastebasket. I had better spend a few hours at the Chicago Public Library, which was about a ten-block walk. This library stuff is one of the things I like least about my job. We had an ogre for a librarian in my high school, and I still think when I'm doing research that somebody is breathing down my neck, about to give me a *D* in citizenship.

But it had to be done.

FIVE

WHEN YOU WORK as a staff reporter, you are always working to deadline. The product always has to be shorter than you think the subject deserves. Well, almost always; there was this rock star once—after nine words I couldn't think of anything else to say about him. He was tall. He was famous. He was loud. But as a staff reporter you are always thinking, Too little time, too little space.

One of the most exciting things about the kind of reporting I do now is that I can really get my teeth into an issue. No, more than that. I have a chance to learn a lot about a subject and find out what really matters.

Before I went freelance, I would get this kind of assignment: "Give me twenty-five hundred words on bag ladies by tomorrow at five." Or: "Judge Letitia Cary in the District Court is rumored as a possible Supreme Court nominee. I need a profile by tonight."

Now, that kind of thing is doable. There are resource materials, and the newspaper morgue, and people can tell you where to look if you really panic, plus if you value your sanity you should have been developing a *wide* network of contacts of all sorts and sizes.

But when I was turning these out I never felt that I had time to do justice to the topic. What if Judge Letitia Cary had interesting opinions on merit selection of judges? What if it would be more interesting to follow one of the women street people on her rounds for a few days, rather than just talk to one or two for an hour, call a couple of patrol officers and welfare people who work with them, and mock up some statistics?

I've always been attracted to issues where society seems to be hypocritical. Why? What is it in my upbringing or nature that wants to ask people in charge to be consistent?

For instance, it bugs the hell out of me that our legal system, with all the power of society behind it, makes certain drugs illegal, and at the same time thinks alcohol is just fine, even kind of (snicker snicker) manly. And prescription drugs are really swell, too. I don't say I know what to do about it, but it certainly is inconsistent.

Inconsistency is surely the case with the lottery. Picture a bunch of guys, unshaven, beer-swilling, shooting craps in a backyard. Appalling, right? But what's wrong with this picture? That they're unshaven? It's the fashion now. That they're drinking beer? Beer is advertised publicly. That they're gambling? Well, okay—and just exactly what is the lottery if not gambling?

To some extent, I believe these areas of discontinuity are where the real values of a society play themselves out. They take off their masks here.

There's something more of context, of who's doing it, than there is an objection to the act itself. Church bingo was always okay. Betting operations were not. Sports betting at country clubs was always okay. Crap games in back alleys were not. Maybe society enforces these laws against people it doesn't like.

Anyhow, I was now feeling the subtle thrill of the chase—the chase as freelance writers know it: As of this moment I knew almost nothing about lotteries, the Illinois State Lottery or any others. But by the end of the week I would know a great deal. I would be a helluva major expert on the lottery.

I love it.

HOWEVER, THAT DOESN'T mean it isn't tiring. By the time I left the library it was maybe five o'clock. My feet were dragging. My back ached. The day had been profitable, but there'd been too much of it. I had discovered one fact that

I knew would be useful, even if I didn't know exactly where.
A person's chance of being struck by lightning is one in
600,000.

I live in a small, really small, North End apartment.
Trudging home, I passed two Korean groceries, a Mexican
grocery, and a couple of supermarkets. None of them
seemed attractive enough for me to stay on my feet any
longer to shop. Maybe there'd be something in the refrigerator.

Mr. Ederle, who lives on the second floor, was not home,
or he'd have grabbed me to talk. He's a nice man, but he has
lots of extra time on his hands.

I'm on the third floor. The building is old. The apartment is small, but it's got a corner, which means two windows in the little bathroom. The realtor was extremely proud
of that. No doubt he was so vocally proud of it in order to
take my mind off the bathroom fixtures and the kitchen
appliances. The oven is so old it has legs. Curved legs. The
refrigerator was probably General Electric's first experi-
mental prototype. The toilet is better not mentioned. Or
looked at.

When I let myself in, my parrot, Long John Silver, was
sulking. Usually he swoops over to meet me. Not today. He
was sitting on my Mickey Mouse table clock. As I walked in,
he said, "Getting and spending we lay waste our powers."

Now, LJ can't possibly know what he's saying. He's a
parrot, not a human. He's an African gray parrot, *Psitta-
cus erithacus*, the best talker in the parrot world. But that
doesn't mean he knows what he's saying. LJ was owned for
some years by a Creole chef from New Orleans who died
and left him to an English professor from Northwestern
University. We don't know how long LJ lived in New Orleans, so we don't know how old he is. At least forty, maybe
as much as fifty. African gray parrots can live to be ninety
years old. The professor lived in this building and owned LJ
for twenty years. Then he left town for Alberta quite suddenly. The professor, not the parrot. Something to do with

a woman. But before that Long John Silver had plenty of time to soak up phrases the prof hurled at him. He therefore has warped ideas about what constitutes conversation.

"Same to you, fella," I said. And I looked around to see why he was miffed at me.

The living room seemed fine. His cage was open, his birdseed dish was not exactly full; obviously he'd taken out his pique by eating—I've been known to do the same—but there was still food left. His water dish was still dispensing water from its inverted bottle as the cup under it was used. The plastic ball he liked to play with was on the floor. It's big, over a foot in diameter, and spongy, like a Nerf ball. For some birdy reason, he likes to fly down, light on it, gripping it with his claws, shout *Awwwk!* or *Braaaaak!* as it rolls over and spills him off, wings flapping so hard you can hear them beat the air. Maybe it's the bird's version of losing and regaining control, like little kids love to slide down slides or spin around until they're dizzy.

"You're just fussing." But I went into the bedroom to see whether anything else in his small world could be amiss. And there it was. When Hal Briskman had called me this morning, he'd suggested I get cracking immediately. Be at his office in twenty minutes was what I remember him saying.

In my haste I'd thrown the bath towel over the floor-standing bedroom mirror.

Horrors!

LJ had spent the whole day without being able to look at himself. This is a big old oval mirror on a swiveling floor stand. LJ likes to sit on the chair, look in the mirror, and talk to himself. I've even seen him fly toward it, and I swear he's admiring how he looks on the wing.

"So *that's* it! If you're so smart, why didn't you peck the towel off?"

The towel removed, LJ hopped over to check himself out. He cocked his head this way and that, evidently pleased. He is definitely not a beautiful bird, by human standards. African gray parrots are a kind of gunmetal color with random splotches of dark red on their lower body and tail, the color of dried blood. And their tails are rather stubby, too. But obviously to himself he was remarkably fine.

The English professor, who had lived downstairs from me in the apartment Mr. Ederle now rented, had apparently taught LJ a special remark to say in front of a mirror.

The bird cocked his head. "Don't say it, LJ," I begged.

"*Braaaak!*" he said. He peered at the reflection, blinked his wide, wrinkled eyes. "*Braaak! Is* this the face that launched a thousand ships?"

"If you've got that out of your system, let's go look in the refrigerator."

The refrigerator was a big disappointment. I like to cook. But when I don't get back for dinner or don't have time to cook, I develop serious guilts about what my mother would call "wasting good food" and so after a while the wrinkled green peppers and moldy cheeses get thrown away and not replaced. The choices right now were tofu, grated cheese, chutney, skimmed milk, and any amount of coffee or tea. And of course, birdseed.

Curried tofu with chutney?

"We've got a problem, LJ." Faithless bird that he was, he flew over to his cage and started eating birdseed. He certainly acts smart.

Weren't there some onions in the bin in the veggie drawer?

Then the doorbell rang.

I don't buzz anybody into the building unless I know who it is. The glass door in the vestibule is visible from the stairs outside my door. I looked. Mike!

He pushed through the buzzing door. Before he even got to the stairs he called, "I know. I know you're upset." He came up the stairs two at a time. "Now just let me explain."

He looked like he does when he's brought a bender under control, under control a little too late. His hair was damp. I assumed that meant a cold shower. His eyes were red. But he was alert, if pale, and apparently full of energy. There was no furrow between his brows to indicate a headache.

"You been eating aspirins?" I asked, letting us both into my apartment. I had closed and locked the door behind me because of Long John Silver. The poor bird knew nothing about the world outside. If he got out, he'd get lost. Plus, it's a jungle out there.

"Give me a minute to explain," Mike said.

Just then LJ came swooping down over Mike's head, ruffling his hair. "You vampire bat!" Mike said.

"Hey, why do you always insult LJ?"

"Cat, listen. I don't dislike that bird."

"Oh?"

"It's just that the way he talks bothers me."

"What's the matter with the way he talks?"

"He doesn't move his lips."

"It's not his fault. He doesn't *have* lips!"

"That's what I mean. It's so eerie. Here's this parrot sitting here, not moving any part of its face, or whatever you call it, and here's this disembodied voice saying clearly—"

"Out, out, damned spot," LJ said.

"See? The voice from nowhere."

"Actually, I have to admit that's true. But it isn't fair to criticize the bird for it. It's eerie, but it's kind of wonderful. It's almost like his mind was speaking to you directly. Not his throat."

"Oh, c'mon, Cat! Whee-ooo! Twilight Zone! Anyhow, just to show Long John that I love him, too, I brought him a flower."

Mike pulled out a miniature yellow rose.

I said, "No! Don't give him that. It's got insecticide on it!"

"It does not. You warned me about that before."

"Flowers are sprayed with all kinds of junk. More than food."

"I got this at an organic flower shop."

"There isn't any such thing."

"All right. All right. Listen. My downstairs neighbor, the elderly woman who keeps giving me cookies?"

"Yes?"

"She has this parakeet. And she's got these pots of miniature roses. Well, I knew about LJ eating flowers, so I asked her if her parakeets ate the roses and she said they didn't. Is that true?"

"I don't know. I don't do parakeets."

"So she wondered why I asked and I explained about LJ, so she gave me a rose to bring to LJ."

"And she doesn't spray her plants?"

"No. They're too sensitive, I guess. She says you can't even keep these miniature roses in a room with a gas stove, they're so sensitive. And she grows them in special potting soil that she mixes with peat moss and crushed eggshells and bone meal and God only knows what other goodies. You could practically eat that soil for a healthful breakfast cereal. I mean, this is a *nutritious* rose."

"In that case," I said grandly, "you may proceed."

Mike held up the rose between thumb and forefinger. LJ flew over and sat on Mike's upper arm, from which he dined eagerly on the rose. I would say that his gusto proved the rose was wholesome, except that he will now and then try to dine on the end of a roll of toilet paper.

"Now," I said to Mike. "You've delayed long enough. Explain. Hal's pissed off and so am I."

"I've gotta take you someplace."

"Now?"

"Now."

"Is there an adequate reason for this? I've had a long day."

"I'll drive."

I studied him. He was sober.

"It's important," he said. "Have I ever lied to you?"

"Well, yes—"

"Other than if I tell you I'm not going to drink and then I do."

"Other than that, no."

"Then let's go."

THERE ARE two old Italian neighborhoods in Chicago—not to mention a lot of new Italian neighborhoods. One of the old ones is on Taylor Street. The other is around where Oakley and Western are cut by Twenty-fourth Street. It's a neighborhood of very small Italian restaurants. Sometimes there are only two or three other diners in these places, and yet they seem to survive, decade after decade.

Mike took me into a tiny restaurant I had never heard of, the Pisa. There was no one in the dining room; on a Monday night that was not surprising.

The round proprietor seated us with a conspiratorial grin and a wink at Mike. Then the man disappeared into the kitchen.

"Mike, what's going on?"

"You'll see. I bet you've forgotten that tomorrow is your birthday."

Well, I *had* forgotten. My mother was coming to Chicago tomorrow, and she wanted me to drive out to pick her up and bring her in. She'd mentioned my birthday. But I'd immediately let it drop from my mind. I was busy.

The proprietor called, "Now." A thin waiter entered and with a flourish flung a red-and-white-checked tablecloth over the white one already in place. Then a candle in a bottle. And a bottle of red wine. Then the waiter brought in—

"A bowl of bones?" I said.

The plump proprietor strode up waving his arms. "Take those away!" he shouted, a mite theatrically. I thought I recognized this—there was a hint somewhere in the back of my head.

In seconds, before I could think of what it was that teased my mind, the thin waiter was back with a big serving bowl of spaghetti and meatballs. Then, behind my back, the proprietor started to play an accordion.

"'Bella Notte'!" I said. "The scene from *Lady and the Tramp*!"

In the movie Lady, who is a beautiful purebred cocker spaniel with lovely long silky ears, is wooed by Tramp, a feisty mutt. Tramp takes her to meet his friend, an Italian restaurant owner, who often gives Tramp bones at the back door. When the Italian sees Lady, he throws away the bones and sets the two a full dinner table, with tablecloth and all the extras.

"'—is the night, it's a beautiful night, and they call it *bella notte*,'" the proprietor sang. He had a warm, full voice, and sang *con brio*.

Mike poured wine for me and not himself. Mike knows I'm a Walt Disney fan. I think that *Snow White* is the best movie every made. Art, music, tight pacing, it's got everything. And while *Lady and the Tramp* isn't up to the best of Disney, it's a darn good movie, too.

"Now," Mike said, "I'll explain." He forked up a ball of spaghetti, wrapping it around his fork, not taking one end of a long noodle and sucking it in the way the mongrel and the cocker spaniel did it in the movie. When he'd eaten it, he went on.

"I want to ask you to move in with me." I started to tell him—again—my reservations, when he held up his hand. "No, Cat, I put it that way intentionally, that I wanted to ask you to move in with me, not 'Please come live with me,' because I knew I couldn't ask you right now. You think I'm too unpredictable."

"Damn right."

"You don't trust me not to—well, you know, go off on a bender."

"You screwed up Hal's assignment."

"Yes, I know I did. When I realized what had happened, I called him and he told me you were already on it."

"Maybe we could work it together."

"No, no. You do it. And by the way, look up old Hector Furman first thing."

"Old Hector? Who's he? I've met a youngish Hector and I've talked with Dorothy Furman."

"Dorothy's old Hector's daughter. There are several Furmans working in the lottery. But Hector was the first. They got him in at the beginning, because the lotteries in the early days hadn't done well. No surprise. State legislators didn't have the foggiest idea about how to make a lottery attractive."

"So why did Hector know?"

"Why? That's my point. He was a mob guy. He'd run numbers and betting parlors for thirty years."

"Oh, Oho!" My mind was racing. "Very interesting. Well, so why don't we work the story together? Obviously you know more than I do."

"We can't."

"Why not? What are you trying to tell me?"

All this time, the fat proprietor and the thin waiter were singing "Bella Notte." With great tact, they had backed over to the far wall, and were now singing softly, almost to themselves.

Mike said, "I'm trying to tell you that I want to do something about the—my problem—before it's too late. The reason I can't do the assignment with you is that I'm going into a treatment program."

"An alcoholism treatment program?"

Mike had never quite said the word "alcoholism." He didn't now, either. But he came close.

He said, "That's right. Here in Chicago. It's a three-week program and you have to live in the unit, so I've passed all my assignments on to other people or postponed them wherever I could. I've spent the whole afternoon working out the scheduling." He reached for my hand and held it. This was not quite what the lovers in *Lady and the Tramp* were thinking about, but for me it was better.

"I'm so happy."

"Cat, listen. I'll be away for three weeks. They won't keep you in the program if you don't stay for the full time. When I get back—don't tell me now, it isn't fair to ask—but when I get back, please think about moving in with me."

"I will. I mean, I'll think about it."

"Always cautious."

"I'm cautious, but I mean what I say. I'll really, seriously, think about it. I'm so happy, Mike. This could be the start of a new life."

"For me or for both of us?"

"Maybe both of us. Let's not push it. Let's just be happy."

He leaned across the table and kissed me. As he did, the singing at the other side of the room picked up added verve and tempo.

"Now!" he said. "Remember the end of the scene?"

There was one meatball left on the serving dish. In the movie, too, the two puppies get to the point where there is one meatball left. Lady wants Tramp to have it; Tramp is still hungry but he wants Lady to have it, and he pushes it over to her with his nose.

"Now watch!" Mike said, bending forward.

"No! Not with your nose!" I looked around at the restaurant owner. He was laughing. The waiter was still singing. Mike rolled the meatball with his nose. "Say you'll wait for me or I'll push it off the dish!"

"No blackmail." I grabbed his hair with my left hand and wiped his nose with my napkin. "Now, that's enough. I've told you we'll see how it goes, and therefore we'll see how it goes."

"Promise you'll be kind," he said, laughing.

SIX

THEY SAY YOU only live once. This is a pity, because here I am in my thirties and I haven't really got the hang of it yet.

Mike's proposal, however iffy, struck some sort of chord. I was getting tired of living alone. It wasn't so much the solitude. It wasn't exactly loneliness; being alone and loneliness are not the same thing. Plus, I am extremely conscious of the fact that I get a lot of work done precisely because I don't have anybody else bothering me, or hanging on me, or needing attention. He travels fastest who travels alone.

But somehow I was getting tired of it. It was becoming wearing that I was always the only person responsible for myself. If I was tired some evening, wouldn't it be nice to say, "Honey, *you* lock up."

Or maybe, "I've got an interview that'll run past six. Can you get me a quart of milk and a tub of egg foo yong on your way home?"

This was sounding like I was looking for a crutch, though, not a relationship. Straighten up, Marsala. What do you really want? How about if somebody says to you, "I'm tired. *You* lock up." Is that just as good?

Well, it didn't sound so terrible, either. Maybe I'd go back to baking my famous hockey-puck-size peanut butter cookies. Or my double-garlic spaghetti sauce. I have a triple-garlic sauce, too, but you have to ask people ahead of time if it's okay, not spring it on them.

It was early Tuesday morning. The philosophizing that occurs before I get my morning coffee is particularly fuzzy, and often some self-pity creeps in. I ate a bowl of extremely healthful and extremely grainy cereal, remembering about

halfway through what Mike had said about his neighbor's
nutritious potting soil.

Mike. He'd be entering the care unit today. Right about
now, in fact. It was going to be hard on his ego.

Bless him.

THE FIRST THING I did after my morning caffeine transfu-
sion was call Captain Harold McCoo. It's not that he knows
everything; it's just that what he doesn't know usually isn't
very important. I call him if possible before I go to see him,
though he tries to act like he's got plenty of time, even when
I drop in unannounced. McCoo is that strange and excellent combination, a very frank and honest man who is also
completely gracious.

I phoned his office at quarter of eight. Somebody came
on the line and asked who I wanted. When I told them, they
forwarded the call, even though I was sure I had the right
number. Must be another of those telephone system re-
structuring things where everybody gets a new number and
then you can't find anybody for a while.

McCoo was there. He was usually there—seven-thirty in
the morning to six or seven or eight at night, most of the
time. Although it was barely eight A.M., he said come now.
He had a morning meeting. I said I'd be there by eight-
fifteen. Which was fine, because I should leave the city by
nine at the latest to get my mother.

THE CHICAGO Police Department—that is to say the main
copshop—is located at 11th and State. It's a strange, half-
gentrified area, some of the sidewalks cracked and tilting
like Lake Michigan icebergs, some new fresh concrete, some
old rattletrap apartment buildings that must have gone up
right after the Chicago fire and some new Yuppie-domes,
some old cop-politician bars, and some brick and fern restaurants with designer water.

I rode up in the elevator with five large male police officers, feeling like I always do, a foot and a half shorter, a hundred pounds less massive. Your basic second-grader on the fifth-graders' playground. I am about at waist level and always think, though never seriously, about what would happen if I stuck my elbow in somebody's stomach. This is not hostility. It's just a natural reaction to being short.

At the thirteenth floor I got out and went into McCoo's outer office. Through the far door I could see his desk. There was a different man at it.

Gripma, McCoo's secretary, stared at me for a couple of seconds and then said laconically, "He's on five."

"Oh. Five where?"

"Five oh seven."

The man's a real talker. I said "Thanks."

McCoo was indeed on five. His door was open and I saw him, so I went in without reading what was written on the glass. "Hey, Captain," I said, "what are you doing down here?"

"It's not captain," he said with a small grin. "It's deputy chief."

"No kidding? Congratulations!" I gave him a hug. "Deputy chief of what?"

"Violent Crimes North." He cocked a thumb at the door. Sure enough, that's what the black paint on the glass said, too.

"Which means?"

"All of the city north of Madison."

"That's half the city."

"Right. We got Violent Crimes North and Violent Crimes South."

Violent Crimes is basically what used to be called Homicide. There is no Homicide anymore. It's all subsumed under Violent Crimes. And this makes sense. A violent incident should be handled by a major crimes unit, even if it doesn't happen to lead to a death.

Harold McCoo is a medium-tall black man. Maybe five-eleven, something like that. I've seen him looking thirty-five years old, but I know he's older. I've also seen him looking sixty-five, when there was a serious problem. Right now he looked forty-five and that was probably about right. He put down his cup.

He'd already set up his office the way he liked it. His coffee machine was bubbling on a metal table at one side. His swivel chair could scoot anyplace in the room, from file cabinets to telephone to coffeepot. McCoo is not a man for luxury. His desk is metal, his chair is old, but it's got good, smooth-rolling casters and a spring back so he can lean back when he wants to. There's no carpet, so the chair can move easily. He likes to keep his own personal files and not depend entirely on his secretary.

But he likes his coffee just right. He has an Italian coffee maker and a Krups grinder.

"What is it this time?" I asked.

"Ethiopian Yirgacheffee." He was pouring out. He knew I liked cream, no sugar. He liked his black.

"I thought you said Ugandan was the best in the world."

"Well, I'll tell you, Cat. It may be, but a man likes a little variety once in a while."

"Right. I've heard that."

"This is the most full-bodied coffee you'll ever taste. But it's especially known for its complex floral bouquet."

"Oh, really? Lay it on me and I'll see for myself. But I still think there's something a little unnatural about this fixation of yours."

He had a dazzling smile. "You find a more harmless addiction, you let me know."

I was tasting the coffee. He raised his eyebrows. I said, "Well, okay. You may be right. This is better than good. Better than great."

He drank, too. "Now, Cat, what trouble are you planning to get into that you want me to get you out of?"

"You've *never* gotten me out of trouble."

"Talk to me, Cat. Don't argue."

"Basically, I just wondered if there was any truth to Hector Furman being an old retired mob guy."

McCoo said, "Mmmm." After a couple more seconds he went on. "This is background?"

"Well, I'm not going to quote you, if that's what you mean." By now, he knew me well enough to believe me. "And I'm not doing anything on Hector himself, anyway. Not as a person. This is a thing on the lottery."

"Um. Well, yeah. The rumor has always been that he was connected."

"Just plain connected."

"Well, when you come right down to it, Cat, if you want the pure inside poop, he was running betting parlors all over the city."

"Aha."

"Aha yourself."

"Is that so different from what he's doing now?"

"Still just background?" he asked.

"Of course. Come on, I'm not a traitor. Or a gossip columnist."

"Same thing. Well, Cat, it's hard to say. The whole lottery business is not exactly what it's cracked up to be."

"What was it cracked up to be?"

"You may be too young to remember, but there was a huge federal uproar in the late fifties about organized crime and gambling. A senator named Estes Kefauver was highly enraged and he wasn't the only one. There were congressional hearings and the whole schmear. The basic idea was that organized crime—meaning the mob—was in charge of gambling coast to coast."

"So?"

"It wasn't true. Just plain wasn't true. The mob was never really able to control gambling in general. Oh, it *liked* gambling and ran it where it could. Nevada, for instance. But every serious law enforcement survey since then has shown that grass-roots gambling, like the numbers game, was local and extremely competitive locally. Even in small towns, nobody was able to get a monopoly, not even by intimidation, unless the numbers people had the cooperation of the local police department. So that they'd run everybody else out and leave one group in control."

"You mean Hector Furman isn't a mob guy?"

"No, no. I'm certain he is. Plus, I'm sure he gave the state advice about how to run a lottery. I'm just saying that you shouldn't get the idea that he was a national kingpin. There weren't any. Not in numbers and policy."

"So he's clean now?"

"Yeah. I think so. Why not? They pay him a hefty enough fee."

"And the lottery is clean?"

"Well, the lottery itself, as far as I know, is clean."

"So why do you say it in that tone of voice?"

"Well, it has its associated problems. For instance, the lottery is an easy way to launder small amounts of illegal money. You buy a ticket, you say you won even though you didn't, you can even declare it on your income tax. That way, by reporting it, you legitimize the money and you can spend it without fear. Who's to know or care, if it isn't a huge amount?"

"I suppose."

"And there are the little fiddles. You're not supposed to be able to buy a lottery ticket on credit or with a credit card. So some stores will sell lottery tickets to customers they know, and write the purchase up as candy or liquor or whatever, so it can go on a credit card."

"Well, at least the lottery must have wiped out a lot of illegal betting parlors."

"Oh, no, Cat. Oh, no, no, no. Policy and numbers and every other form of betting has gone on just like before. There must've been a hundred surveys done, Massachusetts, New York, Illinois, New Jersey, here there and everywhere, and I can tell you policy and numbers are alive and well and all around us."

"Why?"

"Why what?"

"Why would somebody go to them, when they're illegal, if they can get a ticket legally and not have to worry?"

"Three reasons at least. Illegal games are more convenient. They have runners, and they'll practically go house to house and pick up bets. If you're a regular bettor you may not have to move a muscle."

"And?"

"Credit. They'll let you bet on the cuff. You don't see the Illinois State Lottery letting you do that."

"No, but they don't break you legs if you don't come up with the cash to pay off your markers, either."

"No. But for some people credit is more important than what happens tomorrow. And the last thing is, numbers and policy let you make smaller bets. Like a dime. I think the smallest lottery bet right now is fifty cents."

That stopped me. It was somehow inexpressibly sad to think that the difference between fifty cents and ten cents made that much difference to people. And somehow it was disconcerting that, if it did, they would spend that precious little bit of money on gambling.

McCoo, seeing me stare off into space, said, "Want a refresher on your coffee?"

"No, thanks. You've got things to do. Mr. Deputy Chief McCoo. And I'd better get out and earn my money."

"See you later, Cat. You've relieved my mind."

"Why?"

"Sounds like at last you've got a topic that can't possibly get you into trouble."

THAT WAS early morning. I stopped in the lobby of the department, where there are a bunch of pay phones. There's always a slew of uniforms and plainclothes detectives there making calls to home or to informants. I telephoned the Lottery floor at City Hall, where of course there was nobody around this early except an answering machine, and

left a request for an interview with Hector Furman, Sr.,
sometime during the afternoon of the next day, preferably
two o'clock. I could call later to confirm.

Downer's Grove, where my parents live, is about twenty-
five miles from Chicago, but it's a straight shot out the Eisenhower and the East-West Tollway, so it never takes more
than thirty-five minutes except at rush hour. Of course, rush
hour eastbound into the city starts at seven A.M. and goes to
noon, and rush hour westbound starts at three and goes to
seven.

I picked her up at the hairdresser's at nine thirty-five.

"I thought you were going to be here at nine-thirty."

"There was traffic."

"We'll be late."

"No, we won't. It's faster going in." This, of course, was
a lie.

We lucked out somewhat and were in the city by ten-
twenty. Parked at one of those pickpockets cleverly designed as a parking garage, and walked toward the Rehab
Institute. Naturally, we had no idea that we were about to
witness Jack Sligh's death. My mother hobbled along only
half as fast as she had when she was pacing around the block
at the hairdresser's looking for my car. Well, it was her appointment, not mine, that we'd be late for, although I
needed to meet Jack at eleven myself.

The streets were jammed with cars. A traffic officer was
blowing his whistle furiously.

Then Jack Sligh fell to his death on the pavement.

IMMEDIATELY, I looked up at City Hall, but all the windows directly above us were closed and blank. The walls are
basically vertical, except for the very top of the building, the
eleventh floor, which is slightly set back. But they're made
of thick granite, so the windows are therefore recessed possibly a foot from the actual facade of the building. They are
very narrow, too, and because of the recess and narrow-

ness, what goes on behind the glass is not very easily visible from the street.

At one window above us, way up but not quite at the top, I thought I saw a motion. It was not repeated.

The traffic officer, meanwhile, had wisely decided that there were some things more important than gridlock. He was saying, "Move back. But don't leave."

He really didn't have a prayer of holding on to everybody who had been nearby at the time the body hit the pavement. There was one of him and at least one hundred of us. People around the edges were walking away already. It was one thing to be ghoulishly interested in death; it was another to miss your job or your lunch or your next appointment in order to be questioned by the cops. This is a very busy area. City Hall is in the heart of the courts/civic offices/law offices/business area, and in this one block alone there had to be five hundred people on the sidewalks or crossing the streets.

Two of the people who had been right next to us when the body hit were sidling away also. I caught their eyes. "Please stay," I said. "It won't take that long." Once appealed to like that, their public spirit or sense of shame took over, whichever, and they stayed.

My mother, meanwhile, was starting to hyperventilate. Her fingernails were still digging into my arm. We went over to stand with the other "witnesses" near one of the doors. Or I walked over there and she went along because she was attached to me. She pulled back on my arm all the time.

"Come on," I said to her.

"I can't. I'm going to be sick."

"No, you're not."

"I ought to be lying down."

"Hey! Let's do our civic duty here. Then you can faint later."

She gave me a reproachful look. The cop, who had been talking into his radio, as well as gesturing us to stand back and so on, seemed to have made some progress. Two squad cars nosed in, Mars lights flashing, from opposite ends of the street.

The Chicago Police Department is proud of its response time, and you couldn't have faulted this performance. In a matter of just a couple of minutes more, the scene was outlined in yellow barrier tape, the sidewalk was closed off, the crowds who had come wandering over to see what was going on were restrained, the "witness" group was isolated, the older woman who had perhaps been struck by Jack's falling body was being supported by a slender Hispanic officer, and a youngish white officer with a black mustache had been dispatched inside the building to find and tape off the office from which the body had fallen. Or jumped. Or been pushed.

And as if that wasn't enough, by the time I got my mother lowered onto one of the steps so she could sit, some plainclothes detectives turned up. This was pretty good, since they must have come up the four miles from Area One at 5101 South Wentworth. One was Detective Sergeant Derrick Locaster. I had seen him a couple of times while I was visiting my friend Captain McCoo. Locaster, however, didn't know me. His green eyes swept over me and the rest of the "witnesses" without stopping.

None of the police officers made any effort to take the pulse of the man on the pavement. It was scarcely necessary. Not only was the skull split, but I now noticed blood seeping out from under his jacket. Depending on impact, bodies can explode, like a watermelon dropped from a height. Jack Sligh hadn't fallen far enough to explode, but from the look of him, his abdomen must have ruptured.

MUCH AS MY MOTHER annoys me, if another person starts attacking her, I immediately defend her. There's nothing weirder in the world than families.

So when Sergeant Locaster kept badgering her, "Didn't you see him standing at the window? You must have heard something. Did he cry out? Did he shout?" I couldn't stand it after a while.

"Oh, no. No, I didn't," she said, shaking. "I wish I'd never been here at all."

"Leave her alone, can't you?" I barked at him. "Don't you see you're making it worse?"

I had had to admit that my mother had been looking up at the building. Honesty is the best policy. Usually. It appeared she was the only person who would admit to looking up at all, before Jack fell. But she hadn't seen anything important, or hadn't recognized it if she had. Locaster was not pleased.

"I thought I saw something move up there," I said.

"Where?"

"The ninth-floor window, I think." I counted and pointed for him.

"When? You said you weren't looking up."

"A couple of seconds after the man fell."

"You can't see those top windows very well."

"Not very."

"Are you sure you saw anything at all?"

"Moderately," I said, studying the body. It was Jack Sligh, no doubt about it, and I felt guilty. If I'd been a little quicker on the uptake, this might not have happened. And because of the incident of the little gray man yesterday, I also felt I owed Jack something.

Locaster looked at me as if I were an oddball. They always expect civilians to get wobbly at the sight of a violent death. I had spent my early years as a reporter, the paying-your-dues years, going to so many automobile accidents that I just didn't react anymore. But he couldn't know that. Finally he snapped, "Detective Boggs will take down your names. Then you can go."

If he'd been a little nicer, I might have told him I'd had an appointment with his corpse.

SET FREE by Locaster, I got a taxi and trundled my mother
to the Rehab Institute. Only an hour and a quarter late. The
nurse on duty doubted very much that anybody could see
her, since she had "missed her appointment." I explained
what had happened. The nurse said, "I doubt that anybody can see her, since she missed her appointment." This
was a woman who was not going to win the Flexibility of the
Week award. The institute is a full-fledged hospital, so I
asked them to admit my mother for the night. My mother
was letting me hold her up, whimpering softly, and would
have been a healthy color if she were an oyster.

"We can't do that," the nurse said. "She's a knee re-
placement patient and she's three months post-op. She
doesn't have any criteria." ·

Swell.

I let go of Mom, just for a second, to remonstrate with the
nurse. Mom sagged slowly to the floor. "Help me!" I said.

They admitted her for observation.

Did I let my Mom drop on purpose? Let me put it this
way: I would only do such a thing if it was for her own good
and if·I was sure she wouldn't fall fast.

I know my mother well.

IN TEN MINUTES I was back at City Hall.

The body of Jack Sligh may still have been on the sidewalk. Or not. They try to get them moved sooner if they're
in a public place, like this, than if they're in a home or office. Plus, the spot he landed was certainly not the place he
was attacked, so there couldn't have been much evidence to
collect at the street level. The detectives would be upstairs,
trying to make sense of it.

Still, there's a lot of technical work to be done at a death
scene, including getting the doctor to pass on the body, the
photographs, and other odds and ends.

The reason I couldn't tell whether Jack was still there was
that the area was surrounded by three squad cars, a tech
van, an inner perimeter of plainclothes people, an outline of

yellow barrier tape, an outer perimeter of blue uniforms, and a satellite grouping of interested citizens and television minicams. I had been away about an hour.

I didn't stop to look, anyhow. They won't even let a police officer into a crime scene once they've got it buttoned up—only the technical people. They certainly weren't going to let me poke around.

I bypassed the crowd completely and went into the City Hall building.

City Hall, technically the City/County building, is huge, but much broader than it is tall. Inside, it's a fine example of the Intimidate the Public school of interior decoration. The central hall is vast. Its surfaces are entirely coated by unfriendly materials—they are expensive, but there is nothing you want to touch. There is nothing you'd want to lean against, sit down on, or rub with your hand. The floors are made of blocks of marble, mainly two colors, a flesh color and a sidewalk gray. The walls are a cold gold and cream plaster, with soaring arches that join to make groined ceilings, and on the ceilings are mosaics composed of sharp little tiles in pale colors and gold. The arches look like bleached rib bones. You might as well have been swallowed by a rococo whale. The central hall is vast; the main corridor goes on forever, or at least a long city block, lined on both sides with elevators. The elevators are fronted with decorative brass in S-curves and rosette bosses. The transverse corridor goes on just as long at right angles, cutting the floor into quadrants. Inside the quadrants are warrens of city offices. It's not a place you'd want to spend any time in, because it's so cold looking, and it's not a place you'd want to be alone in, because you'd never know what was coming toward you up those corridors you can't see.

Since I'd visited Jack's office yesterday, I knew where it was and I went directly to the elevator. Nobody stopped me. There were a lot of blue uniforms around, but this is the place you go to get your city inspection sticker for your car—not that they inspect it. You get your permits for con-

struction here, zoning changes, all the paper that seems to
be necessary these days. Lord only knows how many envelopes with bribe money have been passed under this roof. So
really, the police were not going to close down any significant part of this building, short of a bomb threat.

In the corridor on the ninth floor leading to Jack's office
it was different. More police. I walked firmly ahead. Jack
had a small office about twenty doors down. I walked toward it as if I was going right in.

"Whaddaya want?"

The officer who stopped me was standing, feet apart, his
hands behind his back, large stomach well to the fore, about
two doors short of Jack's office. I looked around for people I knew—Dorothy Furman, Doris Furman Sligh, or
Hector Furman, Jr., for example—but they weren't there.
Off being questioned, no doubt.

"I have an appointment," I said.

"Not down this corridor you ain't."

"Yes, I have. I had an appointment for eleven. I'm late."

"You're gonna be later. Who do you want to see?"

I had thought I might get close enough by bluff. Now it
looked like I'd get closer yet. I'd be the next interviewee.
"Jack Sligh," I said.

"Oh, is that so?"

"Yes, Officer. Eleven A.M." This gentleman was not one
of their brightest lights.

"You reporters give me a pain. How stupid do you think
I am? Get back downstairs with the rest of 'em, and the
chief'll give you all a statement when he's good and ready."

"I'm not a—" Well, then again, I am a reporter. "I really did have an appointment with Mr. Sligh."

" 'Did have,' huh? So you *do* know he's dead."

Well, so he was only half dumb. "Look, I had a legiti-
mate appointment. Tell somebody about it. You send me
away, they find my name in his appointment book, they
come and ask me about it and I tell them Officer—" I

looked at his name tag and unit designator "—Woldheim from the First District wouldn't let me in."

A couple of seconds went by. Then he bellowed, "Sarge! You wanna talk to this lady?"

If Woldheim was a red-faced white man, Sarge was a tan-faced black man. He had a trace of impatience with Woldheim in his manner as he strode over, but not enough so the public in general would notice. More like "Wait'll I get you home."

Sarge was about to take charge, which he probably did all day every day, when somebody bellowed, "Cat! Yo!"

Woldheim froze. Sarge froze. Not me, though. I knew that voice. I said, "McCoo! Thank goodness."

Woldheim and Sarge—the name on his tag was Smith—stood back with a great deal more respect. McCoo was at the door of an office opposite Jack Sligh's. He waved me inside, saying "Everybody out" to a couple of plainclothes officers, a man and a woman.

"Trust you to find the office with the coffee machine," I said.

"You call this coffee?" McCoo shivered. He'd put on a little weight lately, and when he shivered, it had a lot of body English. The office obviously belonged to somebody who made coffee for everybody else in the wing. There was a large urn, sugar and diet sweetener envelopes, fake cream, a lot of Styrofoam cups, and some pottery mugs with sayings on them: LOTTERY. COFFEE IS ALWAYS A GOOD BET. CAFFEINE TO GO. BOSS. DFS. BINGO! One of them said JACK. This had to be the lottery people's coffeepot. We investigative reporters know how to deduce things.

Deputy Chief McCoo said, "These people don't know how to make coffee."

"Just because Harold McCoo is the greatest coffee brewer in the state of Illinois—"

"In the world."

"In the world, doesn't give him the right to criticize humbler brewers."

"People like this shouldn't be allowed to touch coffee."

He poured a cup and handed it to me. I sipped. "It's bad, but it's not terrible. If you ever visit me, I'll be afraid to make coffee. You're so fussy—"

"If I visit, I'll make the coffee."

"Oh. Deal."

"And I'll bring the ingredients."

"McCoo, aren't you too important to come out to crime scenes?"

"Come on. This isn't just any crime scene. A big lottery official takes a leap in the middle of a multistate lottery conference? In the Loop? At midday? We're talking high-profile case here."

"A leap? You mean you think he committed suicide?"

He closed up on me. "Not necessarily. Maybe yes, maybe no. We'll see what the techs have to tell us." Surprisingly, he became even more serious. "Okay, Cat. Now that the ceremonies are done, tell me this. You were heading toward Jack Sligh's office."

"Right."

"You were going to march right in as if you had an appointment."

"I did have an appointment."

"Oh?"

"Even so, I admit I didn't think I'd actually get in. I thought I might *see* in."

"Mmm-mmm. And why did you want to see in?"

"To find out what had happened to him."

"How did you know anything had happened to him? Somebody talking about it down in the street?"

"No, I saw him fall. You'd have found my name in the reports once they get them all collected, I suppose." I told him about my mother, and what we'd seen.

When I got done, he said, "Uh-hunh. You claim you had an appointment with Jack Sligh?"

"That's what I just said. At eleven." McCoo is a friend. The tone of his question didn't sound friendly.

"Look at this."

He pushed Jack's appointment book toward me. I looked but didn't touch it. The page was open to today, Tuesday. There were the times of day running down the left side of the page, with blank lines next to them for the user to fill in. There was a perfectly understandable note next to nine A.M., reading "Bkfst IA NE IN, Plmr. Hse." Then ten A.M., "Collect ads." There was another note: "Agcy Inch Shmr" opposite the one P.M. time. Apparently it was going to be a long lunch, because there was nothing else noted down during the afternoon. Maybe he was going to the panel on satisfying special interest groups. The last entry was simply "din." opposite seven P.M., and that was it.

There was nothing at all written opposite eleven A.M.

"You're not in here, Cat."

"Well, he made the appointment yesterday and I was meeting him here. At this office. Today."

"All right. How do you read these entries?"

"Pretty obvious, most of them. The first one means the Iowa, Nebraska, and Indiana delegations were meeting with him for breakfast. At the Palmer House. At ten he gets the ads together. Some agency for lunch at one. Probably the agency that actually makes up the ads for the lottery. The dinner has to be some big conference function, probably the scheduled one in Greek Town, or else he'd say who it was with. Unless it was with a woman friend. He's in the middle of a divorce."

"We know that."

"Oh."

"What about 'Shmr'?"

"Beats me. But since it's lunch, and we're at—um— LaSalle and Randolph, I would call up the Shamrock Lounge on Randolph and see if he had lunch reservations. It's walking distance."

"How well do you know Jack Sligh?"

"What is this, McCoo? I've met him twice. Both times yesterday. Monday. Once to interview him more or less in depth, once just in passing to talk to."

"That's all?"

"Yes, that's all."

McCoo moved papers around on his borrowed desk until he got the one he wanted. It was a small sheet, maybe three by five inches, torn from a notepad. It was inside a polyethylene protective sleeve, the kind the evidence techs carry around for preserving flat evidence like papers. "This was found in an inside pocket on the body. In Sligh's vest. A watch pocket. You can touch the plastic sleeve," McCoo said.

I pulled it toward me. Half of the paper inside was soaked with blood, but the black pencil notation was still readable. It said: "RLP Marsala n. attrib."

McCoo said, "Okay. Wanta explain this?"

SEVEN

"I CAN'T."

"What's RLP?"

"I haven't the foggiest idea."

"You deciphered the calendar entries."

"Well, I can't decipher this! 'N. attrib.' must mean 'not for attribution.' RLP is probably somebody's initials. But if I don't know the name, I can't guess it from the initials, damn it!"

"You sure you *don't* know those initials?"

"Hey! What do you think I am? I'm not trying to sabotage you, and I'm not trying to solve the case myself and spring the solution on you! I've never heard of RLP, whatever he, she, or it is! What's the matter with you anyway? You weren't acting like this when I saw you this morning."

"We hadn't had a murder this morning."

"You have murders every morning!"

He sighed and frowned. "Cat, you'd best get out of here and let me work."

I left.

WHAT WAS *that* all about? He was angry about something or other, plus he wasn't the expansive, open person he had been as long as I'd known him. Had I done something to tick him off? I couldn't think of anything.

Of course, if he hadn't been so crabby I might have remembered to tell him about Jack catching me on the street and asking if I did exposés. And hinting at theft from the lottery. Which definitely would be something McCoo would want to know about. Which meant that, even if he didn't have any reason to be crabby at me before, he sure as hell had now.

However, I could worry about that later. I was here on the ninth floor, nobody was asking me to leave (in fact, the session with McCoo probably validated me in the eyes of the rest of the cops), and if I didn't actually force my way into Jack's office, they probably wouldn't send me away.

Which put me ahead of the rest of the Chicago press. This might come in handy. For a while I hung around the central pool where the four secretaries' desks were. The casual conference-goers and press had been kicked out, so it wasn't nearly as crowded as the day before.

It was one-thirty now. I had missed lunch, and I didn't see any vending machines on this floor. But I couldn't leave, or they might never let me back up.

After talking with McCoo in the morning I had made an appointment with old Hector Furman, Sr., for two P.M. Maybe he'd still be here, or maybe he'd been so shocked by the murder that he'd gone home.

Plus the four-thirty appointment with Hector Junior. I had better hang around this wing, starvation or no starvation.

I WALKED DOWN the farther of the two Lottery corridors—not the one that led to Jack's office, but the matching one on the other side. I was careful to stop short of the elevator area in the middle of the building, thinking that if I got that far away and tried to come back the cops would think I was coming from the Cook County Engineers section, or worse, downstairs, and they might not let me back in. I passed a uniformed police officer, sitting on one of the guard's stools. He had stood up when he heard me coming, probably thinking I was a sergeant. He sat down again when he saw it was me.

I passed him again as I came back. "Walking off some tension," I said. He nodded but didn't speak.

Back in the central Lottery pool, I stood quietly next to the secretaries' artificial ficus tree, pretending to read notes on my pad, and eavesdropped on three secretaries talking, two across the desks between them, while a third sat on the edge of one of the desks. Judging by their voices, one was sedate and properly funereal. The other two were fascinated.

"Well, that's what they *say* it was."

"That's right. 'Probable suicide,' the cute one said."

"Not Jack."

"Why not?"

"Well, they must know he wasn't the type."

"How would they know that? They never met him," said the sedate voice.

"Maybe somebody told them."

"The police never believe what people say, anyhow."

"Anybody can commit suicide. Get a fit of despondency, a sudden desire to end it all—"

"Oh, bull!"

"Well—"

"Only sudden desire that man ever got was *sudden desire*."

Whispering: "Did he ever come on to you?"

"You kidding? Didn't he come on to everybody?"

"Well, I certainly didn't take him up on it."

"I thought he was just talking—" the sedate one said. Somebody giggled.

"No, you didn't take him up on it?"

"Cheryl!" said the sedate one.

"Well, I'm not telling!"

"Jeez! You moron!" said one of the cheerful ones.

"Yeah?" said Cheryl. "And what about you?"

Silence.

Maybe they saw me standing there. Maybe they were just shocked at Cheryl. Anyway, I didn't turn around. Casually, I made a few squiggles with my pen on my pad, then sauntered off to see how close I could get to Jack's office without being headed off by the gendarmes.

Naturally, when I was there the day before, I had not been looking at Jack's office as a potential murder scene. But I remembered the narrow, rather tall sash window. Probably accident had been dismissed by the detectives mainly because of that window. It wasn't any wider than a pair of human shoulders—too narrow for anybody falling toward it to be unable to grab the frame. Besides that, the lower window probably only went up eighteen inches or two feet. Sash windows with counterweights in the frame will only go up as far as the point where the rope that's attached to the window reaches the pulley in the frame. Every old building I'd ever lived in had windows like those.

So the choice was suicide or murder.

I couldn't get near Jack's office anyhow. The police had strung yellow barrier tape across the hall, starting five feet on either side of his office door. People who worked in the offices beyond this part of the hall had to go away, toward the other side of the building, to the elevators between us and the Cook County Engineers side, and come back around if they wanted to get to the secretaries' pool or anyplace else in this end of the building.

What all my corridor exploration brought home to me, though, was this: You could get to Jack's office, if you wanted to kill him, from anywhere else in the building. From downstairs, no problem. From the offices around on the other corridor, even from the Cook County Engineers side. Say your office was near the secretaries' pool. You could go toward his office from this side, step in, kill him, step back out, and go *away* from this end of the corridor. Keep walking to the elevators in front of the Engineers, go around to the end of the matching S-corridor and back to the secretaries' pool and from there to your office. Nobody in here would see you coming away from Jack's door.

While I was standing there ruminating, somebody came up behind me and said, ''Boo!''

I knew the voice.

"It had to be you, Bramble. I hope you noticed I didn't jump."

It was Officer Bramble, a woman who had been secretary to McCoo a year ago, and judging from the fact that she was here, probably still was secretary or some such. Bramble was tall, slender, black, and wore her hair *very* short and her uniform *very* crisp. She had always seemed to regard me as McCoo's Folly, sort of a retarded media pet that he indulged. She had never told me her first name.

"Detecting?" she said.

"Deducing, anyway."

"What've you figured out?"

"With the crowd in here yesterday, just about anybody in the building could have slipped in and murdered him. From either direction."

"Haven't you heard? It was suicide."

"Oh? That's apparently what the co—you people are telling the civilians."

"Okay."

"But McCoo said murder. Even the secretaries know Jack wasn't the suicide type."

"Mmm." She peered at me from her greater height, trying to decide if I was lying to pump her or if McCoo had really told me murder. She apparently decided that while I was a civilian, I was a relatively honest civilian. And I was the boss's little buddy. She nodded grudgingly.

"Also," I said, "I would personally doubt suicide. This guy thought he was the bee's knees. The real McCoy. Better than good."

"Mmm," she said.

"But the cops don't know that. So what makes them know he didn't defenestrate himself?"

"Figured he wouldn't've hit himself with the telephone first," she said, patting her gun.

"How did you know somebody hit him with the telephone?" I asked her. "Blood or hairs?"

"On the phone? No. We knew because it was clean."

"What do you mean?"

"No fingerprints. Not one. Not even Jack Sligh's. How many people you know wipe the telephone every time they use it? Every part?"

Matter of fact, nobody I know.

I had weaseled this information out of Bramble. And it was information that McCoo hadn't been willing to tell me—in fact, had intentionally not told me when I asked directly. Bramble had walked into what could have been a bad situation for her. But even though I may have been unscrupulous in getting the information out of her by trickery— lying, actually—I would never use it against her. I would be extremely careful not to let on to McCoo that I knew it was murder until he told me himself or revealed it to the press.

I have my scruples, in my own way.

EIGHT

PART OF THE TIME I spent in the library yesterday had been basics—confirming what Dorothy Furman had told me. You can get into serious trouble taking the uncorroborated word of an interested party and printing it. But she was completely accurate wherever I could check her out.

The other part of what I was doing was trying to get an idea of what the odds were of winning various lottery games. An hour of that made me wish I'd taken more math courses in college.

So I thought I might get the down-and-dirty version of the odds from the elder Hector Furman.

Plus, everything else about gambling was a mystery to me, too. What was "policy"? What was or were "numbers"? What were "numbers runners"?

I walked down the hall to Hector Furman's office, thinking he might not be there. He was said to be semiretired anyhow. If he'd been very shocked by the apparent suicide, he might have gone home to rest. After all, he was an elderly man.

Hector Furman looked all of seventy-five. He was slightly stooped as if he'd had back problems, and his skin was pale and yellowish. He looked frail but mentally he was full of vigor. And he had the most beautiful head of silky white hair I had ever seen. There was no gray in it, no pepper-and-salt. It fitted his head like a wavy helmet. I knew he was vain about it, because he had it cut a little longer than was the style for men his age, and it was freshly combed, the tooth marks of the comb still showing. He waved me into his office with a wide gesture from an arm clad in shirt-sleeves and old-style sleeve garters. I guessed he liked to put on a gambler's appearance.

"You object to this?" he said, waving his cigar.

"It's your office, Mr. Furman."

"I like that answer."

"I was surprised to find you here. I thought you might want to go home after—you know, the accident."

"You think it was an accident?"

"No."

"Well, then don't be a mealymouth, girl. The man was a wimp and he offed himself. Anyway, why would I go home? You want me to miss all the excitement?"

This was not a deeply shocked elderly man. "But he was your son-in-law."

"Was is right. Doris was about to shuck him off. You want me to be upset? I'm upset he treated her bad. Okay?"

"Okay with me." I matched him, tone for tone. He seemed pleased. He grinned and punched his cigar toward me two or three times, making little lopsided smoke rings. "Now tell me what you've heard about me."

"Um." This wasn't what I wanted to talk about.

"You've heard I used to run book, betting parlors, all that crap, right?"

"Yes. So it's not the truth?"

"Oh, it's the *truth*, all right. But don't print it or I'll sue." He laughed. Laughed so hard he cackled. "Actually, I wouldn't give a tinker's damn. My children would, though. *They'd* sue. So you'd better not do it."

"I don't intend to. It's the lottery I want to know about." I liked him, and I felt it would work to ask him straight out. "They say you came in and fixed it. That the—the managers, whatever—didn't know how to run a lottery."

"Oh, hell, girl. They didn't know shit. This started—legal lotteries—in New Hampshire, New Jersey first. They were bookkeepers and businessmen. What did they know about how to get people to bet?"

"Didn't know beans, I imagine."

"They thought, Well, we'll have a few nice ticket outlets, people will seek them out. Sure! And we'll have three-dollar tickets. That's cheap enough. Sure! And a drawing once a week. Oh, yeah, *that's* gonna work great! First few years of the New Jersey lottery, sales went in the toilet. We lent 'em a little advice when New Jersey started up. Fifty-cent ticket, none of this three-dollar shit, and it helped. The Illinois lottery had *dismal* sales at first, flatliners for years, but I straightened them up."

"How?"

"More outlets. You think some guy gets off work he's gonna take a bus, change buses, to go buy a lottery ticket? Hell, no! Cheaper tickets! More games! More frequent drawings. Some of these people buy tickets, they aren't the type want to wait to dinnertime, much less the end of the week. Instant game. Bigger payouts. Plus play value. Choosing your own numbers. The first lotteries were completely passive. Take a number. Shit! People want to bet their lucky numbers! Plus, believe it or not, people liked it when we increased the physical size of the ticket itself. Besides, what I said to these guys first thing I walked in, I said, *Think about what you gotta compete with!*"

"What do you compete with?"

"Oh, girl, you have not been around. Well, numbers is the main thing. The most popular illegal bet."

"What is numbers?"

He cocked his eyebrow at me as if I were a fool. Somehow, coming from him, I wasn't annoyed.

"See, numbers is kind of like policy, but simpler. It's just what it says. Every day there's a three-digit number, drawn at random."

"Yes, but this is an illegal game, isn't it? How do people who play it know it isn't fixed?"

"It's taken from something the local people can't fix. Like the first three digits of the exact cash payout at a local race-track. Bolita is the Hispanic version, and it's the number drawn by the Puerto Rican lottery."

"Oh. Okay."

"Numbers been around seventy, eighty years. See, you pick three digits, either in the exact order you bet they'll come up, or in certain combinations. Say your lucky number is—"

"I don't have one."

His eyebrows shot up. "Everybody has one."

I had noticed his room number coming in. "Nine one four."

"Cute. You may be ignorant, but you're smart. Say you pick 914 in that exact order. Your probability of winning is one in a thousand."

"I don't see that."

"What are they teaching you kids these days? There are a thousand possible combinations from 000 to 999. You've just picked one of them."

"Oh. When you put it that way, I get it."

"But now say you want to bet a 'box.' Your lucky number is 914, but you'll take it as a box, which means all six possible combinations of nine, one, and four—914, 941, 149, 194, 419, and 491. See? Six. Or you do a 'bolita.' That's two digits. Or 'single action,' which is one digit. Single action they give you seven to one."

"You're much more likely to win with a box."

"Sure. But you win less money. That's the thing. The more likely the combo is of winning, the less it pays off."

"Makes sense."

"Now with numbers they'll let you make small daily bets, five cents even, every day, if you want, on your favorite combination. They'll even give you credit. Numbers runners'll come to you for the bet. Take telephone bets. These guys take a ten percent tip, plus they collect on commission."

"Tips? Really?" A detail I was sure would come in handy.

"Plus there's a whole industry grown up around this business. Dream books."

"*Dream books?* What on earth are they?"

"Patience, little girl. Dream books are little books people buy to help them translate their life experiences, and their dreams, and their names, and so on into lucky numbers."

"Like what?"

"Take a simple one. Your nickname you said is Cat. *C* is the third letter of the alphabet, *A* is the first letter, *T* is the—"

I counted on my fingers. "Twentieth."

"You add the two and zero of twenty, 'cause you can't use it otherwise. Except in four-number lotteries. So one of your lucky numbers is 312. That's also your area code, so it's doubly lucky. Another lucky number for you is six."

"Six?"

"Three and one and two added. There's numbers for the devil, like 666. There's numbers for death—in most dream books it's 769. If you dream of death, you bet them. Plus, people bet media events. When Hank Aaron was about to break Babe Ruth's record of 714 home runs, every numbers game in the country was swamped with 715. In four-digit lotteries in 1982, people were betting the lot number of the cyanide-laced Tylenol pills, 2880."

"That's ghoulish!"

"That's folks for you, girl, and folks are ghoulish. They bet 2880 up to the lottery limit and the officials had to halt betting. Now let's see. On July Fourth, you get a lot of 1776. Generally, the most popular numbers are things like 333, 777, and 555. Or 711."

"What are the least popular?"

"Oh, like 893, 091, 887, 968. They don't mean anything to most people. Of course, if one of 'em was your office number, now—" he laughed.

"What do these things pay off?"

"The illegal numbers pay about five or six hundred to one, except for the really popular numbers that pay maybe three hundred to one."

"What's 'policy,' then?"

"Policy started out as bets on the lottery outcomes. Main thing about it is it's very cheap. I mean *cheap*, you can bet pennies. Policy is real popular in Chicago. There's a lot of wheels—"

"Wheels?"

"Wheels are the shops. They've got pickup men who take bets. You pick three numbers. You make, say, a ten-cent investment, you might collect twenty dollars."

"If people are betting pennies, the wheels can't make much."

"Oh, hell, girl! Some of the policy wheels in Chicago gross twenty million dollars a year. And there are a lot of them, too. This is serious business."

My mind was whirling. "You used to do this? Run these policy wheels? Or numbers?"

"Hey! Let me put it this way. I had my house in Northbrook with the swimming pool fifteen years before the state had a lottery."

"And they're still doing well? I thought one of the reasons for the state lotteries was to close down the illegal betting." McCoo had said it still went on, but who could be sure?

"Oh, sweetheart, not nearly. Look at it from the consumer's point of view. Not only in the legal game he gets no credit, no bets under fifty cents, and no runners, but on top of that, if he wins big, his winnings can be *taxed*!"

"Oh." That last reason made a lot of sense.

"And plus, illegal lotteries have a better payout."

"What's payout?"

"It's the percentage of the pot that's paid to winners. Illegal lotteries pay out maybe ninety percent. That's called 'action.' It's the opposite of 'takeout.' Takeout is what the commission or whoever removes for themselves before awarding prizes. If takeout is fifty-one percent, payout is forty-nine percent. See? Legal lotteries pay out forty-five, fifty, fifty-two percent, tops. Less action. Their takeout is say, fifty percent. Illegal lotteries, takeout is ten per cent.

You tell me this, girl—it's Illinois that's really skimming serious money. So why are the illegal numbers and policy so evil?"

"You got me there. Are the games really the same, though?"

"Carbon copies. You got your front pair bets, your back pair bets, four-way box, six-way box, twelve-way box. Twenty-four-way box, combos, straights—"

"Hold it. Go back to front pair."

"Nothing to it. Just means you're betting your two numbers will be the first two drawn. Back pair's the last two. Boxes, like I was saying before. Like twenty-four-way box is the twenty-four different combinations of four numerals. Straight, like in poker, exact order."

"What are the big winning games?"

"Lotto."

"Which one is that?"

"You kidding? No, you're not kidding. You may be naive, but you're honest. Well, most states, Illinois too, let you pick your own numbers, like this: Choose six different numbers between one and fifty-four. You register your numbers. They draw the winning numbers on television, 'cause this is the big game. I mean your Quick Cash instant stuff they just pay you at the retailer. But not these. Okay— to be the big winner you gotta get all six."

"What are the chances of that?"

He grinned. "One in fourteen million."

"Jeez."

"Six out of six, the big winner, wins half the whole prize pool. But the rest of the prize pool gets divided up. It goes to the people who got four out of six and five out of six. If you get four out of six you win a smaller prize, and five out of six a not-so-small prize."

"What if nobody gets it right?"

"It rolls over." He waved his hand. "Don't ask. Rollover means that week's grand prize gets added to next week's. That's where you get your *tremendous* prizes.

Which is good for the game. Which is why lotteries don't tell the most popular numbers. You get bigger prizes with less coverage.''

"What's—"

"Coverage? Right. It's the percent of possible number choices that actually get chosen by at least one player. A random-number lottery increases the coverage. See why?"

"Because people won't cluster on popular numbers."

"Good. You may be uninformed, but you pay attention. Lotteries don't tell people that betting certain numbers reduces the chance of a big pot. But it does, see, because it's a pari-mutuel system. *Which means* everyone who bets on a number shares in the pot if that number wins. It's like horse race winnings. Racetracks have pari-mutuel betting. So at least if you want to improve your odds of winning big, you don't play 777 or 7777 or 711. See? Play something like 831.''

"But is it a good bet?"

"A good *bet*? Girl, there's no such thing. Why, there's slot machines in Vegas they claim have a ninety-five percent payout, and you still lose more money the longer you play. Plus, that's casino puffery. But Vegas, Atlantic City, those places, the gambling commission comes around and tests the machines. They got a minimum—every machine has to pay out seventy percent or else. And even that's better than the lottery. The Illinois lottery returns more to the players than most, and it's still just over fifty percent. But what a handle!"

"What's a handle?"

"Handle is the total amount of bets. The gross."

"And the lottery's handle is—"

"Two billion dollars."

Well, yes. That was hefty.

"I'll tell you this—once we got them to do a real lotto, where you pick your own numbers, and had lots of retail outlets, and got jackpots over a hundred million dollars, growth was explosive. Lotto was the real turnaround. It's megabucks now. The Illinois lottery is big enough to be a Fortune 500 company.''

''Does that mean it's a good bet? You said there's no such thing as a good bet.''

''Well, small winners in any game hardly ever get any-place. Small winners almost all immediately rebet it all. Let alone the odds are against them. Now, the instant games are a pretty bad bet.''

''But?''

''Well, all in all, if you play the lottery *only after* several rollovers, and you bet unpopular numbers so you're not gonna share the prize if you win, then with what you can make if you happen to win, it's not the worst bet in the world.''

''Oh, okay.''

''But I'll tell you this. You put the same amount of money into learning to run a word processor, get a career, you're way better off.''

He barked with laughter, his body jiggling as he did. Suddenly, he said, ''Holy shit!'' and clutched the arms of his chair. He froze and held very still.

''What's the matter, Mr. Furman?'' I had jumped up. Was he having a heart attack?

''Goddamn back! Can you get my daughter?''

I was going to run to Dorothy's office, which was at the farthest end of the floor, when he said, ''Doris. Right there.'' He pointed at the wall to the right of his desk. I took this to mean that she was in the office next door.

She was. ''Your father's having some sort of back spasm,'' I said.

She and I hurried into Furman's office. He was still fro-zen in place, saying ''Damn! Damn! Damndamndamn.''

Doris Furman walked behind him. ''All right. I'm going to tilt you back, now.'' She reached both hands under his armpits and pulled gently upward. Her knee held the seat of the chair in place, and the pulling upward and backward caused the chair to lean back to its reclining position. Hector Furman gritted his teeth until she got him settled in a semi-reclining position. Then he sighed.

"Special chair," he said to me.

Doris was rummaging in the desk. She came out with a bottle of pills. She went to the bookshelves and picked up a bottle of sparkling water, filled a glass, and came back. "One or two?" she asked.

"One. It's not too bad."

She gave him a pill.

"It's a muscle relaxant," she said to me. She probably wondered why I didn't have the good sense to leave, but in my job I've learned to give in to my curiosity. She looked back at her father. "You stay right there at least half an hour. I'll check back."

Then, he closed his eyes; she walked to the door, and naturally, I had to follow.

"He gets over it quickly," she said, closing his door behind us. "It's some sort of disk problem, and he doesn't want to have surgery."

"I can't say I blame him." I held out my hand. "I'm Cat Marsala. I'm writing a story on the lottery." I'd seen her yesterday, but I wasn't sure she'd seen me, and we certainly hadn't been introduced. She'd been busy telling Jack to take a hike.

"Doris Furman Sligh."

So she hadn't gone home this afternoon either, even though her husband had been killed.

"I'm very sorry about your husband's death, Mrs. Sligh."

"Ex-husband." She went into her office and I followed. Here there were no papers on the desk at all, and only two posters on the walls, a Quick Cash ad and a Lotto ad.

"I didn't know you were divorced."

"We weren't quite. Close. We were negotiating." She said the word "negotiating" so bitterly that I let it drop.

"I suppose you've been questioned a lot by the police."

"Why would you suppose that?"

"It's standard operating procedure. You were his wife."

"Hmph. They talked to everybody on the floor."

"I'm doing a story on the lottery. Could I ask you a few questions?"

"I'm in a hurry."

She must have meant in a hurry to go someplace. There wasn't any work in evidence. "Two minutes?"

"All right." In personality, Doris was by no means the same as her sister Dorothy. Where Dorothy was vigorous, Doris was sluggish, where Dorothy was voluble, Doris would hardly talk, where Dorothy was enthusiastic, Doris was all but sullen. Dorothy's black shoe-button eyes were duplicated here in Doris, but in Doris they looked flat and blank. And it wasn't the fact of her husband's death or the investigation. She had looked the same yesterday.

"May I ask what your position is?"

"I am a senior stores coordinator."

"What does that mean?"

"The lottery has retail outlets. They have to be chosen. Not every store that wants to sell lottery tickets gets to sell lottery tickets."

"Why not?"

She smiled. It was a humorless smile. "The stores that already are selling tickets want to keep as much business as possible, of course."

"Well, you also want to get as many outlets as close to the consumer as possible, don't you?"

"Yes. Not just any store, though."

"What do you mean?"

"We want a store that reflects well on the lottery. It doesn't look good if the store is dirty, or dingy and dark. And naturally we don't want anybody with a criminal background selling tickets."

"Could somebody like that rip you off? Go through all the tickets you give him to sell and pick out the winners for himself? Like in Quick Cash, where you rub off the covering over the numbers?"

"No," she snapped. "There is absolutely no way for a store owner to fix the lottery."

"But you just said—"

"The only reason we don't want crooks as store owners is for appearance. It doesn't look good. Suppose somebody bought a winning ticket in the store and it turned out later the owner had a record? You press people would have a field day."

"I see."

"Now, Ms. Marsala, I'm sorry, but I've got to get to a meeting. This is a busy week."

That was true. But she wasn't sorry to get rid of me, and I wondered if there was any special reason. She sure didn't cite Jack's death as upsetting her or making her want to go home and lie down with a damp towel on her forehead. Maybe she just didn't like talking with reporters. As much as some people love to talk to writers and hope to see their words and their names in print, others cringe at the idea.

"Thank you," I said, holding out my hand.

She shook it, very briefly, very limply.

AT FOUR-THIRTY I was at the door of Hector Furman, Jr.'s office. I knocked.

Without calling "Come in" or anything else, he threw the door open. Hector Junior was like a negative of his father. But where Hector Senior had a helmet of beautiful white hair, Junior's was black. Where the elder Hector was sallow-skinned, Hector Junior was tanned. Well, he had told me he'd just come back from the Bahamas, or was it Trinidad?

He barked, "What is it?"

"We had an appointment. Four-thirty."

"Well, you can't possibly expect me to talk with you now!"

"Why not?"

"Good God! My brother-in-law has just killed himself. We're in a complete uproar here. And right in the middle of the conference, and we can't even leave the building—"

"I just came from Doris's office. She didn't seem too upset." I didn't mention that his father wasn't upset, either.

He peered closely at me. "Doris is very good at concealing her emotions."

"Well, but they were getting a divorce, too."

"They were separated. Nothing final had been done. They might have gotten back together."

While I was thinking that a possibility of reconciliation looked farfetched to me, he said, "Thursday. Eleven."

"What?"

"I'll see you Thursday at eleven." And he closed the door. Eleven A.M., I thought, was an ill-omened time for an appointment.

NINE

I WAS BEING TORN by two separate and partly opposing needs.

I had to write the article, but I also wanted to find Jack's murderer. I wanted revenge. Whoever killed Jack had thrown him out of a window nine floors above a busy street. It was an extra level of callousness, beyond whatever conflict the murderer had with Jack, to take a chance on killing innocent, uninvolved people. It was sheer luck Jack's falling body hadn't killed somebody. If he'd fallen a second later, the older woman whose arm was injured could easily have died.

I had more personal reasons, too. My mother didn't receive any physical impact from the body. But the emotional impact on her was severe. She has kept strictly away from violence all her life and was truly shocked. I may have forced her into the hospital, but I did it because I knew she needed the reassurance right then; going home with the image of Jack in her mind would have been a nightmare for her. A night in the hospital would put a little space between the event and her normal life.

And I owed Jack something, too. I went to find the person most likely to have killed him.

"I'D LIKE to talk with you."

"You are—" Seymour Dennisovitch eyed me warily. He remembered me, but he had that look on his face of a person who couldn't remember quite where he had seen me before.

"Cat Marsala," I said. "I'm doing a story on the lottery."

"Oh. Of course!" He said of course, but he still didn't remember that I had been one of the people separating him and Jack after the fight. I didn't want to remind him, either. The less he knew about what I knew the better.

We were in the anteroom of the Stratford Hotel meeting room where most of the panels were being held. I'd figured I could find him there, because he had been a speaker on the four o'clock panel, "Satisfying Special Interest Groups."

Two women wearing badges that identified them as Kentucky delegates came toward us, but veered off when they saw Dennisovitch turn away from them to focus on me. A Wyoming delegate passed carrying his Stetson in his hand, said, "Good points you made," and kept walking.

"Were you representing Gamblers Anonymous on the panel?" I asked.

"No, no. Absolutely not. Gamblers Anonymous is nonpolitical."

"Really?"

"We don't take stands on any political issue. Not as a group. I'm here as a private citizen."

"So you came to explain your view on what? Whether there ought to be a lottery at all?" I was working up to my big question. What I wanted was to know where he'd been this morning about ten-thirty when Jack was killed. There'd been a panel at the time that ran from ten A.M. to noon. I knew that Dorothy, Doris, and the two Hectors had been in the Lottery hall from the fact that they were still there when I arrived after the police had buttoned it up. But I didn't know about my leading suspect, Dennisovitch.

He said, "No. I haven't got anything against the lottery. What I would like to see is a percentage of lottery profits set aside for the treatment of compulsive gamblers."

"Oh." I readied my question. "Then why didn't you go to the double panel today on lotteries, pro and con?"

"How did you—I didn't go because I was going to say what I wanted to say here this afternoon."

"So why did you hang around the Lottery wing at City Hall?"

"I wanted to talk with some of the delegates. Informally. What's it to you, anyway?"

"Nothing, really. Sorry to be nosy." So he had been there. I wondered whether McCoo knew. Had Dennisovitch left before the police showed up?

I said, "Mainly I want to understand how compulsive gamblers feel about all this. What does Gamblers Anonymous do for gamblers, anyway? Is it like Alcoholics Anonymous?" I was familiar with AA because of Mike.

"We're a lot like them. GA is based on the AA formula. The first Gamblers Anonymous meeting was in 1957 in Los Angeles. We have the twelve steps, like they do, only worded a little differently. We sometimes say that we really have two steps, though."

"What are they?"

"First, to recognize that we are powerless against gambling. Second, to stop thinking like a gambler."

"But how can you do that in practice?"

"We have to stay away from any place where gambling is taking place. It's just like taking that first drink."

"Do the members help each other? Do you go to somebody's house when he's in trouble, like AA does?"

"Not very often. It's not really the same as ingesting a chemical, like alcohol. We have meetings, and the idea is, come to meetings, get with the program, and don't gamble between meetings."

"It's a big group?"

"Not anywhere near as big as AA. We have fourteen meeting places in the Chicago area. Usually about fifteen to twenty people at a meeting. Sometimes as many as forty."

"Could I go to one?"

"Certainly not! It's anonymous. Unless you're a compulsive gambler?"

"No. I'm not. You hear a lot these days about alcoholism having a chemical basis, maybe a genetic cause. Do you think there's any such thing in compulsive gambling?"

"Who knows? There's zero research on this stuff. Personally, I think there's a kind of addictive personality. I've known too many people we've got off gambling and they go on alcohol or drugs or start overeating. What we say, though, at GA is the reason why we gamble doesn't make any difference."

"Okay. So what *do* you tell your people?"

"Our philosophy is to stop everything that's got a gambling element. Don't gamble on *anything*. Don't flip a coin to see who buys the coffee. Don't leave your business card in one of those fishbowls at restaurants where they draw to see who gets a free dinner. Don't even go on a company golf outing where other people are betting."

"What about the stock market?"

"Well, see," he said with a slight grin, "I used to be a commodities broker."

"Oh."

"We can own bonds and stable—you might say dull—stocks. But we can't buy options or play the commodities markets."

"Why so strict?"

"Well, see, you have to understand gamblers' psychology. Most of us have had a big win sometime or other, early on. If we didn't, we wouldn't have gotten hooked. If you lost your first bet and every bet you ever made, you'd stop soon. But what usually has happened is what psychologists call intermittent reinforcement. You get a big win now and then, 'big' being a relative term, of course. What's big to one person might be small to somebody else. And that's what hooks you. That's why these poker machines are getting a lot of people hooked. But every one of us, if we gamble on some small thing, like I was saying even if we just flip for who pays for the coffee, if we win, we'll tell ourselves, maybe the bad luck is over. We think Lady Luck has come back. And we'll be right into it again.''

"That's very interesting.'' He certainly sounded rational. I was writing as fast as he talked. "It's pretty clear you think the lottery will create new gamblers.''

"Yes, I do. Frankly, I wish we didn't have a lottery. But I don't oppose it. I think opposition is hopeless. We do need help, though, for people who are gambling their families' livelihoods away.''

"So that's why you were so furious at Jack Sligh?''

He blinked as if I had clapped my hands in front of his face. "No.''

"No?''

"There are plenty of people involved in the lottery. What infuriated me about Jack was that he thought I was funny. He thought the whole business of being a compulsive gambler was funny. As if we could just stop whenever we wanted to and we were just doing some psychobabble thing to—to glamorize our hobby!''

"I can see why that would get to you. So did you kill him?''

"Kill him? It was suicide.''

Did I believe him? Maybe. Maybe not. "What if it wasn't suicide?''

"I wouldn't have killed him. I despise him too much.''

AM I THE ONLY PERSON in the state of Illinois who has never bought a lottery ticket? Everybody looks at me as if I'm strange when I say I don't even know *how* to buy one.

So obviously that was the next step this Tuesday afternoon. I had to know what I was talking about here. Buy a lottery ticket. Do my research.

The sign in the window was a rainbow, a pot of gold, and the words *WE SELL LOTTERY TICKETS*! It was an ordinary convenience store, with snack foods, some canned goods, beer, wine, liquor, condoms, plastic-wrapped sandwiches, disposable diapers, toilet paper, magazines, paperback novels, a cooler with milk, juice, juice drinks, cold beer—just your basic end-of-the-twentieth-century necessities place.

Unfortunately, the clerk on duty was a girl in her late teens, or maybe as old as twenty-one but very young for her age. This was going to be difficult.

I waved a hand at the cheerfully bright lottery display.

"I'd like to buy a ticket."

"'ich wonyawant?"

"Uh. The—what is the one with the biggest prize?"

She looked at me with that special pity youngsters have for people over thirty. Obviously, my mind was going with age, along with the body-softening and general systems failure. But she was kind.

"Grand Lotto. That'sa biggest pot."

"Okay. And while you're at it, give me one of those."

"S'Quick Cash."

I gave her two dollars, which gave me a Quick Cash ticket and a Grand Lotto ticket.

"You get two games."

"What?"

"Lotto," she said patiently. "Ya got two games for a dollar. You c'n pick your numbers. Or Instant Pick picks 'em for you. There." She stabbed a finger at the boxes on the slip. She had very long fingernails, painted pale fuchsia.

"I'll pick my own." Apparently you filled in six two-digit numbers between 01 and 54 per game.

"Do ya lucky number," she urged.

"Right." Not having one, I followed Hector Furman's advice. Pick unpopular numbers, so that if you're lucky enough to win, you won't be likely to have to share the pot. So ruling out such numbers as 33, 44, 22, 07, and so on, I grabbed:

26-03-19-47-35-48 for the first drawing.

And 04-36-27-17-38-51 for the second drawing.

Okay. What could be more meaningless than that? The young woman entered the numbers on a computer terminal and handed me my ticket.

"Seven million this week. Hope ya win," she said cheerfully, snapping her bubble gum. "If ya do, ya c'n always gimme a tip."

We both laughed a lot.

I pocketed the Grand Lotto slip. The Quick Cash ticket was about two by three and a half inches. It was brightly printed in red, white, and blue. There was a serial number at the bottom. There were three rows of three spots each that I was supposed to scratch off. It happily informed me that if I found three bells in a row I would win $250, which would be paid to me immediately by the vendor. Three cherries would get me $100; three stars would get me $10, three apples $2, and three oranges would win a new ticket.

On the back was some miscellaneous information, including a statement of the odds. Apparently my chance of winning was exactly one in 3.7.

Well, gee. You can't say fairer than that. That's not so bad.

Right there in the store, I scratched the stuff off the spots. In the first row I got a bell, another bell—wow!—and an apple. Blast. Was this what Jack had meant about "heart-stoppers"?

Row two: an orange, a bell, and an orange.

Row three: an orange, an orange, and an orange! Yay! I had at least won a free ticket. I was about to claim it from the agent when I realized that taking the ticket home so I'd remember what it was like for purposes of the article would make more sense. No, that was silly. Turn it in, get another, and another chance of winning. I could take the second ticket home. I handed it in, got another, and crapped out.

Then I started to wonder just what a one in 3.7 chance of winning actually meant. After all, even if they gave out a free ticket with every single ticket, if every single ticket held three oranges, the chance of winning would be 100 percent, but *I wouldn't actually win anything*.

So really, the odds statement on the ticket didn't tell me anything, as long as it didn't tell how many "free ticket" wins were included in that figure. As long as it didn't tell how much chance there was of winning real cash money.

I took the tickets to the Clam, not far from City Hall, to study them while I ate a clam roll. The Grand Lotto said that if my six numbers came up, in any order, I would win the grand prize, which was 70 percent of the total prize pool. The young woman with the fuchsia nails had said it was seven million this week.

If I got five of the six, I'd get 10 percent of the total prize pool. If I got four of the six, I'd get 20 percent of the total prize pool. This seemed very strange to me until I realized that guessing four of the six right was certainly much easier to do, so there'd probably be several people who won. Therefore, this being a pari-mutuel system, they would share it out, and the shares wouldn't be as big as the person or persons who got five right and won 10 percent of the total pool.

Hot dog! For somebody who knew zero about this stuff a week before, I was learning!

WITH THE TICKETS in my pocket, I walked to the Rehab Institute, where my mother was eating dinner in bed. She seemed to enjoy this luxury, but didn't admit it. From her room phone I called my father again to report that she was okay and I'd have her home tomorrow morning. Then I dragged myself north fifteen blocks to my place.

What a day. And before I went to bed, I decided I'd better get a couple of pages done on the project I had put aside to take Hal's lottery assignment.

I was carrying my guilt about Jack Sligh around with me, too. I kept going over that last, hurried talk with him on the street. If I had been available to meet with him right then, would he still be alive? What had he wanted to talk about?

"Misappropriation of public funds" could mean almost anything from outright theft through fraud all the way down to plain incompetence.

I had kind of liked Jack. He was slick and maybe even shallow, but he was a bright face. So many people go around long-faced and sour; I really appreciate somebody who meets the day as if it's going to be interesting.

All these reflections on Jack were making *me* long-faced. As I rounded the corner to my street, I intentionally put on a jaunty walk and a bright look. Not quite a smile; put on a smile in the city and somebody will offer you fifty bucks for the night.

That was when I saw the dark blue Mercedes parked in front of my building. John, my other almost significant other.

"Hi, John," I said, peering in the car window. He was already getting out.

"Cat, did you forget it was your birthday?"

WHEN WE GOT inside my apartment, John took a box wrapped in blue paper out of a brown bag where he'd been hiding it. Long John Silver immediately swooped down and clawed at the ribbon.

"Hiya, LJ," John said.

I poured us each a glass of wine and we sat down. I sipped very slowly. After the day I'd had there was a chance of falling asleep on the spot.

LJ hopped off the package and flew up to the top of John's head, where he bent forward and pecked at John's horn-rimmed glasses. John laughed at him. John was always so nice to the bird. How was I going to tell him that I'd made a partial, iffy, semicommitment to Mike?

Like a coward, I said, "I'm working on a story about the lottery."

"No kidding? What aspect?"

"I'm not sure yet, but I think something about how it really works."

"You should talk to Bob Powers."

"Who's he?"

"He's the lottery attorney."

"They have their own attorney?"

"No. He's in a firm. One of the big LaSalle firms. Powers, Potenza and Ginsberg. Most of the city and county departments hire big-firm attorneys on retainer. The Board of Education, the Chicago Housing Authority, Parks, Streets and San, all that stuff. And a lot of these lawyers make a very sweet deal out of it, too."

"What does that mean? They overbill? They're paid for work they don't do?"

"Some of them. They get a PR advantage for the firm from it, too."

"Politics as usual. Chicago style."

"Happens everywhere. Are you going to open the present?"

"Oh." I unwrapped it. When I took the inside paper away from the thing, I still couldn't figure out what it was. It was about twelve inches in diameter, like a ball, but was really a dodecahedron or some such multisided figure, and the sides were mirrored.

"Gee. It's really excellent! A very nice thingish sort of thing!"

John laughed. "It's really for Long John Silver. Your present is coming, but it has to be scheduled."

I put the ball on the floor and rolled it toward LJ. He flew up, squawked, *braaaked* at it, and settled down. He eyed it, first with one wrinkled eye, then turning his head, tried looking at it with the other eye to see if it had changed.

Awwwaaaak!

He jumped up on it, which made it roll. He hopped down next to it and suddenly, from being an erudite, educated bird, returned to his infancy. "Pretty bird! Pretty bird!" he said. It must have been all those visions of himself in the mirrored facets that blew his mind.

Finally, recollecting his dignity, he stood more sedately, cocked his head, and said, "Is this the face that launched—"

I said, "Please!" to LJ and to John. "We've really got to talk."

"I know that expression on your face, Cat. It's your bad news expression."

John is a stockbroker. He's a very quiet, organized person, not at all like Mike. He is not impulsive. He not only makes a lot of money in his business, but his family has money. I have wondered whether the money, not his staid nature, makes me back off. In some perverse way, I know I don't want to be paid for—not that he would see it like that. But I like some aspects of the struggle. What I have, I've *earned*.

"John, listen. I've sort of told Mike that I'd consider moving in with him."

"What does 'sort of' mean?"

"Well, I guess it means I'm going to think about it."

"That means you're not sure."

"That's right."

"Then why is that any different from where we were before?"

"Well—" Yes, why was it any different? "It seemed different to me."

"At the time?"

"At the time. And now, too, I think. I want to be sure."

"Cat, listen. I think I've gone on too long being myself in a stuck-in-a-rut kind of way."

"No, that's wrong. Don't say that. You have to be the kind of person you feel like."

"I don't mean I'm going to put on some new coat of many colors. I mean I've just been myself, as if that were good enough, without ever explaining."

"You shouldn't have to explain yourself."

"Would you let me do this?" He smiled. "Sometimes you talk too much."

"And you don't talk enough?"

"Exactly. I know I'm traditional. I'm probably too quiet. Or—don't interrupt—not too quiet exactly, but too unclear. I'm well aware that other men are sometimes flamboyantly romantic. They send flowers or come over carrying candy, or do some bizarre, romantic gesture—"

I thought about Mike's "Bella Notte" dinner, of course.

"—and I don't," John went on. "But it's not that I can't think of these things. It's that somehow they seem demeaning, to me and to you. A fancy, useless gesture has a quality of treating you like a child, and you're not a child. It's like I'd be saying, 'Here's your cotton candy and roller-coaster ride.' But it's not real. Real is what you do that actually helps a person. Real caring isn't getting you a fantastic whatnot, but seeing a need and stepping in. It's like I'm saying, 'Here we are, two adults. I don't baby you, you don't baby me.' I suppose at bottom I think there's something insincere about the foolish but romantic gesture."

He shrugged and became quiet.

"I don't know what to say. Except, adult to adult, you've got a good point."

"Well, there it is, then. Anyhow, I hope you accept my birthday present. When it gets here."

"I don't know what you're planning to send me, but I really don't think you should. I have to think about this relationship."

"It's already done."

"But, see—"

"It's a toilet."

"It's a *what*?"

"It's a toilet. You need a new toilet."

I started to giggle, then laughed, then I howled, tears running down my cheeks. "Oh, John, you're priceless!"

"But look at this!" Jumping up, he strode to the bathroom. I had to follow; it was the only courteous thing to do.

"Look at that. It's permanently stained inside. It's horrible! And the seat's peeling."

"Oh, I know it's baaaad—" I couldn't finish. I started laughing again.

"The landlord won't replace it. You've called him."

"Every month since I moved in."

"This new one is dark blue, with an oak seat. It'll go with the walls."

"John, John." I took his hand and led him back to the sofa while I giggled.

He said, "They'll call in the morning and set up an installation time."

AFTER JOHN LEFT, I forced myself to write three pages of the other article. This was about a group of Chicago aldermen who were objecting to the displays in certain underwear store windows. The aldermen thought the displays were too "explicit." No kidding. It was supposed to run next week—with lots of pictures—in a local Streeterville paper, so I'd best get it done.

Somebody or other said that if you're a reporter, writer's block is what gets you fired. In my job, freelance, it's what makes you starve. I got those three pages done, thinking they'd have to be heavily revised. It was like squeezing toothpaste out of a dry tube. I was just too tired for it.

Then I fell into bed still wearing my sweatshirt.

I was dreaming about burning leaves in the autumn, a practice now outlawed in Chicago and most suburbs, but one that I loved as a child. I could smell the sweet odor of smoke. I could hear the crackle of the leaves.

Then quite suddenly my dream developed an ambulance. No, it was a siren that my dream was trying to incorporate.

It was my fire alarm!

I jumped out of bed.

The smoke around me was so thick I couldn't see the streetlights through the window. But I knew what you were supposed to do. I grabbed up the phone first and dialed 911 by feel. When they came on I shouted "Fire!" and my address.

Now I had to find LJ and get out of here.

There were flames coming from the kitchen. I ran for his cage in the living room, but he wasn't in it, and since I always let him fly around at night, he could be anyplace. I grabbed some sweatpants, thinking probably I was being stupid taking an extra ten seconds to get dressed, but I would be on the street in the next couple of minutes and didn't want to be out there in underwear.

"LJ!" By now I was getting more panicky. My throat was closing up from inhaling smoke. It was somewhat less thick near the floor, and I ran on all fours into the kitchen looking for the bird, but screaming and yelling "LJ!" didn't get any response.

A surge of flame hit me on the shoulder, singeing my hair. The fire was much worse in the kitchen. I ran on all fours to the front door. Would I die here looking for my parrot? I stood up, opened the apartment door, and jumped out. I abandoned LJ.

What about the people upstairs? I had to wake them. And Mr. Ederle downstairs. They were human, after all. The bird would have to wait.

With my eyes watering, or maybe I was crying about LJ, I raced up to the fourth floor barefoot and pounded on the door. I yelled *"Fire! Fire! Fire!"* Finally somebody came to the door.

Somebody opened it. I didn't wait to see who it was. They were up now and they'd know by the smoke that was now surging up the stairs like an inverted tornado that they had to get out.

I raced down, stumbling in my hurry, through the smoke to Mr. Ederle's door on two. I pounded and pounded again. He was somewhat hard of hearing. He wouldn't wake! I pounded and screamed.

Abruptly, I was pushed aside. It was a man in a black-and-yellow slicker and helmet. "Somebody in there?" he said.

"Yes! An old man. Please!"

"Get outdoors," he said. He reared back and smashed the bottom of one big foot against the door near the knob. It flew back. Way inside, I saw Mr. Ederle staggering out of his bedroom.

I turned to go back up to my apartment on three and find LJ.

An arm went around my waist.

It was a different fireman. "Don't do it," he said.

"I've got to get LJ!"

"Who is he?"

Behind this man, I could see the other fireman leading Mr. Ederle out.

"He's my parrot."

Other men were tramping up the stairs with a fire hose and some axes.

"Are there any people still up there?"

"Not on my floor. On four. But I have to get my parrot."

"No, you don't, lady," he said, and he started to pull me out. I fought back, and he pulled harder. Then the stair lights went out.

In half a minute he had me on the street. I ran over to the side the kitchen window opened on, not realizing I was barefoot and stepping on pieces of glass. There were orange flames just beginning to lick out through the window and up the outside wall.

I ran to the side where the bedroom window was, just in time to see a fireman break the glass with his ax. Smoke and black paper blew out. My article.

From one of the engines, a stream of water arched up, the fireman in my bedroom window ducked back, and the water reached my bedroom window and played back and forth inside it.

Long John Silver. Forty years old at least, he had lived through three owners. African gray parrots can live to be ninety years old. Did he have to die like this?

TEN

STANDING ON THE CURB, about to run to the other side of the building and look up again, I felt somebody put his arm around my waist. It was Mr. Ederle. He was an old man in a droopy, much-washed, dingy terrycloth bathrobe with the hem hanging down, and he stood in the middle of the street in the middle of the night. What little hair he had was sticking sideways out from the fringe around his bald dome. And he was a kind of angel.

He grabbed me and said, "Don't keep running back and forth, Cat. Come on, honey, that's broken glass."

"Mr. Ederle, Long John Silver's inside!"

"Oh, Lord. Well, they're not going to let you in there, and cutting your feet won't help."

I put my hands up to my face, wiping the tears around, making ink out of the soot that was already there.

The flames were going out, except for a glow on the kitchen wall. The firefighters had thrown a bunch of flaming fabric and papers out the kitchen window. Other people squirted foam over them as they fell into the gutter. My manuscript. My notes! More papers, black as carbon paper, came floating out the window. There was a glob of sooty, wet papers that fell straight down with a thwack like a wet sponge. Then more paper came fluttering down.

And landed on my shoulder!

"*LJ!*"

He was coated with soot, black as the papers that still came raining down around us. He wasn't happy, either. In fact, he was madder than hell.

"*Accccchhh!*" he said. His voice was scratchier than mine. I grabbed him in both hands.

"Oh, LJ! Mr. Ederle, look!"

"Good evening, Long John," Mr. Ederle said. "Possibly we have all survived. And you, like Phoenix from the ashes, eh? Or aren't you a mortal bird?"

"*Braak!* Here came a mortal, but faithless was she!"

"Mr. Ederle. He means me! I left him behind!"

"My dear girl, he heard me say mortal, and he's repeating it."

"He said I was faithless."

"You're overwrought. He's quoting Matthew Arnold."

"Really?"

"My word, what do they teach your generation in school these days?"

I CALLED JOHN from the drugstore across the street. The man in the drugstore was very kind about loaning a quarter to a barefoot, sooty woman carrying a parrot wrapped in a dirty towel. In fact, he nodded at the phone and implied he'd already seen everything and this was nothing new. His actual words were "If they don't shoot or bleed, it's no problem to me."

Inside of twenty minutes John was there to pick up LJ and me. He'd brought two damp towels, two dry towels, and a shot of brandy in a screw-top jar. It wasn't until we got to his house that I realized it had never crossed my mind to call Mike. For a while I tried to convince myself that down deep I knew Mike was in the treatment program, but that wasn't it. Mike was not the kind of person you turned to in a crisis.

John's mother, Mrs. Banks, put me in a spare room and LJ in the greenhouse. The Banks's house is a *pile*. It has four floors, a second-floor ballroom, and a turret on top, and was built in the 1890s by a farm implement magnate. Attached to the house but facing toward the backyard is a small greenhouse. I checked its windows and screens to be sure LJ couldn't get out. Then I showered off the soot, discovered that some good angel had kept my feet from being badly cut, and went to bed, well aware that Mrs. Banks, true to her past form, considered LJ a much more welcome guest than me.

It's nice to have some things in life you can be sure of.

I DIDN'T WANT my mother to know what had happened. I'd never hear the end of it, for one thing, but mostly she'd worry. And worry. And complain that worry was making her upset. But I'd promised to drive her home when the hospital released her Wednesday morning, after her overnight stay. She was waiting for me when I got there.

"How are you feeling, Mom?"

"Catherine, you can't imagine what they served me this morning. French toast. You know I can't eat fried foods—"

"But how are you feeling?"

"And I didn't have my cosmetics with me. I'm afraid to go out on the street."

Well, really, she looked far more normal. Hers is the generation that likes their eyelids blue at all times, unless they have green eyes, in which case they like their eyelids green, or brown eyes, in which case they seem to be able to deal with both blue *and* green.

"You look fine, Mom," and I meant it. I had a dozen things to do, including finding a temporary place to live, calling the insurance agent to find out what they would do about my furnishings and especially the word processor, and finding out from somebody how the fire had started. Let alone the fact that I still had to get the lottery article researched and written and reconstruct the one on the underwear stores. Plus, I had not been allowed back into the apartment yet, and I was in an agony to find out what was destroyed and what was saved. I had to find the arson investigator or whoever was keeping me out and yell at him until he relented.

"Mom, I can't take you home. But I'll get you a taxi—" which would blow a hefty part of what I was making on this story.

"Catherine! No! It's too expensive!"

"I've had a job crisis—"

"No, never mind. I'll call your father."

"Mom, come on. You know he'll be furious. He'll be at work by now."

"We'll just have to put up with that, won't we?"

"Look—"

"I know that my children have their own lives to lead. It's very hard for young people to be tied down to older people. God knows I try never to interfere."

"That isn't the reason."

"Ann Landers had such a nice letter the other day. It was about letting our children go. Understanding that they have to go away from us and being glad, even if we don't hear from them very much, that they aren't clinging and dependent and staying around—"

"Damn it! I'll drive you home!"

"Now, I don't want you to do it if you feel that way."

"I'd enjoy it," I said, gritting my teeth.

When we were in my old Bronco, she said, "Catherine? Have you taken up smoking?" She used her cautionary tone, making sure she had the facts before she started to criticize.

"No."

"Well, isn't that strange! You smell like smoke."

MY MOTHER GREW UP on a small farm in Illinois, what used to be called a truck farm. Just after the end of World War II, after high school, she went to a teachers college in Normal, Illinois, intending to teach grade school. She taught a couple of years and met my father there. He was working as an auto mechanic at the time.

They were married a few months later, and although she taught another year or so, she soon had so many children she couldn't afford to leave home and she certainly couldn't afford to hire help on a teacher's salary. There were six kids. My father was not a cruel man, and not even exactly harsh, but he believed that you teach kids about the difficulties of the outside world by making the world at home equally Darwinian. He didn't "mollycoddle" his children, and he didn't want his wife to, either. He was equally unyielding with her. Gentleness to him was weakness. She, for her part, had fallen into a kind of psychological pattern that involved doing her basic job and then claiming weakness or lack of knowledge when she wanted him to do things for her.

My mother's generation thought you met the man you would marry, knew it at once, and stayed married for the rest of your life. She simply did not believe my generation had any idea what life was really like. And she disapproved of how we lived.

I looked at her now. Her hands were getting corded with age, the blue veins starting to show. Soon she would be old.

Somehow I had never been able to build a bridge to her.

"Mom. What if you hadn't married Dad? What would you have done?"

"Why wouldn't I have married him?"

"I mean, what if you'd never met him?"

"We were fated to meet."

Fate. That kind of fate takes a lot of responsibility off the individual. I didn't believe in it.

"What I mean, Mom, is what if you'd lived someplace else? Or not gone to teach in Des Plaines? What if you'd never met him?"

"I was fated to teach in Des Plaines."

"But just *suppose* things had been different. What would you have liked to do?"

"Catherine, the world is full of people who want to become princesses or movie stars. And if it's not your fate, thinking about it is foolish. All you will get from wishful thinking is discontent."

She wouldn't make the plunge. Wouldn't suppose. And I thought she knew all there was to know about discontent.

When I let her out at home, she said sadly, "We didn't even get to have your birthday luncheon."

"We'll do it next year."

ELEVEN

AFTER I DROPPED MY mother off and started back to the city, I was surprised to find myself getting angrier and angrier about the fire. Why the delayed reaction? Probably last night I was just too shocked and too tired to react fully. And I hit the deck running this morning, with too much to do and the problem of my mother hanging over me. I have never been able to think straight when she was upset. It always seemed important to settle her down first.

But by the time I got to the East-West Tollway junction with the Eisenhower, and could see the skyline of Chicago, the John Hancock and the Sears Tower gleaming several miles ahead in the morning sun, I was shaking with fury.

There was nothing in my kitchen that could start a fire that fast. People's toasters have been known to catch fire, but mine wasn't working and I'd unplugged it, planning to take it to a repair place or buy a new one, whichever was cheaper. And I just hadn't gotten around to it.

There had been no burner left on; I hadn't cooked last night. Unless the aged refrigerator or stove had done something weird, this was arson.

It was a clear, cool, beautiful morning, and I became hotter and more furious the closer I got to town. Somebody had been willing to kill me, and a harmless parrot, and a harmless old man, and everybody else in the building besides.

THE GUTTER WAS BLACK with soot and pieces of burned paper. There were puddles of black water in the potholes and black streaks down the side of the building. Yellow barrier tape outlined the front, but ended at two sawhorses

on either side of the front door, where a uniformed policeman stood. Two of my streetside windows were empty of
glass. One of Mr. Ederle's windows was boarded up, the
other was undamaged.

I walked up to the front door.

"Hold it," the officer said.

"I live here."

"Mind showing me your driver's license?"

I held it out. It confirmed that I lived here. "Can I go
in?"

"Yeah. Be careful. There's glass all over."

"Okay."

"I'm here for your protection, you know," he said.
"Your door's open. Anybody could get in."

"Yeah. Okay, thanks."

"Sightseers. They'll go look at anything."

"Right."

As I walked away I heard him add, "They're bored.
Sightseers. Don't have anything better to do with their
time."

Mr. Ederle's door was not damaged. The stairs, though,
were soggy with sooty water. My footsteps slapped wetly as
I climbed to my floor.

No door. Just splinters. The hinges held just the upright
part of the frame of the door, nothing else. No panels, no
doorknob. The locks—parts of them—stuck out from the
doorjamb on the other side. I walked in.

It was horrible.

The walls of the living room were streaked with soot as if
spray-painted. The rug, which had been a blue-and-white
tweed, was gray, and down the middle it was covered with
black footprints. Half of it was wet. The sofa was wet.
When I pushed on it, it felt spongy. In the middle of the
floor lay the mirror ball that John had given LJ, squashed
flat.

The kitchen was much worse. The fire must have started
here. Everything combustible was burned—the curtains, the

stool near the stove. The entire top of the stove and a big frying pan sitting on it were so black that they were shiny. Even the wall behind the stove had that peculiar alligator-skin appearance that wood takes on when it's burned. The fire must have raced up the wall and spread out along the ceiling, because the ceiling was black, with some of the paint melted and other parts of the paint blistered. Many of the blisters had popped from gases beneath, and patches of sooty paint hung down like dead skin.

My word processor on the kitchen table had been totaled. Part of the table had burned. The keyboard and hard drive were blackened and wet, and the monitor had exploded. There were windrows of burned paper scraps all over the floor. A pile of unused paper had slid off onto the floor, and the top pages had burned. The pages underneath had not burned, but they were now soaked and useless. There were some sheets of my earlier hard copies that were only wet, not burned, and probably some of the text could be reconstructed. But right now all I could do was look at the fragments of the rest and think, All that work. All that work.

The only good news seemed to be that the ceiling looked sound. The fire had not had a chance to burn through into the apartment above. And the floor was dirty but not burned.

My small bedroom was chaos. It was sooty—even the mirror was soot blown, but while I could not see my face in it because it was so soiled, it was not broken. I looked at my clothes in the little closet. Most of them were dry, and the smoke had been less here, but they smelled like burned paint. LJ's cage was somewhat bent and very sooty, but I could clean it up and take it to the Banks's house when I went over to pick him up. And fortunately, I always keep my notebooks with me, so they were in the bedroom, not the kitchen, where they would surely have been burned.

Suddenly a thought hit me. *What frying pan?*

I ran back to the kitchen. I hadn't been cooking in that kitchen yesterday at all. And while I am not in competition for the Suzy Homemaker of the Year award, I don't leave pans on the stove when I'm not using them.

The frying pan was blackened and the handle had been burned beyond guessing even whether it had been made of wood, or plastic or whatever, but one thing I was sure of.

It wasn't mine.

I PUT EVERYTHING usable in my car. Some clothes, LJ's cage. My notebooks. A pile of soggy but potentially readable papers. My wallet, which had been kicked under the bed. By then the car smelled like a fire, too. I drove to Eleventh and State. McCoo would have to see me even though I hadn't called ahead.

McCOO'S POLICY is to leave his door open unless some officer has a problem so embarrassing or so sensitive that it's impossible. So he saw me coming from the moment I turned into his hall. The officer in his anteroom saw that McCoo accepted my approach, and therefore didn't stop me.

"Hi," I said.

"Hello yourself." He nodded and gestured at a chair, but there was something different about him. His face was closed. He wasn't happy.

"I've been burned out of my apartment."

"I heard. Word got back to me."

"It wasn't an accident."

"No?"

"No. If the fire started on the stove, like I think, and not in some electrical wiring, then it wasn't an accident."

"I hear it started inside. There wasn't anybody inside with you, was there?"

"No. John had been over, but he'd left."

"Light it yourself?"

"What are you talking about?"

"People do things for insurance."

"My insurance won't begin to cover the loss. I didn't have enough insurance, and what I had included a big deductible. Like everybody else in the world. And I lost yea number of hours of work. I mean like *hundreds*. What is this, McCoo? You think I'm a fraud? Do you seriously think I'd take a chance of burning up Long John Silver?"

"You sure you don't know what 'RLP n. attrib.' means?"

Wasn't he going to offer me coffee? What was the matter here? This was a different man. His hands lay on his desk as balled fists. He looked fifteen years older.

I pulled over my chair, grabbed one of the fists, and covered it with my hand.

"McCoo, this isn't right. It isn't you. What's going on?"

He got up, shook off my hand, and stalked over to the window. I followed him. I wasn't willing to give up. "You know me better than all this. I'm not an insurance scammer! What's the matter?"

For several seconds he didn't answer. I thought he was stonewalling me. Or maybe so mad at me, for whatever it was, that he wouldn't talk. Then he said, "Susanne probably has cancer."

"What? Susanne?" Susanne was his wife. I had never met her, but had heard about her a lot.

"She had a mammogram last week. Yesterday they called and told her it was positive."

Positive. A word that used to be nice. "Oh, Lord. You heard this yesterday?"

"Susanne called me here in the morning. She was scared."

She would be. Anybody would be. That explained his change between eight-thirty A.M. and noon. "But that doesn't mean she definitely—"

"They said it looks pretty typical for cancer. Microcalcifications, whatever they are."

"What's next?"

"A biopsy. Friday morning."

"Oh, jeez! McCoo."

Suddenly he started crying, and then I started crying, and I put my arms around him, reaching around his waist because he was taller by a lot. He draped his arms over my shoulders and cried.

Just then Bramble came in the office. I only saw her through wavy tear-lines in my eyes, and because I was facing toward the door. For a minute I think she believed she had walked in on some sort of romantic tryst, but then she heard me sniffle and saw the tears on my face. I backed up.

McCoo wiped his face with one big hand. He pulled a Kleenex from a box and handed it to me. He pulled another and wiped his eyes. Bramble stood there, tall and slender and patient all the while. Finally McCoo spoke. Patiently.

"Yes, Bramble?"

She didn't miss a beat. Someday, I thought, I'd like to see her caught off stride. "We have the lab results," she said.

"Stick 'em on the desk."

She rightly interpreted this as a cue to leave the papers and then go.

McCoo stood still a few seconds longer, heavy with worry, and then ponderously walked to his desk and sat back down. I sat opposite him and waited. He sighed. If I waited long enough he would speak. He did.

"I'm mad at the world," he said.

"I don't blame you."

"I'm mad at the people who aren't sick."

"Yeah."

"But it isn't the world's fault. It's just the—the goddamn luck of the draw."

"Chance."

"Chance . . . Well, it's not your fault." He took a large breath. "No, I don't think you torched your apartment."

"I didn't. But I realized there is something I forgot to tell you."

"Oh? And what would that be?" The way he said "Oh?" was halfway to his usual self.

"Jack came out of City Hall after I had talked to him that day—Monday—was that only day before yesterday? I mean he intentionally followed me and caught me outside. He asked me if I do exposés and I said not exactly, and he said he'd been asking around about me. Probably after I left and before he caught me, which was maybe twenty minutes because I talked with some of the demonstrators on the street."

"What if he hadn't been able to catch you?"

"I guess he would have called Hal and got my phone number and then called me for an appointment at eleven."

"The appointment he didn't note down."

"The very same. Anyhow, he said he wanted to talk about theft of money from the lottery."

"Were those his exact words?"

"Umm—let me think."

"Cat. Come on. You report people's exact words for a living."

"Yes, but he wasn't an interviewee. I didn't write it down. Why do you think I carry all these pens and pencils? What he said—yes, he said 'misappropriation of public funds.'"

"Misappropriation."

"Which isn't exactly theft, is it?"

"Sounds like he meant somebody connected to the lottery siphoned some off some way."

"Yeah."

"And you forgot to tell me this?"

"Well, things were happening fast, and I was busy, and you were so crabby."

"Oy!"

"I know. I know." I stood up. "McCoo, let me know how she comes out."

He shook his head back and forth like a baffled buffalo. "There's nothing I can *do*. I can't affect this." McCoo was a doer, and it must have infuriated him.

Then he realized what we had talked about earlier.

"I'm sorry, Cat. It can't be easy for you, being burned out of your apartment. Did you lose important papers?"

"Work in progress. Papers. Belongings. At least LJ wasn't killed. But I'm telling you, McCoo, it was done deliberately."

"Bomb and Arson doesn't think so."

"Then Bomb and Arson is wrong."

"Go see Flash."

"Who?"

"Freddy Murphy. They call him Flash. Here." He scribbled a note on a piece of stationery that said it was from the desk of Deputy Chief Harold McCoo.

"Chin up, McCoo. There's gotta be at least an even chance that it's not malignant."

"I want it to go away. I want to *make* it go away by sheer force. I want to *shoot* it."

FLASH DIDN'T LOOK so flashy. He was a big, bulky, redhaired man with heavy shoulders. Somehow I always think of this type as being stubborn and hard to convince of another position when they've settled on an opinion. Which probably isn't fair. Appearance is not reflected in the mind.

"You're damn lucky you got out of there," he said. "One of the kitchen cabinets was starting to catch. Another five minutes and the whole place would have gone up."

"Right. Lucky."

"I'm sure you don't feel that way right now."

"I had a fire alarm."

"So many people don't. Or they forget to replace the battery."

"It wasn't bad luck that there was a fire, either. The place was torched."

"Listen, Ms. Marsala. I hear this all the time. There was no evidence of arson. No accelerant. Accelerants leave characteristic patterns on floors. No matches. No fuses. I know that people don't want to believe they've left a pan on the stove—"

"I didn't leave a pan on the stove."

"People forget."

"Will you *listen* a minute? I didn't cook there yesterday at all. I don't leave pans on the stove when I'm done with them anyway; I stick 'em in the sink to soak."

"This one was left on the stove, full of oil. You were going to fry something and you've just forgotten in all the uproar. People have a drink before they start dinner—"

"*Hold it!* I haven't deep-fried anything in years! Sauté, yes. Listen to me a minute. That is *not* my frying pan. That pan was rounded on the sides! If you want, I can show you the other pans in the cupboard. My mother gave me this set of five pans. A little saucepan, a big saucepan, a big pot, a small skillet, and a large skillet." And when she gave them to me she had said, that, well, if I was not going to get married then she couldn't give them to me at a nice bridal shower, but she supposed I was going to need something to cook in, anyway. "The pans she gave me were stainless steel and they have squared bottoms. They are all the pans I've ever had. The frying pan on the stove is not mine and I've never seen it before!"

He looked at me without speaking for a few seconds. Probably he was wondering whether it was worth it to me, for insurance reasons, to lie about this. In a few more seconds he shrugged.

"So how'd it get there?"

"Through the window."

"The window? Lady, you got bars on your window. Plus, you're on the third floor."

"I've been thinking about that. The fire escape runs past the living room and the kitchen window. The living room window is the one you're supposed to use if the stairs are on fire and you can't get out that way. So I don't have bars on that window. I just keep it locked. But the kitchen window has bars, so I don't lock it."

"Right. Nobody can get in."

"Right. But last night—most of the time, in fact, I have it open a couple of inches for air. In that position, it can be pushed up farther."

"Fine. But no human being could get in."

"I've been thinking about that, too. The stove is right near the window. Look." I got out of the chair. The chair had a slat back. I grabbed an in-tray from his desk. The tray was about ten inches wide, twelve long, and two inches deep. Not exactly a frying pan, but close. I dumped two or three papers out of the tray. He winced, but was a good sport enough not to say anything.

"Watch. Now I'm standing out on the fire escape."

I took the tray and slotted it vertically in between the chair slats. Plenty of room, and the bars on my window were farther apart than that. With my arm through the slats, I placed the tray on the desk. I pulled back my arm. "Now I'm getting a bottle of cooking oil out of my pocket," I said, miming it. "Now I'm pouring the skillet full of oil. Maybe I splash a little lighter fluid on top, just to help it along."

I put the pretend oil bottle back in my pocket. "Now, I'm turning on the heat. My stove is gas with a pilot light. It goes on. Now I wait a minute or two while the oil gets really hot. Now—it's hot. I light it with my cigarette lighter. When it flames up, I spill a little on the floor, hold the curtain over the flames for it to catch fire, and then I'm out of there."

He tapped his fingers on the desk. "So how did he get up on the fire escape? If he'd pulled down the end section, everybody would have heard it. Those things shriek like the damned."

"You know perfectly well how. It's done by burglars all the time. Drive a car or a van under it, and climb from the car roof to the fire escape at the second-floor level."

"Wouldn't the people on two have heard something?"

"Mr. Ederle is mildly deaf. But even so—why would they? The guy wouldn't make much noise. He'd just be walking up the fire escape in running shoes. Not moving any part of the fire escape."

"Hmm."

I let him think about it. You push people, they push back. But if you let them come to their own conclusions, assuming you have the facts on your side, then they may not only agree with you, but do it enthusiastically.

"Tell you one thing," he said, finally.

"Yes?"

"There seemed to have been more oil burned on the floor in front of the stove than would ordinarily spatter out of a pan."

"Aha!"

"Also, the fire started late at night. This wasn't a smoldering situation. It has to have started about one-thirty A.M. Which isn't a time most people cook."

"You're right. I hadn't thought of that."

More silence and thinking. Then he slid a sheaf of black-and-white photographs out of a big manila envelope, one of four or five similar envelopes on his desk. He sat there dealing the photos out on the desk, like they were big playing cards, then pulling them toward himself and doing it again. Once he dealt one over to me. It showed, I guess, a small section of the linoleum floor of my kitchen in front of the stove. There was a ruler lying in the photo also. Of that one pictured part of the floor, a smaller part, maybe eighteen inches by twenty-four, was very black. So black that in the photo it looked shiny.

Still he went on thinking, putting one photo behind the stack, studying the next. Abruptly he chucked the bunch on the desk.

"I'm willing to put it down as possible arson," he said.

"Possible? Arson is the *only* possibility."

"I don't know that."

"But that frying pan did not levitate itself into the kitchen!"

"Hey. You say you know it wasn't your frying pan. I don't know it wasn't."

"You don't believe me? Why should I burn up all my notes? And my word processor? And my—"

"Lady, mellow out. Take what you can get."

"I'm getting nothing. I've been burned out of my home and I can't even get a sensible description from the police."

"Does it make a difference to your insurance coverage?"

"I—no, not that I know of."

"Well, then? What's the beef?"

What, indeed, was the beef? I like things to be logical; I like the world to call a spade a spade. Well, join the club of people who find that the world isn't constituted to their exact prescription. My main reason, though, was to know where I stood. Basically, I wanted to know if whoever killed Jack was after me, too. But did I need the word "arson" instead of "possible arson" on a police report to tell me that? Nope. I knew now.

"Okay. Okay. Just for my own information, or my own peace of mind, tell me this. If you knew of your own knowledge that the frying pan appeared there in the night, would you call it arson?"

"Of course. What else could it be?"

"Thanks."

"Only I can't see why that would add to your peace of mind. Me, it would make me real nervous."

TWELVE

ME IT WOULD MAKE real nervous, too. Only, not knowing and going around in a state of unjustified feelings of security would make me even more nervous. If I knew about it. In which case—well, anyway, the point was, if I knew there was a problem I would be more thorough about protecting myself.

BY THE TIME I left Eleventh and State it was a few minutes past noon. I had not eaten anything except a cup of coffee and half a roll at John's house, mainly because I didn't want to run into his mother. Not before I had my metabolism up to speed. She was served breakfast in her room by the staff, but I didn't know when she would come downstairs, so I'd been up and out before anybody but the housekeeper.

Long John Silver had seemed happy in the greenhouse. He had a full water dish and a full food dish, and as far as I could tell, no poisonous plants to nibble on.

I was cruising up LaSalle when I realized that I now had no apartment, no phone, and nobody in the world knew where I was or how to reach me. If somebody was trying to kill me, maybe that wasn't so bad. On the other hand, I was also trying to run a freelance business, so maybe that wasn't so good. Living in my car was only a temporary option. Writers need word processors or typewriters and paper and electrical outlets.

What to do?

One: I had to be able to get my mail. Somebody might be sending me on a $10,000 assignment. Sure. I'll hold my breath. Would mail be delivered at the apartment, even if I was temporarily not allowed to live there? Check with the post office.

Two: Would the apartment be cleaned and fixed by the landlord, Graniteheart Pennypincher III? Call him and find out.

Three: Where could I get temporary use of a word processor?

Four: What if Hal wanted to get in touch with me? Go see Hal and explain.

If yesterday I was behind on the article I had put aside, plus set back on the lottery article by Jack's death and driving my mother around, I was now *seriously* set back.

Hold it.

What my mind was doing was bouncing around from one worry to another. If somebody was out to get me it was time to be systematic. I did not have to visit Hal *this instant*. I pulled over to the side of the road—no, not here, I'd get a ticket even for standing. Around the corner? No, that's too busy. Up ahead? Loading zone. Restaurant traffic all over. I nearly wiped out a bicycle messenger. They shouldn't allow those things on the road unless they obey traffic laws. Pull into a parking lot and *pay* just to park and think? Not on your life! By now I was northbound on Franklin, under the El. No places to park. Took a turn right, then left. North Sedgewick. Aha! Storefront drop-ins for street people. Broken windows. Seedy bars. Great! Nobody wanted to leave their cars here, so there were a few places to park.

I slammed the brakes on at the curb. A wino started toward me, saw the way I slammed the gear into park, looked at my face, and walked away. Jeez! Now I was taking my problems out on the homeless. At least the car wouldn't get mugged.

Okay.

Let's start with the obvious. If somebody wanted to kill me, they must think I have something or know something I shouldn't. Since I don't have anything—wait. Could they think Jack passed me some piece of important paper?

Wouldn't they have sent a burglar instead of an arsonist, if so? Fire was unpredictable. I could have been killed by smoke inhalation and the paper might never have burned.

And what did "RLP Marsala n. attrib." mean?

I was getting distracted again. It didn't matter whether he passed me a physical piece of paper or a verbal piece of information. Though I'd bet it was the latter they were worried about. The question was, Who would think I had it?

Not just anybody. Not that many people knew I had even met Jack on Monday. It had not been an appointment. I only talked with him at all because I bumped the door into him when I was leaving Dorothy's office.

So Dorothy knew. She was number one.

Then Jack and I stopped at Doris's office. I wasn't introduced to Doris at that point. She was too mad at Jack. But I introduced myself the next day when I was talking with Hector Furman, Sr., and his back went out and we had to call Doris. So if she had been looking for me, I walked right into it then and gave her my name. Number two.

I had told Hector Senior that I'd met Jack, too. Number three.

After Jack and I talked in his office Monday, we walked out into the central pool. And then he got into a fight. Who was out there in the central area? Almost everybody in the city of Chicago! Don't give up. Who, really? It was extremely crowded—so much so that if you were ten feet away you couldn't even see the fight through the people standing between.

Seymour Dennisovitch? This let Seymour Dennisovitch out, didn't it? Distaste for Jack Sligh wouldn't make him kill me. Dennisovitch had not seemed like an arrogant enough type to kill. When I met him, I thought he probably would have killed Jack only if Jack infuriated him at the time. A rush of red anger and then it's over. It did not suggest that he'd creep up on my fire escape and torch my place and me. An unlikely number four.

Hector Furman, Jr. Five.

The white-haired gentleman who held Jack back. Six.

Media people? Not likely. The secretaries? Well, maybe he romanced and then dumped one. None of the secretaries I'd overheard seemed to take his flirtation very seriously. Still, if one had, she'd certainly put on a casual front in self-defense. And why would Jack tell me about that kind of thing? Still, the secretaries were very unlikely suspects. Out-of-state representatives in town for the conference? Oh, really!

What about the little gray man? The one on the street who wouldn't give me his name?

That took me the next step. Jack had been mentally jogged by meeting me. He thought he could use me for something. An exposé. He wanted to ask me to do an exposé. But he hadn't mentioned that until he caught me on the street. He was lucky to catch me there at all. Well, only so-so. If he hadn't, I suppose he would just have telephoned Hal for my number and set up an appointment anyway.

The important part was, Who could have been on the street and overheard him ask me about doing exposés? Who was nearby? The little gray man had seen Jack. He knew the lottery people, too. But had he stayed around to hear what Jack said?

Sure he could. All he had to do in the crowd on the street was back up enough so that he was behind somebody else and we'd never have noticed he was there. He was the sort of person you might not notice was there even if he was standing right in front of you. Two feet away he was not even background.

But this applied to a lesser extent to anybody else, if they were willing to keep back out of sight.

I was seeing it in my mind: Jack and I come out of his office. Jack and I are talking. Jack gets into a fight. I leave to talk with Hector Junior in his office. Meanwhile, Jack wipes the blood off in the men's room, goes back to his office, and makes one or two phone calls about me. Meanwhile, I've been talking with Dorothy. Jack comes back out looking for me, either sees me going down in the elevator or asks somebody who says I just left. He follows. He catches up to me right in front of the building, after I've tried to talk with the man from Carbondale and the woman from the West Side. I'm now talking with the little gray man. He shoos the little gray man away and asks me whether I do exposés. I say not exactly. I ask him what he has in mind.

"Misappropriation of public funds."

And now in my mind's eye I see a shadow. Whoever it is, the shadow sees Jack talking with me up in the Lottery wing. It follows him to his office, maybe lounges outside his door and hears the phone calls. It follows him out of the Lottery wing.

The shadow sees him catch up with me on the street. It lurks behind other people, hoping to catch what Jack is saying. It hears "misappropriation of public funds." Or it does not hear that, but hears "exposés."

But it can't hear everything. Just fragments. The shadow does not know how much I am being told. Then, like a gift, we start to walk apart and I called back that I'd get there tomorrow as early as I could after leaving my mother. When Jack yelled back "Eleven!" the shadow had it all.

He knew then that either Jack had told me what it was about, and was just giving me the proof tomorrow, or maybe he hadn't but it was going to be too risky to take a chance. We both had to go.

If there was any chance that he hadn't told me yet, then Jack had to be killed before our meeting.

So by shouting back at Jack, I had got him killed. For Jack that shadow was the shadow of death.

"YOU HAVE TO HAVE an address and a phone," Hal said, pushing out a chair for me.

"Well, I know that."

"No, I mean you *have* to. And now. You can't live out of your car. People you're interviewing have to confirm or cancel. You need a typewriter at the very least, Stone Age technology though it may be."

"Yes, yes, yes."

"What about staying at John's?"

Now, Hal Briskman is a lovely person. All the stories about hardhearted editors do not refer to Hal. But he has this appalling avuncular streak. It wouldn't be so bad, either, if he weren't usually right.

"I don't think I want to stay with John. It's not fair to him."

"Don't want to give him false hope, huh?" Hal said, hitting the nail on the head.

"Hey. Leave me be. I'm a grown-up."

"Sometimes I wonder."

"I will call you by five P.M. with an address, damn it!"

I had told Hal about Jack's death before I told him about my apartment being torched. It seemed to make more sense chronologically. Now, referring back to that, he said, "Cat, living with a family right now might not be such a bad idea. I don't want you killed."

"Don't worry. Forewarned is forearmed."

"Sure. Have a mint?" Hal is addicted to hard candy. He quit smoking two years ago.

"No, thanks. Do you know any dirt about the lottery I don't know?"

"Not dirt exactly. There was talk when the next-door neighbor of one of the people—let me think a minute— yeah, the next-door neighbor to Hector Junior won a jackpot. Must've been, oh, five months ago." He picked up the phone. "Belinda? Remember that business with Hector Furman, Jr., and the neighbor who won the lottery?"

Belinda has a more photographic memory than Hal, if that's possible, and I was sure on the other end she was saying, "Are you kidding? I remember every word."

"Can you Xerox me anything on it, chop-chop?"

Hal is also addicted to old slang. He hung up the phone. "She'll have it for you before you leave. Now, listen, Cat."

"Yes, boss."

"We are already four days behind on this piece because of Mike's little—ah, setback."

"I know."

"We need the thing by Monday. I realize you didn't burn down your place in order to get out of the deadline, but our paper goes on the stand despite flood, civil insurrection, plague, or arson."

"Yes, boss."

"I am afraid you will get distracted by this murder and try to solve it, instead of keeping your hand to the plough."

"Or nose to the grindstone."

"Or shoulder to the wheel."

Fortunately, Belinda came in with the stuff.

"That was fast," Hal said.

Belinda said, "I knew where to look."

He thanked her and she left.

"Suppose the solution to the murder makes a good story?"

"Then it will make a good story *after* the lottery story. Now, Cat," he went on, handing me the Xeroxes after a brief glance, "write me the piece. Don't get distracted. Don't go off on a tangent."

"Is it okay if I also don't get killed?"

"Yeah, sure. That, too."

I LEFT THE OFFICE with my priorities straight. I had thought it was one, don't get killed. Two, write the article. Three, find the killer.

Now I knew write the article was number one.

FIRST THING, I stopped at a seedy hotel that was near the Loop. What most cities need is more single-room-occupancy residence hotels. For one thing, some of the homeless could be housed in SROs if there were inexpensive rooms available. However, the trend is going the other way. New,

breathtakingly expensive hotels with enough marble to pave
Versailles.

That's why the seedy places are hard to find. This was like
something out of a 1940s skid-row movie, which was about
when the carpet had been laid down. About when it had last
been cleaned, too. But unless my insurance company decided to pay for my interim lodging, this was it.

Having placed my paper bag of smoky clothing in the
room (this was the sort of hotel where a paper bag of clothes
was absolutely unremarkable) and called Hal from the room
to tell him where I was, I paid as much at a lot to stash my
car as I'd paid for the room. Then I walked over to John
Banks's office.

Speaking of marble, John's company is in a LaSalle Street
financial building, where you get on the elevator, and instead of pushing the twenty-sixth-floor button, you push a
brass plaque that says "Biller, Trueblood and Banks."
When the elevator opens its portals, not doors, on twenty-
six, you see before you, chiseled into great blocks of Italian
marble, BILLER TRUEBLOOD & BANKS.

It always makes me giggle. I asked the receptionist once
which block Biller was buried under, but she looked at me
and with one hand felt for the security call button, so I shut
up. Today she recognized me and nodded, as if confirming
a dread suspicion.

I walked into the hushed central room, currently paneled
in dove-gray suede, where a forty-foot-long video display
stock market ticker runs all during the trading day on the
wall. Come to think of it, maybe it does overseas markets
even at night, when Wall Street is closed. Must remember to
ask about that. Several senior citizens sat quietly watching
the numbers and letters go from right to left on the screen.

Past the plush seats I walked, trailing smoke perfume, and
into John's office. I was having a moral dilemma.

"Cat!" He got up from his desk, looking so happy I
wondered why I didn't just marry him today. He gave me a

hug. "Sit down. You left so early this morning I didn't see you."

"I had to take Mom home."

"Oh. Right. Well, I have news."

"Um, I should tell you something, too. Also, I should admit I have a favor to ask."

"Let me tell this first. I called your landlord."

"Mr. Lance Hope?"

"What? Oh, I see. Yes, Mr. Welsh. He was quite upset, saying that your carelessness had burned the place."

"It was torched."

"I told him that."

"How did you know? I didn't know myself until a little while ago."

"You said last night you hadn't left anything burning. You said it didn't look like an electrical fire. I took the liberty of calling the police department investigator before I called Mr. Welsh. You had just left. The investigator told me what you said and admitted he was putting it down as a possible arson. I called Mr. Welsh and told him I thought that constructing the building in such a way that the fire escape permitted access to the kitchen window and bars that were so wide apart that a person could insert flammable materials might constitute negligence. And that I was advising you to contact your attorney."

"I don't have an attorney."

"You would if you needed one. I also said that the age of the stove suggested some other distressing possibilities. He then said that a lawsuit would cost him more than a coat of paint and some new kitchen appliances. By new I think he means he'll buy them used, but they'll be new to your apartment."

"Great! He'll never be able to find any as old as the ones he had before!"

"Right. He said that as far as your own contents were concerned, you should talk to your insurance agent."

"Oh."

"I called him. He says you're covered for loss of contents—"

"Great!"

"—but you have a five-hundred-dollar deductible. And it doesn't cover things that are not destroyed, like clothing that gets smoke smell."

"Oh."

"Best I could do. It means you get a new word processor, at least."

I was thinking I'm out $500 already, plus the temporary room, plus parking the car. I would never be able to make up the losses. Determined not to show him how difficult this would be, I smiled cheerfully.

"Still working on the lottery story?" he said. So far he had done really well at not telling me I should go on vacation in Sri Lanka with him for a few weeks. He was surprising me.

"Working harder. I'm falling behind."

"You've got to go see Bob Powers, if you're interested in the real workings of the lottery."

"The lottery attorney?"

"Right. I don't say he's the most scrupulous person in the world, but he knows how the thing works. Hey! Want me to call him?"

"Oh. Well, sure. Thank you." I was giving out markers here like dealing cards. How was I going to repay John?

"Bob Powers, please." John had a speakerphone, so the conversation was hardly private. Powers came on. "John! Got a new OTC gamble for me?"

"No, Bob. I wondered if you'd talk with a friend of mine. She's Cat Marsala. You must have seen her byline around. She's writing a story on the lottery."

There was a half-second pause. It doesn't sound like much, but among these movers and shakers, heartiness is very big. He should have responded instantly. It meant something. Wish I knew what.

"Great! When would she like to come over?"

"Tomorrow afternoon?" I mouthed. I was seeing Hector Furman, Jr., in the morning.

"Tomorrow afternoon sometime work for you?" John said.

"Sure. Say...two?"

I nodded at John.

"Good."

"Tell her I'll see her then. And John, buy you a drink out of the IBM puts. Okay?"

"Okay."

When John hung up, I said, "Money talks, I guess."

He looked at me oddly. "It's my job. I try to buy low and sell high."

"Hey, I understand. God knows you might as well bet on the stock market as on the lottery."

"Better. Or money funds. Or even just put the pennies in the bank."

"The lottery gives people hope."

"False hope. Look at it this way. Your chances of winning the lottery are what—one in thirteen million. Right?"

"That's what they say." I added brightly, "Your chance of being struck by lightning is twenty times that."

"People just don't picture how big a million really is. Say you plan to buy a one-dollar ticket every week until you win. There are fifty-two weeks in a year. Okay." He punched at his calculator. "Divide fifty-two into thirteen million. That means you have one chance in winning every two hundred fifty thousand years."

"Gee, I'd be too old to get much out of it."

"Right. Plus, the average grand prize is what? Six million dollars?"

"Roughly. That's why your chance is one in thirteen million. The money is pooled, and about half goes to the state for schools and so forth and expenses."

"Okay. So it takes you two hundred fifty thousand years to have a one-in-one chance of winning six million dollars and you would have spent thirteen million dollars to do it."

"I suppose so. Must be, or the state wouldn't be making any money."

"But that's not all. Each of those dollars as you went along could have been earning you interest if it was invested."

"Like how much?"

"Well, let's imagine you put fifty-two dollars in the bank instead of buying a one-dollar lottery ticket a week for fifty-two weeks. If it's compounded at six percent, and they actually compound continuously now, then the money doubles every twelve years."

"In twelve years it's only $104."

"Right. But when things double they get to a point where they're going up fast. In twenty-four years it's $208. In thirty-six years it's $416. In forty-eight it's $832. In sixty years it's $1664." He pulled over his calculator. "By a hundred years it's $20,178. At a hundred and sixty it's $425,984. In two hundred years it's six million dollars. In other words, by just investing $52, you make as much in two hundred years as you would win on the lottery in an average of two hundred fifty thousand years, and in the case of the lottery you would have invested thirteen million dollars to do it."

"That's amazing. That's really fascinating."

"After three hundred years it's three trillion dollars, which is more money than there is on earth. By a thousand years it's six followed by twenty-seven zeros. And then— jeez! My calculator won't do it! If you let it run two hundred fifty thousand years, you'd have more dollars than the universe could hold."

"But, see, people don't think that way. A one-in-thirteen-million chance of winning six million dollars in their lifetime is much more attractive than having twenty thousand dollars in a hundred years."

"Well, I realize that. After all, people buy lottery tickets. But suppose you were talking to somebody sensible and you said—" he punched at the calculator a few seconds—"that if they put a dollar a day in the bank they'd have—umm— a hundred thousand dollars in fifty years, which would help in their old age for sure, or a million in ninety years, if they want to leave something to their children."

He was really into it now. I let him go at it.

John said, "Did you know that Benjamin Franklin, as a kind of stunt, put a dollar in the bank with instructions that after he died it should go on earning interest indefinitely?"

"And what happened?"

"Well, a few years ago even the *interest* on the money got to be so much the bank couldn't handle it. It was humongous! It was finally broken up and made into several separate funds."

"Yeah, but see, if a person has to wait—when did Franklin die? Late seventeen hundreds?—two hundred years, it loses a lot of its appeal."

"Of course. I'd rather put you in money funds."

"Thanks."

"And we haven't even figured out what you would make at a dollar a week every week through the years, the way people really play the lottery. All we did was the first fifty-two dollars."

I put my hand over the calculator.

"Hey, John! Are you opposed to gambling?"

"No." He smiled. Once in a great while something a little devilish comes through his businessman exterior, and I love it. He said, "How could a stockbroker really be opposed to gambling?"

I nodded.

"Plus, gambling is going all-American. Disney is planning a television lottery show. With a national lottery."

"*What?* Mickey Mouse is going to spin a lottery wheel?"

"I don't know. It's a proposed television program. Disney has given stories on it to the *Wall Street Journal* and the *New York Times*."

"Is nothing sacred?"

John shrugged. "It's a natural enough development. The lottery drawings in most states are televised already. But they aren't very showbiz. I mean, they just blow these little numbered Ping-Pong balls up into tubes. It was only a matter of time until somebody put more pizzazz into it."

"I can see it now. Glitter balls. Snow White spins the wheel and Tinkerbell waves her wand—showers of gold coins—a magic paintbrush paints a rainbow in the background—"

John said, "Enough. Let's plan to do dinner."

"Wait a minute. John, I wanted to tell you that I've taken a hotel room temporarily. While my landlord is getting the place in shape."

"Why not stay with me?"

"Your mother, partly. And John, I can't lean on you like that until I decide what to work out with Mike. It isn't right."

"It isn't wrong."

"Look, I have to do it this way. You have to tell me to get lost if I take advantage of you. Okay?"

"Yes. I am an adult, Cat. You can't take any advantage I don't give."

I nodded. When he said it, it sounded all right. Plus, I was under such pressure that the only way I could survive was to swallow my misgivings. "Fair enough. But that's not all. I wondered if I could use a word processor here until I get things together. Welsh may not move very fast. I mean, he collects rent faster than he dispenses paint and appliances."

"Work here as long as you like. There's an extra machine or two in the reference library."

"And that's not all, either."

"Go ahead. I can stand it."

"Can you keep Long John Silver awhile?"

"I'd be glad to," he said, manfully. "Long John and I are old friends. I feed him birdseed and he tells me all your secrets."

"What? He *doesn't*!"

"Oh, come on. He couldn't. Birds can't really think, can they?"

THIRTEEN

THERE WAS TIME to trek back to City Hall and catch a few people before the end of the working day. I found the Lottery hall unusually empty. The secretary, Cheryl Weeks, said, "Most of 'em are at the symposium."

I looked at my schedule. "'How the Lottery Generates Jobs'?"

"Should be into 'Typical Expected State Revenue' by now."

"Where's that being held?"

"The—um, let's see—Macedonia Room at the Stratford."

The Stratford was only three or three and a half blocks away, but I didn't see much point in going. Unless you're assigned to report on the symposium itself, it is very rare that a reporter learns much of anything useful about a subject at a symposium. People are too guarded. Plus, even if there's a question-and-answer period, you don't really get to pursue questions the way you do one on one. I decided to walk around and see who was still here in the building.

Neither Doris, nor Dorothy, nor Hector Furman, Sr. or Jr., responded to knocks at their doors. According to the schedule she had given me, Dorothy was busy chairing the symposium.

I wandered down the corridor opposite to Jack's and came to a door that was ajar. It had the name HOWARD RINGWALD on it, and under that LOTTERY STORES CO-ORDINATOR. I tapped.

"Come in."

I introduced myself. The man had a pile of papers in front of him and was punching at a calculator. What did we do before calculators? He quit punching out of courtesy, but he eyed the calculator hungrily as I spoke, and he did not ask me to sit down.

"What does 'store coordinator' mean?" I asked. "Is that something to do with what Doris Furman does?"

"I'm the head stores coordinator," he said primly. "Doris is a senior stores coordinator."

Taking the cue from his tone, I said, "Then you're her boss?"

"Yes."

"Didn't you want to go over to the symposium?"

"Certainly not. I already know about the lottery. What's more important, I have work to do."

"Isn't that where everybody else is? I couldn't find Doris."

"Oh, Doris! She'll be in the bar at the Stratford if you want her. Drinking gin and tonic. Unless she's in a brandy mood."

This was a new insight into Doris. She had been rather sullen and unhelpful when I first met her, even before Jack died. At the time, it seemed maybe the divorce was the reason, but then again maybe that was too simple an explanation. Howard Ringwald gave no impression that Doris's behavior was recent in origin, nor did he suggest he had any sympathy toward her as a result of the impending divorce or even Jack's death. This might have been more Howard Ringwald's psychological problem than Doris's, except that it was consistent with her behavior. Maybe she was a problem drinker. Maybe she was just a grouch who drank. Anyway, Howard was not in the mood to be a chatty interviewee. I puttered along the hall, passed a guard resting on one of the guard stools, felt like a burglar as he followed me with his eyes, and found myself in the center of the building, where Lottery becomes Cook County Engineers, and went back into the other Lottery hall. There was a clattering coming from two offices on the inner side of the building.

Two larger than ordinary offices had been combined, making the largest single room I had seen on this floor. The ceiling was studded with fluorescent light bars hanging between the ubiquitous air delivery system ducts. Two lines of four desks took up most of the room, and two larger desks near the windows used the rest. Every desk had a computer terminal and monitor. In fact, while I'm no expert, these desks looked like the latest thing in workstations. Every one was occupied. Every person was either pecking away at a keyboard or ticking things off on hard copy printout.

A woman at the further big desk blinked at me, with the faraway gaze of a person who has been staring at a video monitor all day. She stood up.

I told her who I was.

"Beverly Krakus," she said, staring at me wide-eyed, asking wordlessly what I wanted.

I explained why I was asking around, getting ideas about how the lottery worked. Could she talk a little while?

"Oh, not now. I'm going to be here an hour overtime as it is. This stuff has to be done tonight."

"What is this place?"

She gave me another stare. "Accounting." As should be obvious to any idiot, she meant.

"I suppose, with one lottery game after another all week, and money coming in all week, the accounting never stops."

She smiled at this oversimplification. "One thing we can't allow to happen. We just can't *ever* start getting behind." She was already edging one foot back toward her desk. I waved and left.

Everybody was too busy to talk with me? Okay, I'd go to the Stratford.

DORIS FURMAN WAS DRUNK.

She didn't respond to my greeting, but when I said, "Doris, we ought to do something. Jack didn't kill himself; he was murdered."

"Murdered? You think you're telling me something I don't know?"

"The police haven't said so, have they?"

"Fuck the police. It's been obvious from the beginning."

"You knew he was murdered? Why didn't you tell the police so, then?"

"Why should I? That's their job."

"They usually appreciate a word or two from the next of kin."

"Not if you don't have facts, they don't. Suppose I said, 'Jack's the kind of bastard that gets himself murdered.' You figure they're gonna be grateful?"

"Um, maybe not."

She was at the Stratford lobby bar, called the Bar Association, probably because of its proximity to the Daley Center, where the Cook County civil courts were located, the Dirksen Federal Building, where the federal courts were located, and LaSalle Street, which was lawyers' row. The place was cheerfully decorated with prints of British judges in white wigs, court reporters' sketches of defendants and attorneys in famous Chicago cases. The bartenders wore three-piece suits. Cute, huh? There were judges' gavels with which you could rap on the bar for a drink. Fortunately, Doris Furman wasn't sitting near any of these. She was sour enough to rap my fingers or the bartender's, just for fun.

"See, I don't have any facts," she said.

"So why do you think it's murder?"

"Do you seri—seriously think he wanted to die?"

"No. But I didn't know him."

"If you knew him more, you'd even be more oblivio—it'd be more obvious."

"I see. Don't you think we should do something about it?"

"We? You and me? Not our business."

"He was your husband."

"Well, I'll tell you this. I don't care. Saved me a lot of trouble, whoever—you know." She waved a hand at the bartender. Waved it sideways like Queen Elizabeth waves at cheering crowds, but the bartender got the meaning and came over.

"Another brandy?" I said, to Doris, deducing what she drank from the shape of her glass. She nodded sagely. "And a bourbon and water." This was the moment to spend a couple of bucks. I also briefly felt a pang of guilt. I wouldn't want somebody to ply Mike with liquor in a bar. So was I wrong to do this? Well, maybe. But even AA says the drinker has to make his own decisions. And I didn't know for sure whether she was a problem drinker or a person with problems who sometimes drank. Besides that, my goal was to decide whether she had murdered her husband. That took precedent over the pros or cons of one single drink.

"Well, so the killer did you a favor?"

Doris looked funny at me, but the drinks arrived almost immediately and a gulp moved her to a more friendly place, socially speaking. "Bastard wanted everything."

"You mean the divorce settlement?"

She mumbled unintelligibly, but nodded her head again. Nodding her head got her lips closer to the glass without having to raise her arm so far.

"But Doris, he can't. There are community property laws in this state."

"'Zactly."

"'Zactly?"

"See, my dad gave me things. My dad loved all his kids."

I had met Hector Senior, and while I think he probably really did love his kids—Lord knows he kept them all close around him—my leading candidate for the reason he gave them things now was inheritance taxes. Hector Senior was not a man to miss playing the odds.

"I'm sure he loves you, Doris."

When they get soggy, you use words of one syllable.

"See, he gave us all houses. I have this nice six-bourbon—six-bedroom house. Gave me a car. Gave me some of his mule—mutual funds. And Famy—Fanny Mae. See? So those are mine."

"Well, sure."

"Jack wanted it."

"If it's after you were married, I think he's entitled to half."

"Fuck half. They're *mine*. My father gave 'em to me."

"Oh. But I think the law says that's community property."

"Fuck the law."

I was afraid I'd antagonized her by even mentioning the law, much less appearing to be on the side of the law. "Well, I'm sure it would have been more gentlemanly of Jack to think of your father's gifts as your—"

"Ha! Jack? Gentlemanly?"

"Well—"

"And I'll tell you this. He's a greedy bastard, too."

Of course, I was asking myself whether a woman who had killed her husband would talk like this. Was Doris smart enough to try a double bluff? To admit that she had a substantial financial motive to kill Jack? To admit, even encourage, the idea that it was murder, when whoever had done it must have hoped it would pass as suicide? Doris Furman was no Dorothy Furman. Actually, Doris was probably smart enough. She struck me as a person who was not so slow-witted as she was mentally lazy. She might not want to be *bothered* with making up a double bluff of that sort. Smash him over the head, pitch him out the window, wipe any fingerprints off the telephone, and just rest on the probability that nobody would ever be the wiser. It would look like suicide.

Besides, even if the cops found the telephone had been cleaned, and even if they were morally certain that Jack didn't polish his phone after every call, Doris could still rest on the comfortable assumption that that didn't mean *she* had killed him.

She was amply justified, if so.

At least she didn't ask me what possible relevance any of my questions could have to an article on the lottery.

Pressing my luck, a strategy that has worked before, I said, "Is that why your divorce was so unfriendly?"

"You ever heard of a friendly divorce?"

"Yeah, actually. But what I mean is, I get the impression you wanted the split."

"You bet I did."

"And Jack wanted to stay married?"

"Well, no—" She didn't like this line of questions, but she was too indolent to get up and walk away. "Not exactly. He woulda gone along with it. Christ, he's been one foot outta the marriage for years! Bastard."

"But then why?"

"Hey! These things never come easy, you know? Le' me alone."

THAT WAS ALL I could get out of her. She was becoming soggier by the minute. I stopped in at the back door to the symposium, which was just coming to an end.

"But does this mean lotteries are just going to go on getting bigger and bigger indefinitely?" asked a woman whom I could only see from the back. She was wearing a flowered hat. Obviously not a Chicagoan.

Dorothy Furman, the moderator, turned to her panel. "Who would like to answer that?"

Hector Furman, Sr., was standing outside the door talking with two women. His big thatch of silky white hair was visible across the room. When I went over, he introduced the women as part of the Iowa delegation. Then he excused himself to them and took me aside.

"How's my best girl?"

"Wait a minute. We're just friends. I don't kiss on the first date."

"People told me there'd been a revolution in dating habits."

"That was twenty years ago. It's revolved back."

"I don't believe it. I know how you media people can play with words."

"Not me. I'm not that kind of girl."

"Come see me in my office. I'll teach you how the pros play poker."

"You promise?"

"Shake on it," he said.

There were no other people I knew from the lottery around, and I had agreed to meet John for dinner, so I left and trekked to my hotel. In sad little damp piles on the bathroom sink, tub edge, toilet tank, and floor lay all the hard copy of various notes and articles that were unburned. I sat down for a few minutes and peeled the almost-dry sheets off the tops and placed the cheap hotel's thin towels under the piles to absorb more water from the bottoms of the piles. If they dried in a clump, the pages would probably stick together, but what could I do? Peeled apart wet, they tended to tear. The few pages that were already dry were curled and stiff, but later they could probably be pressed reasonably flat. I wasn't planning to hand them in to anybody, just copy from them. They didn't have to look good.

John and I ate corned beef and cabbage at Binyon's. I told him I wanted to work at the office for the rest of the evening. There were two notebooks of material that had to be transcribed. And the old underwear article. It had to be finished tonight or else. What I didn't tell him was that I was pressing so hard on this paperwork tonight because there would be research time wasted tomorrow, if "wasted" was the right word, on searching for Jack's killer.

I had a right. The bastard had tried to kill me and a perfectly innocent parrot. But John wouldn't be pleased.

He didn't even like the idea that I was going to work late, but he dropped me off at his office. He wanted to come up and work, too, but I knew then he'd nag me to quit at a reasonable hour and go home, and that wasn't going to work. We were edging toward an argument. We both backed off before it happened.

I said, "Is Long John Silver happy?"

"Judging by his appetite, yes."

"Does he miss me?"

"Well, when I left this morning, he made it clear that he did."

"Really?"

"He said, 'How sharper than a serpent's tooth is man's ingratitude.'"

"That's inaccurate. It's 'How sharper than a serpent's tooth it is to have a thankless child.' *King Lear*. Otherwise it's 'Blow, blow, thou winter wind, Thou art not so un-kind—'"

"'—As man's ingratitude.' *As You Like It*. I know that, Cat. Aren't you the one who always said that Long John Silver talks, but he doesn't know what he's talking about? This time he's proved it."

I always said so, but I didn't believe it. Now I believed it even less.

FOURTEEN

THERE WAS A whining noise, getting closer. A giant mosquito, the size of your average Michigan Avenue pigeon, was coming in to suck my blood. It hovered at some distance, looking for the carotid artery, then swooped closer, whining louder and louder and—

—and said, "What are you doin' here?"

"Mmmp?"

The cleaning woman snapped off the vacuum. "You bin here all night workin'? Don't you know any better? You'll get a crick in your neck, sleeping like that."

"Oh." I looked around. No mosquito. Thursday morning had crept in on little vacuum wheels. "I'm sorry."

"I didn't say you need to be sorry. I said you need to take better care of yourself."

Hey. I have other people who do this to me on a regular basis. But she meant well. "There was this work that had to get done."

Work. I looked at the workstation. The cursor was still blinking patiently on the screen. The evening was coming back to me. I had just put my head down for a minute, someplace around two A.M. But the first article, the article on the aldermen and the underwear stores, was done. I would read it again tonight, after it had settled down in my mind and I could be objective. But thank goodness it was out of the way.

Nothing on the lottery, though.

I rubbed my neck.

"See?" she said. "You know, the most important thing you can do is take good care of your spinal column. If you're comfortable in your backbone, you're comfortable everywhere.''

"You know, that's very true.''

"Sure is. You once get a crick in your neck, or you get your spinal column out of line, it's maybe out of line permanently.''

I stretched. "It seems to be straightening out.''

"You gonna leave now? I gotta do this room.''

It was seven A.M. Time to get to the hotel for a shower and then breakfast. A big breakfast! My body knows an emergency when it sees one.

JACK SLIGH was killed because he was going to tell me something. Did that theory fly? Yes, otherwise nobody would have tried to burn down my apartment. So that meant Doris wouldn't have killed him just because she was angry that he wanted a divorce or angry that he forced her to divorce him by sleeping around with other women. Okay.

What Jack was going to tell me had something to do with "RLP Marsala n. attrib." That was certain, too. There could be more, but that was part of it, otherwise why make the note? And it could be the whole explanation. Whatever that was.

"RLP Marsala n. attrib." was partly decodable. "N. attrib." meant not for attribution. He was going to tell me something that he wanted me to use—to print in some kind of article or exposé—but not to attribute to him. He wanted to feed me some scandalous data, but not be quoted.

Why? Why not be quoted? Because he was a state official and it wouldn't look good? Because he was going to be stabbing a friend or acquaintance in the back? Or maybe because it was dangerous?

So who or what was RLP?

Richard L. Parker? Robert L. Peebles? Rebecca Louise Plotz? Why did it have to be a name? The fact that it was in capitals didn't make that a sure thing.

Robbing Lottery—what? What started with a P? Prize? Robbing Lottery Prizes? Ripping off Lottery Prizes? Robbing Lottery Paper? What would that mean? Of course, it only had to mean something to Jack. A note to jog memory.

Rigging Lottery Prize!

I liked that one. It sounded juicy. If this was a note worth killing for, that is, if whatever Jack was going to tell me was important enough to kill him and try to kill me, it had to be something like lottery rigging.

Who could rig the lottery? Maybe Hector Furman, Jr., in his role as security director. As a matter of fact, that would place him just perfectly for some sort of slick trick.

Thirty million dollars, the prize last week, was certainly enough to be worth killing Jack for. Even a slice of that would whet most people's appetites.

I had the appointment with Hector Furman, Jr., at eleven. I could hardly wait.

BY THE TIME I finished pancakes, sausage, orange juice, and a lot of coffee at Hermione's, it was barely eight. Hermione had come by the table several times, pouring extra coffee, urging another glass of juice. Finally she said, "Hey, Cat honey. You look tired."

"Don't mother me. Somebody already did that today."

Hermione is five feet five or so and weighs three hundred pounds. And she doesn't want to hear any bullshit about it. She lives her life her own way. She runs her restaurant that way, too, with an exuberant mixture of health foods and such items as Trucker's Breakfast (eggs and sausage with a second, fresh, hot plate of eggs and sausage when you finish the first) and the Debutante's Nightmare (ribs slathered in barbecue sauce and corn on the cob—food you can hardly help getting on your clothes). She has one called the Cardiologist's Friend. Don't ask.

And she lets her friends be themselves. Which made it strange that she went on. "You been pushing it a little too hard?" she said.

"Hermione, my business is so wasteful of time. I bet I get ten times as much information as I ever use in an article. The rest is just thrown away. I mean, I learn something from the other ninety percent, but from a direct-use standpoint, it's just thrown away."

"Why don't you just shove it all in the story?"

"It doesn't work. If you put everything you researched into an article, it doesn't hang together. It'll have all these ugly bumps and lumps all over it."

"Maybe you're too sensitive about it. You could work faster and do more articles and get paid more if you used more of what you get."

"No. The best people, the really good writers, work this way. I can see it in their product."

"Yeah, but you got to make a living, child."

"A piece of writing has to be unified and have its own special form, or shape."

"You mean it's not a salad. It's more like a cake?"

"Right. Only I think of it as a house in the dark."

"Oh, really?" She poured me coffee as if I were cracking up and needed help.

"When you're first collecting material, and you know what some of it is, but not all of it or even where to find all of it, it's like being transported to the center of a dark house on a dark night. You start feeling your way around with your hands. Is there a wall here? Is this a pillar that supports a lot of weight? How big is it? And after a while, even though it's still dark, you get a feel for the shape of the thing. Then you start asking yourself where's the circuit breaker to turn on the lights and really illuminate it. And where's the furnace to warm it up and make it live. They're all just separate little details, but when you get them right you have something that stands alone and lives."

She was nodding at me. "I can see that. All right. You have to do it right or not at all."

"I think so."

"So you want to know the solution to being tired?"

"Sure."

"Carbohydrate loading," she said, giving me a dough-nut.

MY APPOINTMENT with Hector Furman, Jr., wasn't until eleven and it was still before nine.

On an off chance, I walked over to the Stratford and found a friendly face behind the desk. He was a young black man who smiled at me, and did not say I looked tired or was ruining my neck by sleeping on tables.

"Is there any way to know whether the Utah delegation to the lottery conference is awake yet? I don't want to wake them up, but I'd like to catch them before all the day's events get started."

"Easiest thing in the world. They have an office adjoining their suite. I'll ring the office and see if they're in."

He did and they were. And they'd talk with a reporter.

The Utah delegation was courteous. That's about the best I can say for the interview.

John Scott was wearing a navy gabardine suit with a white shirt and dark blue tie. Henry Smith, ringing wild changes on Scott, was wearing a navy polyester suit with a blue-and-black tie. Their conversation was of a type to suit the suits.

"It's hard for me to understand what you wanted to see us about, Miss Marsala," Scott said. "We're just delegates. We're not putting on the programs."

"Actually, Dorothy Furman suggested I see you."

"That's very odd. She's pro-lottery, of course."

"Of course," Smith said.

"And she must know we're not."

"She would, of course, know we're not."

I said, "Well, that was why she told me about you. She wanted me to get a balanced view."

Scott said, "How interesting."

Smith said, "That's very interesting."

This was going to be a problem. "Would you care to tell me why you're against lotteries?"

"Why, certainly. People waste money playing them."

"They waste money," Smith said, "and even when they win, which most never do, they haven't earned it."

"So it's a bad example either way," Scott said.

"And sets a bad example for our young people," Smith said.

Scott said, "Do you want young people to think they don't need to work?"

"Or don't need to learn?"

"Or don't need to be educated?"

"Or don't need to save their money?"

"And just wait for a bolt from the blue?"

It was like watching a tennis match. "But don't they gamble anyway?" I asked. "Whether it's legal or not?"

They gave me the standard answer on that, too—namely that the government should set a good example.

There are some interviews that are total zeros from the first word. Mainly it's people like these, who talk to the press a lot and have answers ready for everything. I used to fool myself that if I thought of a question they hadn't anticipated, then I'd get something fresh. The chances of that are about as good as winning the lottery; 999,999 out of a million times, they will either say, "That's a good question, I'll have to think about it," or even more annoying, pretend to misunderstand the question and answer something you haven't asked that they have a good answer all ready for. Watch politicians talk to the press. They do it all the time:

"What about your indictment on charges of fraud and corruption, Senator Foghorn?"

"Our criminal justice system is the best in the world. I have always said that anyone in this country can be proud of the court system and the guarantees so movingly rendered for us in our Bill of Rights. And I hope you will all support my bill to make the first week of February National Bill of Rights Week.''

I HADN'T SLEPT WELL, or long enough, and my eyes felt hot. Also, I kept wondering how much I ought to watch my back. It didn't seem likely that anybody was going to try to kill me out here on the street, but who knows? Personally, I thought that it would be fairly easy to drive by in a car with a partner at the wheel, stop a few seconds, and shoot anybody on the street at a little distance, say half a block. With the traffic noise, most of the passersby wouldn't hear the shot anyhow. They'd think the victim was having a heart attack. Meanwhile, the car never gets any closer to the target, turns the corner, and drives away. Maybe one chance in a hundred that anybody would get the license number, and that could be faked. A borrowed plate, or a borrowed car.

However, there was nothing I could do about this except stay in crowds. And keep an eye open. And worry.

With over an hour before I had to see Hector Junior, I decided there was a piece of research I had been forgetting to do. It was a natural, and I thought it was important.

It was not hard to find a lottery store, because Hector Senior had had his way all those years ago and the retail outlets were conveniently located. However, I was carrying the list of places Dorothy's son Fred was supposed to inspect, so I walked to one, hoping to catch him. It was mainly a drugstore. The manager was a man with thin, mouse-colored hair and bulging eyes. I asked if Fred had been there yet. It was a little past nine, and he was supposed to be here first thing. But the manager said nope, not here yet. Then I showed him my press card and explained that I wanted to interview a couple of people who bought lottery tickets.

"I don't think that's a good idea. We don't want our customers harassed."

"I'm not going to bother them or chase them. If they don't want to talk with me, that's fine."

"I don't like it."

"I can always catch them outside as they leave, I guess."
I didn't mention that it would be much harder for me to see
from out there whether they bought tickets.

"Oh, never mind. Go ahead."

Obviously this man was going to win the Mr. Graciousness of the Year award.

Cold interviews are not necessarily difficult. You hope
that people want to talk. And in fact, this is often the case.
Most people don't often get to talk about their lives and
about why they do things. Their families already know how
they live, and they either think they know why the person
does the things he or she does, or they don't care. An interviewer really wants to find out, and people are flattered by
media attention.

The first person who bought a Grand Lottery ticket was
a young Hispanic woman. She was overweight, but not as
much as Hermione. And by the limited standards of beauty
in the United States in the closing years of the twentieth
century, she was not beautiful. Her face was broad and her
eyebrows met over her nose. She was as short as I am, and
very squarely built.

Her clothes were trendy—aqua and pink T-shirt with
surfing shorts—but they were cheap. The fabric of the shirt
had started to pill, and the shorts showed a bending at the
seam that was characteristic of one piece of the fabric going through the sewing machine faster than the other. Hasty
manufacture.

"Could I talk with you?" I asked, showing her my press
ID and holding my notebook and pen in the same hand as a
kind of backup ID. "I'm writing a story on the lottery for
Chicago Today and I notice you just bought a lottery
ticket."

"Why, sure." Her voice was musical and pleasant.

"Do you buy lottery tickets often?"

"Why, I guess it's often. I buy a Quick Cash ticket on
Mondays and Tuesdays, usually. And I buy a Grand Lotto

toward the end of the week, so I can watch the drawing on Saturday night.''

"Have you ever won?"

"Oh, yes.'' Her eyes lit up. "I won fifty dollars last March in the Quick Cash.''

"How much do you think you spent in order to win the fifty dollars?''

Her pleasant mouth sobered for a few seconds. "I don't know, not for sure.'' She didn't like to think of it that way.

"Have you been playing for a long time?''

"A couple of years.''

"Win anything else?''

"Free tickets, quite often free tickets. And one time, maybe two years ago, I won twenty-five dollars.''

Now I was feeling guilty for raining on her parade. "Say, I guess that's pretty good.''

"Yeah.''

"Why do you like to play the lottery?'' I was going to ask "Why do you play the lottery?'' but it sounded accusatory, and adding the words "like to'' seemed to put it in the realm of entertainment. She paused before answering, though, and studied my face.

"It's just fun,'' she said finally.

"But you were going to tell me something else.''

"Well. Sure. It's a feeling I get. It's like, when I buy a ticket, I have as much chance of winning as anybody else. My ticket is as good as anybody else's ticket.''

"It's equal?''

"Yes. So you do understand. My ticket is the equal of anybody's else's.''

Yes, I understood. "What do you figure your chances are of winning the Grand Lottery?''

"Oh, not good. I'm reasonable about that.''

"What would you guess?''

"Uh, maybe one in a thousand. No, several thousand. Maybe, like, one in fifty thousand.''

"What do you do? What's your work?''

"I make salads."

"Salads?"

"At the hospital. Northwestern Memorial. I make up salads for the trays."

I thanked her. She smiled her sweet smile and walked away toward Michigan Avenue. My next victim was already buying a ticket. He was an elderly black man with pepper-and-salt hair. He had to be seventy, but he was wearing a denim work jacket and billed cap and was carrying a toolbox. He listened to my opening spiel courteously. When I finished, he had a quizzical look.

"You really want to find out whether people are wasting their money, right?"

"Well, not necessarily. I want to find out what they get out of it."

"Dreams."

"What do you mean?"

"Every time you buy your ticket and you wait for that drawing, you get a ticket to dream. That's why folks buy 'em. You sit there watching the TV and dream what you'd do with ten million dollars. That's what everybody does."

"I suppose you're right."

"Yes, I'm right."

"What do you figure the odds of winning are?"

"*Real* small. Millions and millions to one against you. Doesn't matter to the dream, though."

"What line of work are you in?"

"Days I'm a handyman. Nights I'm night manager at a gas station. Self-serve. Pay before you pump. I sit in my booth and eat Milky Way bars."

I thanked him. "Good luck," he said.

"Good luck to you, too."

I was doing just great. People talking to me, telling me useful material. What a hotshot interviewer I was. And pride goeth before a fall.

The third purchaser was maybe twenty-five, a slightly pudgy young white man, going prematurely bald on top. I was just barely into my spiel when he said angrily, "Why do you want to know?"

"I told you, I'm doing an article. But you don't have to say anything to me."

"Thanks a hell of a lot. Then I won't."

I nodded what I hoped was pleasantly. There wasn't any point in getting into an argument. And anyway, I was asking him for a favor he didn't have to grant.

He'd half turned, then he said, "Nothin' wrong with it, anyhow!"

"Never said there was."

"Goddamn do-gooders."

"I don't have any objection to the lottery." I saw the store manager glancing our way.

"Oh, sure!"

"Really not."

"Really not." He mimicked my tone in a more goody-goody way than I hope I used.

"Well, it's legal and you women can just go fuck yourselves! Hear me? It's *my* life!"

I backed away, hoping he'd stomp out. Fortunately, he did exactly that. The manager eased his way back to mouthwashes and toothbrushes.

"How many tickets did he buy?" I asked the clerk, on impulse.

"Twenty. Twenty Instant Picks. He's a regular."

It seemed a good idea to leave the store now.

UNABLE TO contain myself any longer, I arrived at City Hall at ten for an eleven o'clock appointment. The place was beginning to look like home. It wasn't warm and user friendly, but it was familiar.

I had stopped by my unwholesome hotel room to pick up the Xeroxes Hal's researcher Belinda had made for me yesterday about the time a neighbor of Hector Junior's had won the lottery. While I was in my room, I peeled a few more sheets from the tops of the piles of drying paper. It's a good thing laser printer letters are not water soluble.

The news stories were skimpy enough. A man named Howard Driesenga had won the lottery. Not the biggest of big jackpots. Nine million dollars. He was quoted as having a surefire system: the ages of his father, mother, self, wife, and two daughters—68, 66, 42, 40, 15 and 09 respectively. His wife was quoted as saying she would just as soon he hadn't revealed it, having not yet got used to being forty.

At any rate, in one paper it was simply mentioned that Driesenga lived next door to Hector Furman, Jr., lottery security official, in Evanston. The slightly more muckraking *Downtown Register* allowed as how it did not look good to have neighbors of lottery officials win. Driesenga was quoted as saying that he and the Furmans had been friends for years, and their children played together when they were little. Then Roger Boykins, sometimes pundit and regular syndicated columnist, took it up, and made a joke out of it.

If we are to prohibit neighbors of Lottery officials from winning the Lottery, I predict a new class of pariahs. Picture it. All over the state of Illinois—a dead zone, a no-man's-land, a scorched earth around any house where any Lottery official is unfortunate enough to reside. There, in isolated sorrow, his children friendless, he ponders where his career decision went so horribly wrong.

There was more, in the same jocular vein.

Having reviewed the stories, I still had not decided whether to ask Hector Junior about them or not. Some things are best played by ear.

Hector Junior's door was ajar. I tapped and looked in, but he was not there. His desk was clean except for a colorful brochure on Trinidad. I backed out.

And almost stepped back on his foot.

"Sorry! I know I'm early."

"No problem. Come on in." He waved me to a chair.

I noticed now that his nameplate said DEPUTY CHIEF OF SECURITY. He had been mentioned to me as chief or supervisor of security. Oh, well; people don't necessarily put all the detail in during casual conversation.

Why is it I distrust sleek men? His hair was beautifully cut, thick and dark, and he was as freshly shaved as if he'd just come from his razor. His nails were filed and either buffed or coated with a light polish. He crossed his legs, revealing silk socks and some very pricy Mario Blanik shoe leather.

"What can I do for you?"

"I want to know how the lottery actually works. Most people know a lot about the prizes and some people have a fair sense of the odds, but almost nobody knows how it all gets done. How do the tickets get to the vendors? How do you make sure the drawings are fair? What security is there to prevent somebody from rigging the lottery?"

"They can't rig it. It's impossible."

"You don't mean that."

"We've taken every precaution in the world."

"Come on. You and I both know that anything that can be devised by man can be broken by man."

"Not this one." He wasn't being very communicative.

"It's only a matter of how many people you get into the scam. Eighty million dollars could buy a lot of people."

He shook his head.

I said, "Really? Wasn't it the New Jersey State Lottery that somebody rigged by injecting a small amount of water into some of the Ping-Pong balls? Which made those balls a little heavier. That would take collusion among several people."

"That wasn't in Illinois!"

"Could've been, though."

"Do you have any idea how carefully we guard those goddamn balls?" He was almost shouting.

"No. How would I?" I said sweetly. "That's what I want you to tell me."

"We have maybe two hundred sets of balls at a given time. Ten in a set, numbers 0 to 9. Or 01 to 54 for the Grand Lotto. The sets are kept in a bank vault until they're going to be used."

"Couldn't somebody steal them and substitute rigged balls?"

"The bank vault can't be broken into—"

"Oh, sure."

"Fort Knox is a piece of cake by comparison! But if it were," he said, gritting his teeth, "the alarm would go off. There are other fail-safes to let us know if the containers or balls have been moved. The balls themselves are in a container with a seal and we would know if the seals had been broken."

"What about switching balls between the time they're removed from the vault and the time they're put into the apparatus for the drawing?"

"They're under continuous armed guard and the guard is under the eye of a state official and a lottery rep—" he held up his hand before I could make any objection—"*and* these officials rotate on a random basis. So nobody knows when he's going to be observer and he doesn't know who's going to be observer *with* him."

"I like that."

"I'm delighted you're pleased with it."

"But how do you know the balls are all the same weight to begin with?"

"You know physicists weigh things down to the electron level these days?"

"Maybe. But I'll bet not without some seriously sophisticated equipment."

"My point is, you can weigh things very exactly. I'm no scientist, either, but I'm told we can weigh the balls down to a microgram with the equipment our own techs have."

"Uh-huh."

"I can tell you this. They got it to the point where they were dealing with the differences caused by the paint—you know that the numbers are painted on the balls?"

"I suppose they would be."

"Well, the number '8' has more paint than number '1' so it weighs more. The '8' weighs 2.7 times the weight of '1'."

"Oh. Now that's interesting." I wrote it down.

"So the techs have to shave the Ping-Pong ball with the '8' on it enough to make up for the difference. The '6' weighs just twice the '1', for example."

"Thanks. This is great stuff."

"Then they don't allow anybody to physically touch the balls before they're dumped into the clear plastic containers. You've seen drawings?"

"On television."

"Right. Ten balls are dumped into each of the plastic containers, four containers for the Lucky Four Game, six for Grand Lotto, or whatever, and they're blown up and around by compressed air. Then the drawer, who usually is a television personality, takes a cap off a little tube at the top end of the container and a ball is forced up into it and held there. And the television personality turns the ball so the viewers can see the numbers."

"I know that."

"Well, the television personality doesn't touch the balls before they're drawn, and nobody else does either. Because you could have natural skin oils on your hands, or if somebody really wanted to pull off a scam, maybe he could conceivably have something sticky on his hands that would adhere to certain balls and make them heavier. So they're poured right from the transport container into the clear plastic containers."

"I see."

"And after that one drawing, they aren't used again. Because the television personality could inadvertently have left some substance on the ones he or she touched."

Hector Furman, Jr., lounged back with an air of having trumped my ace.

"Basically, you're saying that every time any of the Ping-Pong balls are painted or moved there's half a dozen people watching."

"More than that. I can't think of any time they move that fewer than ten people are on top of them. Except when they're in the safe, and that's heavily guarded and alarmed, and they're weighed under the eye of another ten or a dozen people when they're taken out, just before they're used."

"So why was everybody so bent out of shape when your neighbor won?"

"People are nuts. Ms. Marsala, suppose there are a hundred top lottery officials. Suppose each one has six close neighbors—one behind, one on each side, one across the street, two whose backyards corner on his backyard. Suppose each neighboring house has a family of four. That's six times four or twenty-four neighbors for a hundred people, or twenty-four hundred people total. Now suppose each lottery official has ten friends and ten relatives. That's twenty times a hundred, or two thousand people. Which adds up to forty-four hundred people already who can't play the lottery without looking like crooks. Now what about work colleagues of the lottery employee's spouse? People at school with their children? Members of the same church? Where do you draw the line?"

Had he thought about this, or had he thought about this?

"You've got it all worked out."

"Wouldn't you, in my place?"

"I guess I would." Naturally, I was trying to guess if this character was bold enough to have hit Jack with a telephone and thrown him out the window. He seemed coolheaded. If he'd been caught setting up a lottery scam, how coolheaded and ruthless would he have been? I tried to catch him off balance. "So why do you carry a gun?"

He answered with a kind of lazy grace. "Would you believe there are people stupid enough to think I carry part of the prize money around with me?"

"Yes. Unfortunately, I *would* believe there are people like that."

"So you see, we've thought of everything."

"Well, actually I've been doing some thinking, too." Mainly about what kinds of scam Jack would have been likely to discover. I wasn't giving up this easily. "I believe you. I believe that the multimillion-dollar jackpot would probably be very, very, seriously double-checked and guarded. The Quick Cash would be much easier to run a scam on. There's less money involved because no individual ticket is worth an obscene amount of money, so the process wouldn't be so carefully eyeballed. But it would make a nice little scam all the same. Say somebody siphons off a few winning tickets every week or two. Maybe one or two thousand dollars a week in hundred- or two-hundred-fifty-dollar wins.

"I was thinking, in the Quick Cash game, the one with the three rows of three spots that you rub or scrape off, you can win as much as two hundred fifty dollars. Do that here and there on a regular basis and you have a tidy source of income. Besides, two hundred fifty dollars is below the amount the lottery agency reports to the IRS. A lot of people think you have to cash the ticket in where you buy it, but that's not true. You can walk into any lottery vendor and be paid. No one vendor would see you often enough to remember you."

"It's impossible! The winner has to write down his name and address. If we saw the same name and address pop up week after week, we'd go after the guy." He was firm but unflustered.

"You telling me you don't get false names all the time?"

"Well, naturally, some people don't want—"

"The vendor doesn't check. He pays the money to the ticket holder immediately."

"That's true—"

"After all, lots of people probably don't report lottery winnings for taxes. Maybe *most* people don't report them for taxes."

"We are aware that that happens."

"You can't seriously be telling me that you copy all the names off the little cramped lines at the bottom of those tickets, and have clerks to figure out the handwriting, and put all these names on computers, and rotate them through every previous set of winners after every single game to see if some people win a lot. Do you?"

Grudgingly, "No."

"There must be thousands of two-hundred-fifty-dollar winners, all over the state."

"Look, Ms. Marsala, you got the wrong end of the stick!"

"Why do people always say 'Look, Ms. Marsala' when they run out of arguments?"

"The point is, you can't tell which ones are winning tickets. You are plain *dead* wrong and I can prove it to you!"

THE RUMBLING HISS of the printing press made it almost impossible to hear what Roy Otterstrom was saying. I cupped my hand behind my ear, miming that I couldn't hear, while Hector Furman, Jr., stood by with his arms folded, smiling, miming smug satisfaction. We were in Naperville, fifteen miles from Chicago.

"*Called a web!*" Otterstrom yelled. "Because it's a continuous roll that feeds into the press."

"Paper?" I shouted.

"No. Paper backing with aluminum foil bonded onto it. The aluminum foil makes it completely opaque."

The gigantic printing press stretched away so far into the distance that I couldn't see what was going on at the end.

"How long is this thing?" I shouted.

"Two city blocks!"

"Gee!" My notepad was out and my dozen pens and pencils were ready in my pocket. I picked one and made notes.

"Let's step over here for just a second," Otterstrom said. He waved a big hand at the wall and walked away from the press into a room with a glass window facing toward the press. When we got inside, he closed the door. The noise decreased. Some.

"We can talk easier," he said. "Also, I wanted to show you the computer."

In a side room with no outdoor window was a completely uninteresting computer. For all the fascination that people over the whole state of Illinois would have in its output, the thing itself couldn't have been more ordinary. Its case was drab green. Its buttons were slate gray. It was about two feet by two feet and either sat on a closed stand or had more of its guts inside the stand. A power cable went into it. An output cable went out of it, up the ceiling, out through the wall and over, presumably to the press, which we could see through the interior window.

"Mathematicians develop algorithms for us that generate random sets of symbols for the game."

"Then the mathematicians know what will come out?" I asked.

"No, no. They generate the formulas that allow the computer to generate them. Neither the mathematicians nor anybody else would know what the computer was going to do."

Didn't seem to be any loophole there.

"Do you get any printout of what it's doing?"

"No. The symbols are printed directly on the tickets and no place else."

"Then how do you know it's printing the right proportion of winners and free tickets and so on?"

"It's designed to."

"But how do you *know*?"

"We don't, I suppose, before we send a given batch of tickets out. But we know later from payouts. If there were a major screwup, we'd know when the tickets were cashed in. Or weren't. If it printed no winners at all, or too many winners, we'd know pretty damn fast. It's never happened, though. Mathematicians have been working out random-number-generator algorithms for years, long before we needed it for this."

"Okay. Say the configuration of symbols is generated randomly. What about when they're actually printed on the tickets? Can't somebody see them at that point? Before you cover them up with that stuff that gets scratched off?" I pointed at the printing press. "You've got several workers out there."

"In the old days the ticket-printing process was done in three steps. First the color graphics were printed on the aluminum, then the numbers or symbols went on, and then the covering—it's latex and aluminum oxide, by the way—went over it. So there were times when the numbers were exposed. In fact, at one time the process was done in three different plants by three different suppliers. It was intended as a security precaution, but really it was a security nightmare."

"What do you do now?"

"Come see this."

We walked back out onto the floor and up to the press. The aluminum/paper web came rumbling out of the roll and onto a printing bed. It went under rollers. When it came out of the first one, white letters and borders were on the foil. I couldn't exactly see what the white was, because the future tickets were moving too fast to see. I suppose that was one major safety factor right there. But I remembered from my own ticket what the white stuff was. We walked farther down the press.

In the intervening distance, the white must have dried. The next roller overlaid the tickets with blue. We walked farther and the red color was applied. I happened to look up. There were videocameras trained on us, and it looked like there were others all along the route the tickets took.

Then we came to a fence that forced us to walk fifteen feet back from the press. Here the continuous roll of paper ducked under a more complex machine. I looked up and saw that the cable from the computer room ran to this machine. Somewhere under this hood, the computer was randomizing the symbols—bells, oranges, whatever—onto the future tickets. These symbols, I remembered, would be in black.

We walked a little farther, still held fifteen feet away from the press by the railing. Inside the random-symbol printer, some process must have dried the black ink quickly. There was a loud hissing as if air were being forced through, and the odor of chemicals was strong. At the far end of the symbol printer, the tickets rolled out and almost immediately went back under another roller.

I couldn't see the symbols on the tickets.

"That one lays on the opaque latex cover," Otterstrom shouted.

A little farther along, the latex covering was itself overprinted with blue squares, indicating to the customer where to scrape to reveal the symbols.

Hector Junior turned and looked smugly at me.

Ahead was the cutting process, where the continuous roll became real tickets. First the sheet was cut in long strips. Then, before the final cutting into ticket size, quality control people inspected them. Naturally, they couldn't see under the latex covering, either.

"If there's a single defective ticket in a roll of a thousand," Otterstrom said, "the inspector rejects the whole roll."

Beyond this point the rolls were cut into individual tickets, which were then stacked and shrink-wrapped.

Bricks of shrink-wrapped tickets went into boxes. At the very end of the room, two blocks from where we started, several men were loading the boxes into a truck.

Furman said, "The truck gets locked and sealed here, and the seal on the lock isn't broken until the truck gets to lottery headquarters."

"That's so the tickets themselves can't be stolen."

"Right."

"But even so, they couldn't tell which were the winning tickets until they scratched the covering off."

"Sure. But if somebody steals a big block, he's likely to get winners."

Furman said with satisfaction, "Well, what do you think?"

"I have to admit, it looks pretty safe to me."

Otterstrom smiled.

He said, "Every person who goes into the plant goes through a metal detector."

"I noticed when we walked in."

"Also, we screen everybody for any criminal conviction before we hire them."

He walked us to my car. Like so many people in slightly oddball businesses, he was proud of his work, I figured he'd enjoy giving me extra information.

"Do you print in continuous runs? I mean, game after game?"

"No. One run at a time. For one game. We ship that and start over."

"How many tickets is a run?"

"Varies some. About forty million."

"That's a lot of tickets."

"They're three inches long. If you laid 'em end to end, they'd reach from Chicago to Las Vegas and back."

While we rolled from Naperville to Chicago in my elderly Bronco, I encouraged Hector Furman, Jr., to crow about the security. I said, "Okay, it looks foolproof."

"Absolutely. Once the completely opaque scratch-off covering was invented, we were home free."

"Never had a problem?"

"Well, not at any serious level. We had a couple of vendors who tried to find winning tickets for themselves."

"How'd they do it?"

"Oh, scratch a very thin line across the spots to try to see if there was three of a kind underneath."

"Yeah."

"Or they remove tiny dots of the covering with a pin, to see if they've got a winning line of symbols."

"And?"

"It's just about impossible to do undetectably. And once they're caught, they're out."

FIFTEEN

IT SEEMED BEST to let Hector Furman, Jr., have his little fun. When we parted at the State of Illinois Building, he was still bragging about the splendid security precautions that, as he put it, "surrounded" the lottery. And they were splendid. It was just that, as I had told him earlier, there is nothing that the mind of man can devise that the mind of another man can't scam, evade, con, or hocus. In fact, why *another* man? The person who devised it is probably in the best position to evade it.

What I did accept, however, was that if somebody wanted to rig the lottery, he'd have to bring ten people at a minimum in on the deal, and more probably, upward of twenty. He'd have to make up a team, everybody would have to know the plan, everybody would have to be paid in shares of the pot, and then there was the biggest problem of all: Every one of those members of the team was a possible future leak. A lifetime threat. Like the old saying: If you want to keep a secret, don't tell anybody.

Rigging the lottery would be a very, very risky deal. Not just at first. For the rest of the scammer's life.

Hector Junior had given me great stuff for the article. But as to whether he had killed Jack and given my mother a serious shock and tried to kill me and LJ, I wasn't much farther along. His character was a puzzle to me. He talked a lot and seemed actually proud of the lottery's security, but I wasn't quite sure what he actually *did*. And he had an odd kind of playboy manner about him that puzzled me. Still, I had made one step forward. It was perfectly clear that he was subtle and cool enough to have killed Jack and not give himself away. Put another way, if my intent was to cross some people off the list, Hector Junior was definitely not going to be crossed off.

I'd managed to kill two birds with one stone, which was all right. Now I just had to worry about getting killed.

My appointment with Bob Powers was at two, and I could make it by hiking fast down LaSalle. And missing lunch! Oh, damn. Talk about making sacrifices for your job!

THE LAW OFFICES OF Powers, Potenza and Ginsberg were in the Lafontaine Building on North LaSalle. There are two kinds of beehives for attorneys in this area of town. First are the old buildings with heavy carved cornices, dark wood interior—sometimes beautiful, sometimes ugly. They tend to have too few bathrooms and too few electrical outlets and lots of cachet. The second are the very new, very techy buildings that look as if they were made of transparent bronze. The materials used inside tend to be marble and metal, there are plenty of bathrooms, and enough electrical outlets in every office to power all the Christmas trees in Grand Rapids, Michigan. These buildings are sometimes beautifully simple and sometimes simply ugly.

Powers's building, I had to admit, was beautiful.

The elevator opened directly into the anteroom of Powers, Potenza and Ginsberg. They occupied the whole floor and, judging by the building directory, the two floors below this as well.

A *thin*, blond woman in a champagne-colored Anne Klein suit sat at a table made of a six-foot-long oval of blond wood. There was absolutely nothing on the oval, not a telephone, not a buzzer, not even an intercom.

"May I help you?" she said in a blond voice.

"I'm here to see Bob Powers."

Oh, days of techy elegance! Unobtrusively, she touched a button that was not on top of the desk but on the side facing her, out of the sight of the client. "Won't you sit down?" she asked.

I sat on a soft white sofa, somewhat like rising bread dough. Next to me on the blond-wood side table were *Barron's*, the *Wall Street Journal*, the London *Times*, the *New York Times*, the *Washington Post*, and several foreign financial journals written, of course, in their own languages. I recognized French, German, Dutch, Japanese, and guessed at a couple of others.

I had spent a minute or two looking at one, trying to decide whether it was Hungarian, when the receptionist said, "You may go in now," and gestured at a door.

A door to her left opened and another woman held it for me. I followed her down a corridor to an open door, walked into an office, took one look at the occupant, and said, "Oh, it's you."

He looked puzzled. He held out his hand and said, "Bob Powers. Have we met?"

"Not exactly. You and I were holding Jack Sligh back from destroying that man Dennisovitch on Monday." Powers was the handsome older man with gray hair, but I didn't say that. "You took him to the bathroom to clean him up."

"Uh-huh." We both sat down without ceremony. "Poor Jack. Who would have known he'd kill himself the next day?"

Personally, my brain was reeling. If anybody was in a position to follow Jack and hear him talk with me, this guy was it. For that matter, Jack could have told him something about me while Powers was swabbing him down. People say things when their adrenaline is up and they're angry that they would be too cautious to say otherwise.

Plus, Powers either didn't know or wasn't saying that Jack was murdered. If he killed Jack, he might believe he'd gotten clean away and left everybody thinking it was suicide. Since I knew more about what the police were thinking, I ought to be able to play this guy like a violin—isn't that the expression?

"Mr. Powers, I'm writing an article on the lottery for *Chicago Today*. Which was why I had stopped in to see Jack

Sligh. I understand you're acting as corporation counsel for the lottery."

"Yes, that's right."

"Would you tell me what you do?"

"I can't imagine what I do would be very interesting to your readers," he said, shoving some papers sideways on his desk. He had a trendy blue-and-cream enamel nameplate, saying ROBERT LAYTON POWERS, and the nameplate went sideways, too. Then he piled all the papers in one stack, squared the stack, and straightened the nameplate up. Playing for time?

"Well, for one thing I don't understand whether you're a consultant or you do all their legal work for them."

"The lottery is like a lot of state and local government agencies. They have in-house counsel but have outside counsel on retainer."

"Which one does what?"

"If you ask me, everything gets referred to me." He smiled. "The in-house attorney looks over labor contracts, hiring forms, contracts with ticket retailers, contracts for supplies, leases for the lottery offices, but when you come right down to it, anything that is at all different from what they do every day gets referred to me. Now, the in-house counsel might tell you different." He smiled again.

"Does this mean the lottery takes up a lot of your work time?"

"A lot! It takes up almost all of it."

"All year? Full time?"

"Just about. And I have another partner here and an associate I farm out some of the work to, besides."

"Oh. I hadn't realized there could be so much."

"Stop to think about the number of disputes that can come up in a business like the lottery. Although most of what we do is perfectly routine," he added—hastily, I thought. "Suppliers that don't send materials by the scheduled date, advertising on roadside billboards that peels off in the rain, that kind of thing."

There was something nagging at the back of my mind, but what it was I couldn't tell. It was throwing off my rhythm of questions.

"Um, who chooses you?"

"What do you mean?"

"Who picks you to be counsel? Is this a political appointment?"

"No. The lottery chooses me."

"But who is the lottery?"

"Actually, there is a civilian oversee board, and they choose. They make the decisions relating to top hiring. The legislature has final approval, I believe."

"Where do they get their list of candidates?"

"For what?"

"For counsel?"

"I haven't any idea."

Did I believe that? Nope. Why was he being so difficult? I couldn't guess. And I was still being niggled by some notion in the back of my mind.

"Who would know?" I asked.

"Who would know what?"

"Who would know who makes up the candidate list?"

"Ms. Marsala, your readers can't possibly be interested in trivia like that."

"I can't tell that without knowing the answer, can I?"

"Certainly you can." He pushed the pile of papers farther out of his way, bumping his nameplate.

Robert Layton Powers.

Nameplate. RLP.

RLP?

RLP. Marsala n. attrib.! Jeez!

Powers had said something I'd missed. "Excuse me?"

"I said, is there anything else you'd like to know?"

"Yes. Did you know Jack Sligh well?"

"Hardly at all. Why?"

"Well, there you were, saving him from making a fool of himself and washing him off."

"You pulled him back, too. Did you know him well?"

"Just met him that morning."

"See?"

I was in McCoo's office before you could say "attribution."

Again, I hadn't called first. He saw me coming, though, and waved me in. Probably there was a serious expression on my face, because McCoo got up and leaned forward with concern. "Hey," he said, "I didn't mean to snap at you so much. It was the trouble with—"

"Not so much? You mean to snap at me a little?"

"A little you usually deserve."

"When will you know Susanne's biopsy results?"

"The lab doesn't work on weekends. Except for emergencies," he said bitterly. "To them this isn't an emergency."

"Lord! You have to wait all weekend? Not knowing?"

"Yup. And we'll be lucky if we get the results on Monday."

"Oh, my God. What will you do all weekend?"

"I figure we'll take five-mile walks."

"Right."

"Twice a day."

"Right."

"And again in the evening."

We sat there a few minutes, and it said much for Mc-Coo's distraction that he didn't even offer me any coffee at first. Then he got up and absently made us both a cup and didn't even tell me what part of the world the coffee beans had been grown in. I stuck my index finger in it to see if it was too hot, which McCoo's coffee sometimes is, and found it was tepid. This was a deeply troubled man.

It took him a while to recall what was going on, too.

"You came to me, Cat," he finally said. "What do you want?"

"I've found out what 'RLP Marsala n. attrib.' means."

"Oh? Really?" *That* he remembered. Once a cop, always a cop, some people say. Even in times of personal distress.

I told him about Robert Layton Powers. First the RLP business. Then the fact that Powers had helped hold Jack back from pummeling Dennisovitch.

"You didn't tell me about that."

"I didn't think it was important."

"Swell, Cat."

"Hey! I didn't have the foggiest idea who Powers was, then. Anyway, that put him in a good position to hang around Jack, maybe listen outside his office door if he made a call or two. And follow him down to the street."

"Jack'd have noticed if he took the same elevator."

"Sure. But the building has a dozen. And the lobby was so crowded you couldn't just walk right out as soon as your elevator hit ground level."

"Okay."

"Plus, it was so crowded you could follow somebody and not be noticed."

"Granted."

"So basically, McCoo, what I wondered is whether you found any papers about Powers in Jack's office. Obviously, Jack was going to tell me something about Powers. Something not for attribution to him, that is, to Jack. He had to have found out something about Powers, and whatever it is was probably something to do with the lottery."

"Why not something personal?"

"Remember Jack said 'misappropriation of public funds' when he caught me on the street in front of City Hall."

"Yee-ees. Yes, I think you're probably right. We found two locked file drawers in Jack's office. In a four-drawer file. The top two drawers were unlocked. So we looked through the top ones, but held on to those two bottom drawers. I can't say the detectives going over them have come running in crying 'Huzzah!' though."

"They might not know what to look for. Not having thought of Powers especially."

"Probably not."

"Now we need to look for anything relating to Powers."

He said, "Right," but he didn't move.

"Well, let's go."

"If you mean 'let's' as in 'let us,' Cat, the answer is no. You can't go through the papers. They're evidence in a murder case."

"But I've just told you about them! You wouldn't know anything about this except for me!"

"No. No-no-no. But I'll call the troops and tell them what you said."

"I want—"

"Absolutely not! Get back to me later. I didn't say I wouldn't *talk* with you about the contents of the files. Only that I wouldn't let you physically touch them or get near them right now."

"Jeez, McCoo. Fat lot of gratitude I get."

"Later. I'll praise you later."

I left. He was looking a lot better than he had when I walked in. It hadn't solved any of his personal problems, but there's nothing like a potential lead plus a little controversy to spruce up Harold McCoo.

I WAS TENSE and frustrated at the same time. Deep down, I believed I had the keys to the whole thing in my hands. Maybe I could solve the murder if I had Jack's papers, but as it was I couldn't act on anything. McCoo was shutting me out.

But the answer was in there someplace. Jack had something on Robert Layton Powers. Overcharging the lottery for legal fees, maybe. And he wanted me to expose Powers. And Powers killed him and tried to kill me.

Maybe. But I needed proof.

I walked up State Street so fast I was race-walking, try-ing to use the nervous energy.

Four-thirty in the afternoon, and I hadn't eaten. Had I? I was so excited I could hardly remember. No. But there was the article to deal with, too. First I'd better get the notes I'd made so far transformed into hard copy. Wait. My printer was history. All right. Stop by my hotel room to get another note pad and replenish my pencil and pen supply, even though I'd only used up one pencil, and that a pretty stubby one. If I have fewer than twenty assorted pens and pencils on my person, I feel I may not have one when I need it.

Just as well I did. Another few sheets of my papers had dried and needed to be peeled apart. Unfortunately, the farther down in the stack, the longer they had been wet, and thus it seemed the more holistic they had become. They were starting to pick up layers from each other, producing something very much like a double exposure on a camera film. Nevertheless, I had to keep pulling them apart. No matter how bad it got, some of the stuff might be salvageable.

As I worked at the papers, a cockroach scuttled across the floor toward its own hotel, somewhere in the wall. Hmm. Well, at least I didn't have to worry that the building was dosing me with insecticide.

Then I realized—a little late—that I'd spaced out on something else. My parents might not know where I was. It was one thing not to want to explain to my mother that I'd been burned out intentionally. It was quite another to have them calling a dead phone and worrying. I picked up the telephone.

Once through the preliminaries (Where was I? Did I want to have lunch with my great-aunt as a week-late birthday celebration? Did I know there was a new product available that made stove cleaning even easier than before?) she let me utter my message. I was staying in a hotel while "some repairs" were being done to my apartment.

"It's about time."

"What is?"

"Your apartment needed some fixing."

"Even more so lately."

"Well, you can tell your landlord for me that refrigerator is a disgrace. My aunt had one like that before World War Two."

"I'll tell him."

"Although, if you cleaned it out more often it would help."

"Mom, I have to go now."

"What for? It's five o'clock."

"I don't quit work at five o'clock."

"Well, if you don't, you should."

"This is a competitive job—"

"Which is part of the problem, Catherine. Now that women are getting these competitive jobs, they're getting all the same illnesses men have. I saw it on Geraldo. Or Oprah. Maybe it was Sally Jessy Raphael. The ulcers. High blood pressure. Even lung cancer—"

"I think that's if you smoke, Mom. Listen, I really have to get to work—"

"Well, I understand. It means a lot to you."

Meaning it meant more than she did. "I'll talk with you soon, Mom."

After we hung up, I had just about time to sigh twice, deeply, before the phone rang.

"Cat?"

It was Hal Briskman. "Anything wrong?" I asked.

"No. But the piece on the lottery looks hot."

"How hot?"

"Hot enough to be the lead in the Times & Customs pages on Wednesday."

"*Wednesday?!*" I shrieked. This was already Thursday, which meant it would be on the stands in six days, which meant—

"Which means, as you well know, that we have to have it by Monday."

The Times & Customs section was designed as the antidote to the newspaper's midweek blahs. They liked to run articles in it by nonstaffers. Articles that could cause a little controversy, not too much, of course, wouldn't want to lose advertisers, but enough to generate a few letters and, one hoped, a lot of talk. He had not told me earlier that he wanted the lottery piece for this section.

"All right, Hal. Who bugged out on you?"

"Henrietta."

"Oh, jeez! What this time?"

"She got her hand stuck in her fax machine and sent the skin of four fingers to Omaha."

"That's impossible."

"Well, it's what she said."

"I can't get it done in time."

"You have to. It'll be good—I would have wanted to run it soon anyhow. It's turning out that the lottery conference is getting more play on the tube than we expected."

"I still can't get it done in time."

"You have to."

"You didn't ask me. I never promised to. This is last-minute changing of the assignment."

"Cat?"

"Yes?"

"You're right. I didn't warn you. You never promised. This is changing the assignment at the last minute. *And you have to. I need it.*"

"Oh."

I had to. Need. As in livelihood. Survival in my business. Getting another assignment later. Stuff like that.

"Cat?"

"Okay. Okay."

I sat picking at the damp paper for a couple of minutes. Some of it turned out to be my initial notes from the interview with Dorothy Furman. Early lotteries in colonial times. Half the prize money to the winners. Be sure to see Utah.

I was feeling calmer when the knock came at the door. Swell security they have in this hotel. Although if they're not going to replace worn carpeting, why should they check for visitors? This was an every-man-for-himself kind of place.

Mindful of the fact that somebody had been trying to kill me, I stood to one side of the door. "Who's there?"

"John."

It was really his voice, too. I opened the door.

"I'm glad to see you're at least taking precautions," he said.

I didn't need any other criticism at this point. But he meant well—don't they all?—so I didn't say it.

"Cat, come out to dinner with me."

"I can't, John. I've absolutely got to get some work done."

"Seems to me you've been working all day."

"Oh. My mother just said the same thing. What I meant was writing work. That's the real work. Getting the material together is really only getting ready to work."

"I've planned dinner in the greenhouse. You can visit Long John Silver. He's lonely."

"Sure. He said 'alone, alone, all, all alone,'"

"Not exactly. He said something about 'this delicious solitude.'"

"He didn't!"

"No, he didn't. But he also didn't eat the pea pods I got especially for him."

Well, all right; maybe it was serious.

And then I realized: John's knock was opportunity knocking. Who would know about corporation lawyers and how they could wangle stuff? Who better to tell me what to look for or ask about if I got a chance to study the papers Jack left?

"Sure. Let's do dinner," I said.

SIXTEEN

"YOU KIDDING? There's a thousand ways a lawyer can pad a bill," John said.

"Well, tell me some." I had yummed up the salmon that Lucinda, John's mother's cook, had baked in butter. She'd also made pecan pie, which she always does if she hears I'm coming over. Unlike John's mother, Lucinda is a total romantic, and thinks the best thing in the world would be for me and John to get married tomorrow. Ten to one she's got a wedding cake recipe that she's trying out mentally, just to be prepared. She thinks the way to my heart's through my stomach, and she's not wrong.

Long John Silver sat on my shoulder most of the time, his little claws tickling but not hurting. He liked lettuce, and every so often I'd give him a piece that had escaped the dressing.

"Take phone calls. Lawyers charge a fixed rate for phone calls. The actual rate depends on the lawyer's prominence or expertise, of course, but every firm has a minimum rate. And they charge each call to the client as fifteen minutes, minimum."

"What do you mean? Even if it's one minute?"

"Right. That's pretty much accepted, in fact. Say you talk to your lawyer for an hour. That's at an hour rate. Say you call and he says he'll have to call you back. You've only talked twenty seconds. That's still a fifteen-minute call."

I was disappointed. "If it's accepted, how are we gonna catch him?"

"Who said you were going to catch him?"

"Oh." Hastily, "That wasn't what I meant. I meant how was Jack going to expose him? He must have had more than phone calls."

"Not necessarily. Although where there are phone calls that are seriously overbilled, there'll be other things. What you look for is egregious opportunism."

"Swell."

"Don't be petulant. Like: Powers could have charged for twenty fifteen-minute phone calls in an hour."

"A three-hundred-minute hour?"

"Right. People—by which I mean firms, the bar association, even clients maybe—will accept five or six fifteen-minute charges in an hour. But not twenty. That could get him in trouble."

This was more like it. "Okay. What else could he do?"

"Charge full research price for boilerplate."

"Explain."

"Boilerplate you must know about. It's the paragraphs in standard contracts that are always the same or used in whole chunks. It doesn't take any research time. You must plug in the relevant boilerplate for the relevant contract or papers to file or whatever."

"So?"

"But if you want to finagle, you charge as much as if you had researched and written the whole thing from scratch."

"Every time, you mean?"

"Sure. There was a legal secretary brought up on charges recently of practicing as a lawyer without a degree. Her defense was basically this: She'd been writing all the contracts and wills and filing all the motions and so on for her firm for years, because the lawyers would tell her 'File an X' whatever, and she'd just plug in the boilerplate. They never even looked at what she did. So she thought, Why not open my own office and get paid lawyer's rates for doing this?"

"Enterprising."

"As a matter of fact, firms now have boilerplate paragraphs on their word processors that they can call up and plug in with save/get functions."

"I see. So Powers maybe charges—what?—ten hours of lawyer fees for taking five minutes to tell the secretary to plug in some pieces of boilerplate?"

"Maybe. Then there's the cases themselves."

"Go on."

"Say you're a lawyer and a case comes to you for the first time. You've never seen a whatever before, a certain kind of liability case, maybe, where a school bus was involved. So you really have to research it. Takes you thirty, maybe even fifty lawyer-hours. You charge those hours."

"Sounds fair."

"Is fair. Then the second case like that turns up. If the first one took you fifty hours, this one takes you only maybe fifteen. You check upon certain things that are different, recently decided cases as precedents, maybe. Plus no two fact situations are ever exactly alike, of course. And it takes maybe fifteen hours. You have your original precedents and arguments. But you charge fifty hours."

"Nasty."

"Now suppose you start doing cases like that all the time. You've got it down to a system by then. Except for making sure no new cases have been decided that cause you a problem, you don't need to spend much time on it at all."

"I see. And you still charge fifty hours."

"Right."

"But, John, suppose you're Powers and you argue that the client is paying for expertise. Now you're such an expert on that kind of case that it's *worth* fifty hours' pay. You might even argue that the recent clients are getting more experience and more value than the ones in the first case, the one that actually took you fifty hours."

"Aha! You could argue that. But the bar association won't buy it. Because the greater expertise is supposed to be reflected in your hourly charge, *not* fudged by pretending you did more hours work than you really did.''

I thought about that for a minute. ''So I should look for things Powers does all the time and seems to be charging too many hours for?''

''What's this 'I'? This is a job for the authorities.''

''Well, it's possible they might let me help them.''

John gave me a sideways glance, not totally unlike the way LJ looks at me. But he'd obviously made a decision not to interfere. If he'd started a lecture on me writing my stuff and not getting involved with police business and not taking chances, it would have become a serious argument in less time than it takes to fire off a Fourth of July bottle rocket.

John was learning. Hmm.

AT TEN P.M. John dropped me back at my insalubrious hotel. He was still boarding LJ for me. I thanked him very sincerely and went up to my room alone. But I stopped and peered around every corner and opened the door all the way back and scanned the room before I entered.

And sank down in the bottom-sprung chair, exhausted. At least the day was over without another major disaster! My one thought was to get into bed and sleep like the dead, and hope to finish off both the article and the solution of Jack's murder tomorrow.

Somebody knocked on the door.

It wouldn't be John. He was a genuinely dependable person. If he said he was going home and would take care of LJ, then he was going home and would take care of LJ.

It had to be Powers, or a killer sent by Powers.

At least this stupid room had a telephone. I picked it up and was about to call the desk, or punch nine for an outside line and dial 911 for the cops, but I figured it couldn't hurt to ask who it was.

Standing to one side, *not* in front of the door, I said, ''Who's there?''

''Me.''

"Damn it, who's me?" But apprehension was coming over me. I put down the phone.

"Mike," he said, just as the recognition of his voice hit home and I opened the door.

"What are *you* doing here?" I was tired, I'd been burned out of my house, somebody was trying to kill me, I was behind on my work, and I did *not* need any more hassle. I was seriously pissed off.

"Asked Hal where you were. Hey, aren't you glad to see me?"

"No. You're supposed to be in the treatment center."

"Well, I know I said—"

"You said you had to stay the full three weeks or they wouldn't treat you!"

"See, it was kind of a waste of time."

"Waste of time! You said our whole future was going to—to blossom from—was going to be the result of your treatment."

"See, Cat, there wasn't anything much to do there all day. And plus, I had a lot of work I could be doing out here. We're talking major-league boredom there—"

"It's *treatment*! It isn't supposed to be Disney World!" I could hear myself getting louder and angrier, but I couldn't stop myself. Mike's old AA buddy, Yosemite Sam Yusimele, always said don't make excuses for them, but don't blame them either. I couldn't help it.

"You've been drinking!" I said.

"Just one beer. On my way over."

"It was more than one!"

"Just one. I swear."

"You're lying!" I screamed.

"Well, two."

"I knew it! God damn it, Mike. You promised!"

"Hey." His voice got low and reasonable. "I can handle this myself. Without wasting so much time. I can just cut down on my own."

"You can *not*. That's the whole point! Oh, shit. I can't count on anything with you! I'm fed up. I just want to be able to know that you're going to do what you say you're going to do. And that's obviously too much for you to handle."

"Cat, please—"

"Don't say it! Don't even try! I want you out of here! Right now!"

"Hey, Cat. Come on—"

"No! Out! Outoutoutout!"

"I'll be home if you change your mind," he said quietly.

"No, you'll be in a goddamn bar!"

"Give me a chance."

"I've done that before!"

I slammed the door on him, just at the moment when somebody in the next room started pounding on the wall.

SEVENTEEN

McCoo's DESK was covered with papers. Awash with papers. Laden. Swamped. Piled. A Sergeant Kolodny, who seemed to be a CPD money expert, kept trying to prevent the papers from slipping off onto the floor, but they did anyway. Plus some of them were developing coffee rings. McCoo was still visibly worried about Susanne, but he'd got himself paced enough so that he was brewing some sort of Nigerian coffee this Friday morning. Which was a good thing. I was not in any frame of mind to kid-glove him or anybody else. I'd been seriously pissed off when Mike left last night, and an uneasy sleep, dreaming of smoke and flames, hadn't done anything to sweeten my disposition.

"Don't worry so much," McCoo said, as Kolodny wiped coffee from a sheet of paper. "They're only Xeroxes."

But Kolodny, like a lot of financial people, *respected* paper, and he wiped it anyway.

At least they were letting me look.

"How'd Jack Sligh get this stuff, do you think?" Kolodny asked.

I said, "It's just a wild guess, but if Powers has a youngish, nice-looking secretary or office manager, I'd guess Jack would find a way."

Kolodny had already cottoned on to the excessive phone call charges before I told him about it. He chortled and put one fat finger on the sheet he'd just wiped. "8/18/89. Between ten-fifteen and noon, thirty-eight fifteen-minute phone calls. 8/19/89, eight in an hour. 8/21/89, twelve. Goes on like that. Really gets your attention, yuh?"

"It sure does," I said.

"Plenty more, too."

"What about cases where Powers knew the type of case cold and charged as if he were doing it for the first time?" I had explained what John had told me.

"I don't know how we could tell that," Kolodny said, "unless we went over every case he was working on and found out exactly what it was about. Analyzed the content."

"And that's not a problem for Violent Crimes," McCoo said, keeping us focused, quite properly, on the murder.

I'd been looking at the Xeroxes. "Are these Jack's own Xeroxes, or copies of his copies?"

"Copies of Jack's copies. I keep the originals in a file. Not for working on," Kolodny said in a tone of horror. Like, do you sketch over the Mona Lisa to learn painting?

"Oh. Then these squiggles on these time sheets here may be his?"

"Yuh. They're pencil on the originals, Jack's copies, I mean. They aren't readable, though."

Kolodny was obviously not a man who had to decipher his own notes the way I had to, hastily written in the dark at a political rally—and decipher them two months later when it turns out surprisingly that they were important.

"Do you take notes in full words?" I asked him. Couldn't resist.

"Sure. You wanta be able to read them later, yuh?"

"Look here." I pointed at a couple of squiggles. They looked like "rit disnay," but that made no sense. "There are two of these 'rit disnay' things, one on this page and one a couple of pages back. Where was the one I was looking at a minute ago?"

"On the floor," McCoo said quietly.

"Oh, okay. Well, look for some more of them."

Kolodny said, "Even though we don't know what they mean?"

"Yeah. Because I'll tell you why. When you see several of the same thing, the differences sort of iron themselves out. And then you can see what it means. Sometimes."

He found two. I found one more. Then McCoo, who had been watching us and smiling wryly like an elder statesman, said with surprise, "Here's one, too. Right in front of me."

"Okay. Now look at these. It's not 'rit disnay.' What looks like a 'd' is obviously a 'cl' on this sheet and what looks like a 'y' is a 'g'. And the first 'i' doesn't have a dot over it. Neither does the second one. I'll bet the first one is an 'e' and the second one is the beginning half of an 'o'."

"So?"

"So it's 'ret closing.'"

Kolodny said, "You can't really tell—hey, you know, you may have something there."

"And that means 'retail closing.' Something to do with closing a lottery retail outlet, I'll bet."

"Hey!" said Kolodny, seizing up all the papers with 'ret closing' on them and bringing them to his face to study better. He was a terrier on the scent.

I waited, having done my part. McCoo poured coffee.

"They're all for $15,000. And there's different initials ahead of them on the lines. Plus the dates go all the way from 1986 to the present! I'll bet he was doing retail closings and charging fifteen thou every time, and—"

"—using the same boilerplate every time and doing zero work!" I finished.

"And for this," Kolodny said, "he was making annually—we haven't got all the figures and we haven't talked with the IRS yet—he was making between $250,000 and $350,000 a year."

And at that point, we all sat back and smiled.

After half a minute, though, I started to wonder. "McCoo, how could he get away with it? I mean, doesn't somebody check? Doesn't the state or the city audit this stuff and figure out how much this kind of legal work is supposed to cost?"

"Sure," McCoo said. "Some."

"So why don't they do anything about it?"

"Point one. They don't have the time or the money to audit everything."

"Spot check?"

"Look. City government, Cook County government, state government. Lots of jurisdictions. Take the city. You got hundreds of agencies. You got the Board of Ed, Water, Streets and San, the CTA, Parks, more agencies, as my father would say, than you can shake a stick at. Now they all gotta have legal help. These days everybody's gotta have legal help."

"I know that."

"So they've got guys on retainer. In-house counsel. Take care of routine stuff that comes up. Every damn question has to go to the legal department. They get paid a salary. Then, on top of that there's independent counsel in law firms. Supposed to do more specialized stuff. Take the time a couple years ago when somebody decided to straighten out the S-curve on Lake Shore Drive. Well, that's not just land rights and easements and liability, all that kind of thing, it's also on the lake front so you got air rights and water rights. Lotta legal time. Supposedly."

"Supposedly?"

"These outside firms get thrown a lot of work. Now I'm not saying that project specifically, who wants to cast stones? But suppose there's a major city project going. Or county or state. Who decides what firm to hire? Well, suppose a firm is hired, one they've hired before. Suppose they're overpaid. Suppose some of that overpayment money gets siphoned off, goes back to pay campaign contributions to certain political candidates. Maybe even the very guys who decided to hire them."

"Wait. Wait. There's a federal law that limits campaign contributions."

"Sure there is. Suuu-uuure there is. But now suppose you have a three-hundred-man law firm. Excuse me, three-hundred-*person* law firm. Each lawyer can contribute, say, a thousand dollars to Representative's X's campaign, right? *As individuals*. After all, they got their rights. Don't they?''

"Right."

"And that's three hundred thousand dollars."

"Yes. It is."

"So if that firm pads its bills shamelessly, is the alderman, or the legislature, or whatever, going to say, let's go over that firm's billing practices with a fine-tooth comb?''

"No."

Kolodny also said, "No."

"There's some sweet, sweet deals out there in lawyerland."

John had used those words, too. Sweet deals. "And there isn't anything you can do about these guys!!?" I was outraged. This was my tax money in their pockets.

"Not much. They're insulated."

Kolodny said, "See, everybody really knows this goes on. But nobody has any interest in doing something about it. Even if the Democratic representative from a district knows the Republican rep from his district is doing it, he may not want to say anything because his guys are doing it for him."

"It's an open secret," McCoo said.

"An open secret," I repeated.

"It just lies there," McCoo said.

"But there has to be something—"

"Unless there's a scandal. Then it's a whole new ballgame."

"Suddenly everybody gets moral?"

"Right. And scandal basically means the press."

"Oh. Meaning me in this case?"

"Yup. That's how Jack Sligh intended to use you. To blow Robert Layton Powers out of the water."

OPEN SECRETS, HUH? One that Bob Powers knew that a few people knew about but he didn't want to see in print. Because then something would have to be done about it.

Or to put it another way, if I did an article on Powers ripping off the lottery for hundreds of thousands of excess legal fees, his career was over, his income would stop, and he might even go to jail.

Motive for murder? You bet.

Powers would have seen Jack and me come down the corridor together and into the central pool in the Lottery wing. We were talking, and pretty obviously continuing a conversation. You can tell when people have just started talking, even if you can't hear the words. Then Jack got into his fight with Seymour Dennisovitch and Powers and I helped pull them apart. Then Powers took Jack to the washroom to clean him up.

Did Jack hint at something then?

Or did Powers berate him for the fight and make Jack angry? Then did Jack threaten him with exposure?

After which, it would have been no problem for Powers to hang around Jack's door while Jack phoned some contacts and got information on me. Taking an elevator down, following him to the street was no trouble at all in that crowd. And then he would have seen us talk, maybe even heard Jack ask me about doing exposés, although we were speaking at normal volume then. And he would certainly have heard the shouted words about the appointment for eleven on Tuesday.

No, wait. If he heard the whole conversation, then he would have known that Jack had not told me the content of the story yet. He'd only asked me generally if I did exposés. Therefore, he would not have tried to kill me. Jack, yes, but not me. So Powers must have seen us talking, but being tall, he probably didn't dare get close or he'd be seen. So he didn't hear what we said. Until we loudly made our eleven o'clock appointment.

Which meant Powers thought Jack had told me his name and his game, or couldn't take the chance that *maybe* Jack had told me.

Which meant that when I went to see him yesterday, he must have thought I was playing a very cool, very subtle game. He could even have thought I was trying to black-mail him.

And this meant I was probably in greater danger than before.

TEN O'CLOCK in the morning and no time to start giving in to feelings of tiredness. Working by yourself, you can think of a lot of reasons to take time out. After all, nobody is standing over you. You can easily get to thinking: time for coffee and a *really large* jelly doughnut. This is weakness. (Most reporters, just like cops, know the diners and coffee shops that serve the largest coffees and the largest, juiciest doughnuts.)

Instead, I consulted my Lottery Week schedule. This was Friday, which in terms of the panels provided was advertising day. Television advertising at ten A.M., which I was now missing; radio advertising at eleven. Break for lunch, then point-of-purchase at four. Since this was the last day, there was no evening on the town. Instead, at six there was a delegates-only cocktail party in the Lottery wing at City Hall. For "delegates only," I read between the lines "no press or public." There would certainly be politicians there.

I'd crash it. No problem.

Then at eight was the closing banquet in the Boul' Mich Room at the Stratford. Maybe I could crash that, too. There was always an unclaimed ticket at the last minute. Maybe Hal would pay for it.

THE RADIO ADVERTISING panel was, according to the lobby bulletin board, in the Queen Anne Room, 2C. This proved to be an extremely plain room with no windows and a brown carpet patterned with red paramecia. Some day some hotel will call their meeting rooms Ordinary B and Nothing Special C. And win the Hotel Association Honesty of the Year award.

Right.

A man introduced to the group as Peter Bergendorf of Marks and Sales played us a number of radio lottery ads. He categorized them as narrative, descriptive, and reminders. The reminders apparently didn't give anybody any new information, but just reminded them that the lottery existed or when the drawings took place. A narrative:

WOMAN'S VOICE: I never believed it could happen to us!

MAN'S VOICE: Neither did I.

WOMAN'S VOICE: I was at the store, and I had a little change left over and I just thought I'd pick up a lottery ticket.

MAN'S VOICE: I'm sure glad you did.

DIFFERENT MAN'S VOICE: But how did you choose your numbers, Mrs. Kneeland?

WOMAN'S VOICE: Oh, I used my Social Security number, but I broke it up, you know, and part of my daughter's Social Security number!

OTHER MAN'S VOICE: And what do you plan do do with the eight million dollars?

WOMAN'S VOICE: Oh, my! I'm going to buy a little house in Florida for my father, who's retired, and we're going on a trip to Italy, like we always wanted to do, and my husband wants a riding mower... (*voice continues, fading out as music fades in*).

I listened to this and a musical ad, and then realized I wasn't concentrating. I was worrying about Robert Layton Powers and the murder of Jack Sligh. There was something not quite clear about the sequence of events. I slipped out the door of the meeting room.

A large clipboard came toward me down the hall, with Dorothy Furman behind it. "Cat Marsala," she said. "Getting whatever data you need?"

"I think so. Has the conference been a success?"

"Absolutely. At least everybody we invited came, and what's more, they all stayed." She almost laughed at herself. Obviously, she was half giddy from the relief. You do months of work, leading up to a conference like this. You wake up at night with terrors about what can go wrong. And when it looks like it's all coming to an end without utter catastrophe, the relief makes you silly.

Except there had been one catastrophe. Jack.

"Um, Dorothy. I hate to ask, but I haven't heard anything about a funeral for Jack."

"You haven't heard because we don't know yet. They have to release the body from the morgue."

"Really? Why would they hold it?"

"What they told Doris was that they didn't get to the autopsy until yesterday."

"There's a lot of bodies in Chicago."

"It's so unnecessary to take all this time. They know what he died of. Everybody knows he died from a fall. And we'd like Doris to get it over with. She needs to put the whole thing behind her. Doris is having emotional problems with this."

This or maybe she had them before.

"Well, Dorothy—I'd better let you get to work."

"With any luck, the funeral will be Monday."

I WENT OUT WALKING, but it didn't clear my head. In order not to waste time, I stopped by John's offices and put in an hour and a half on the word processor, getting my thoughts together on the lottery article.

About one o'clock, still restless, I finally gave in to the coffee-and-doughnut urge.

The Jumbo Java is just a block off LaSalle. It's specifically designed to give sugar and caffeine boosts to office-weary executives. The coffee comes in a mug the size of a soup bowl and they'll keep filling it as long as you sit there. The doughnuts are six inches across. I ordered the raspberry jelly-filled yeast-raised doughnut.

My problem was that I couldn't make the motivation behind the events work out in a reasonable way.

I had told Hermione that writing an article was like feeling your way around in a strange, dark house, little by little defining the shape of a house around you. Getting the feel of what had happened to Jack was somewhat the same. And although I didn't know why, exactly, it wasn't coming clear. I was falling over furniture in the dark, and running into walls that were not at right angles to other walls.

In fact, there were walls that didn't fit at all. For a couple of days I had had the feeling of a shadow reason, a half-perceived motive for Jack's death. I couldn't quite touch it, couldn't see it at all. But it was out there all around me, as if it were perceived by the third eye that the ancients believed existed in the center of the head.

McCoo and I had agreed that Robert Layton Powers's need to keep his "open secret" from the press was motive enough. So far so good.

Open secrets I can understand. It's a credit to the power of the press. Nothing mysterious about it, either. The point isn't just that people know there's a problem but nobody does anything until the press gets involved. It's really that very *few* people know there's a problem until the press gets involved, and the ones who know don't necessarily have a reason to make a fuss. Democracy being the populous thing it is, nothing gets done until a lot of voters are up in arms.

This is political reality.

But wouldn't it have been an even bigger, better motive for somebody like Bob Powers in cahoots with others to rig the lottery so he won millions? How did the three hundred thousand dollars or so that Robert Layton Powers made a year compare to that?

I pulled over a paper napkin. The usual lottery grand prize was six or seven million dollars. But it wasn't paid all at once. It was given out in installments over twenty years. So, if an individual won six million, spread out over twenty years that was 6,000,000 divided by 20, or $300,000. Good

God, I hadn't thought of it that way. A guy like Powers was already making as much off the thing as if he'd won the lottery!

I pulled over another paper napkin, having torn through the first one with the point of my pencil in my excitement. The lottery's total handle, the total amount of money that went through it in a year, was two billion dollars. That's a two followed by nine zeroes—$2,000,000,000. That's big money in anybody's book. Half of that's prizes, but most of the prizes are very small amounts to Quick Cash winners, and even the bigger winners don't win so very much money. Five percent of the two billion is salaries, advertising, and costs. Costs like lawyers. Five percent is .05 times 2,000,000,000. I calculated. A hundred million dollars. Say half of that hundred million is paid to individual people who work for the lottery, like Powers. Half is fifty million dollars.

Fifty million dollars to spread around on individuals! They can pay Robert Layton Powers three hundred thousand and hardly notice. His three hundred thousand would be—um—.006. In other words, six-tenths of one per cent of the salaries budget.

And what part of the total handle is that? 300,000 divided by 2,000,000,000. This needs another napkin. Um—it's .00015, or fifteen one-thousandths of one percent of the lottery total. Powers's bite was like that of a gnat.

Now, let me figure it the other way—somebody bringing off a lottery rigging. Say the win is six million dollars. If he was going to do it by, say, injecting water into some of the Ping-Pong balls, he'd need a lot of people in his pocket. And he'd still be taking a terrible risk of discovery. He'd need collaboration from the two people who break the seals on the ball container. He'd need the collaboration of the guards who watch this. He'd probably need the collaboration of half a dozen or so other people who transport, oversee, and dispose of the balls. Maybe fourteen or more people altogether. But for the sake of simplicity, let's suppose he can do it with the collaboration of just ten people, including himself. If the yearly payout on a six-million-dollar prize, $300,000, is divided among ten people, each gets $30,000 a year.

Powers is making ten times that in salary without anywhere near the risk!

Obviously, the real way to rip off the lottery was to get paid by the lottery.

So okay. Forget the prizes. What else was bothering me? McCoo had said Jack was going to use me to blow Robert Layton Powers out of the water. That would work. No problem.

But why? *Why* did he want to get Powers? What did he have, particularly, against Powers? It was the lack of motivation that bothered me.

Nobody, not Powers, not Jack, not even Hector Furman, Sr., who said he didn't like Jack and probably would have told me if Jack were causing trouble with the lottery attorney, had said word one about a grudge between Jack and Powers.

So why did Jack do it?

If Jack was out to get Powers, it was an excellent reason for Powers to kill Jack. No problem there, either. Powers was looking not only at the loss of future financial bonanzas from the lottery account, but possible disbarment, possible prison, and—which was more important to some of these guys—certain disgrace.

Which also gave him an excellent reason to try to kill me, if he thought Jack had sicced me on the case.

But all of this did *not* give Jack a reason to do it in the first place.

Plain meanness?

That was not my take on Jack. He was slick maybe, a womanizer no doubt, and maybe even conniving, but not gratuitously mean.

Let's try it from the top again. Vaguely, I noticed the waiter pouring more coffee. Good. My brain burns about two hundred milligrams of caffeine an hour.

First. Assume Jack has evidence against Powers. Powers has been ripping off the lottery for years.

Two. Meeting me gives him an idea of how to destroy Powers. So he asks me, in a vaguely worded way, whether I'd be interested. Like an idiot, I don't take him to lunch right then, but make an appointment for the next day.

Three. Powers knows about the appointment but does not know that I haven't been given any useful information yet. The police haven't admitted publicly that Jack was murdered—in fact, they haven't even as of today, Friday—so he thinks he got away with Jack's murder clean. Next he needs to kill me.

Four. He burns my apartment, figuring it will go down as another accident.

Great, wonderful. Then why hasn't he tried to wipe me out since then? Because he's figured out I don't know anything, after all? Or because he hasn't had a chance?

Probably he hasn't had a good shot at it. I've been moving around a lot. Okay, I can buy that.

But I'm right back at the beginning on the origin of all this. What did Jack have against Powers? Why did he want so badly to destroy him?

There was only one chance to find out: Go to the cocktail party and ask every living soul until somebody tells me.

I looked down at my plate. There was the end of a cinnamon cruller on it. But I had ordered a raspberry jelly-filled, hadn't I? The waiter, noticing that I was puzzled, came over.

"Would you like the check?"

"Please."

The check said coffee and a jelly-filled doughnut, a chocolate bismarck, and a cruller. I'd ordered and eaten all three without being aware of it.

EIGHTEEN

THE SEMINAR ON point-of-purchase advertising was in full swing when I got back to the Stratford. It actually was neither a lecture nor a panel discussion, but a sort of tour. The lottery people, jointly with Marks and Sales, had arranged a variety of displays around the four walls of the meeting room. These were the sorts of displays that were used on the counters at stores that sold lottery tickets, and they went back several years. They were arranged in chronological order, and on the fourth wall arrived at suggested future displays.

Touchingly, a lot of them were posters, layouts and gadgets I had seen in Jack's office. Even the electronic pinball machine was there, and delegates were playing it, groaning when they lost and groaning when they won, too, because it was not yet set up to pay off real money on bets.

A trio of young people, two men and a woman, were acting as guides. Each had a group of delegates and was walking them from display to display, explaining when and why it had been developed, how well it had worked in terms of sales, and why it was no longer used.

The middle of the room held large posters and counter displays for the projected Central States Lottery. There was even a real store counter, and on it some mocked-up Central States Lottery tickets. They were larger than the lottery ticket Illinois presently had and much more beautifully colored. The usual warnings about the odds were printed on the backs of the tickets in small black type over a glorious four-color print of a highway running between forested mountains with a yellow, orange, pink, red, purple, and cerise sunset in the background.

There were also three or four prototypes of the new point-of-purchase ticket dispenser. The latest thing, as Jack had said, was on-line recording of bets and dispensing of tickets with your own choice of numbers. The designs ranged from the functional—something not much different from a thinking typewriter—to the bizarre—a clown face that spat tickets out of its mouth.

I followed one of the guides around the hall, mainly keeping an eye out for my acquaintances—Dorothy and Doris Furman, Hector Junior or Senior, Robert Layton Powers, Seymour Dennisovitch, and the little gray man with no name. The only one present was the little gray man. The others were probably setting up for the cocktail party and banquet.

When I saw the little gray man, I approached him where he stood in front of a counter display: "It's YOUR lucky day!" The tickets were green and white, with mock-dollar-bill-etched patterns, a discarded motif from six years back.

"Hello," I said, placing myself in front of him.

He blinked.

I said, "How come you're here? I thought you disapproved of the lottery."

"Oh, my, yes. Didn't I make that clear?"

"Yes, you did. But you were listening so carefully to the guide."

"Naturally. I have to keep track of the opposition."

"I hadn't thought of that. That makes sense, of course. What have you learned?"

"The astounding inventiveness of evil."

"Oh. Well, yes, there is that. Uh, Mr.—"

"Yes?" He still wouldn't utter his name.

"You remember Mr. Sligh, who came by on Monday while we were talking?"

"Yes. An evil man. Although, to be generous, it's possible he was deluded, not bad."

"Mmmm. Did you ever hear him refer to Robert Layton Powers?"

"No. I can't say I ever did."

"Do you know Robert Layton Powers?"

"No. Who is he?"

"The attorney for the lottery."

"Oh. Another one of them."

"Distinguished-looking guy. Grayish white hair. Tall. Hawk-nosed sort of profile. Wears navy suits with a chalk stripe?"

"No." He shook his head in what looked like real regret. "Sorry."

"Well, thanks."

I waved, one of those hand gestures that takes the place of meaningless words like "See you later," and started to walk away. He said, "Wait!" Eagerly, I turned back.

He said, "Have you finished your article? Have you done what I advised?"

I smiled through gritted teeth. Another person who wants that damned article done. "I'm working on it. It's not done yet."

"That's good." He blessed me with an approving nod and turned back to the display.

It was now after five P.M., and the display was supposed to close, but a lot of the delegates continued to play with the player-activated machines and the other technical gadgetry. I hung around a little longer. Nothing magically appeared to solve my mystery for me, though. At five-thirty I took off for the Lottery wing of City Hall, where the cocktail party would take place.

I didn't have an invitation and wasn't a delegate. No problem. I waved to an approaching pair of delegates and went up with them in the elevator and chatted my way with them into the hall.

Giddy festivity had taken over. A gaggle of attendants in black suits and white aprons had just finished placing trays of hors d'oeuvres on trestle tables covered with white cloths. They stood back to admire their handiwork. The secretaries' desks had been draped in white, and now other attendants bore in great buckets of ice and trays of glasses. Bottles of vodka, gin, vermouth, bourbon, rye, scotch, a variety of wines, brandies, and bitters were already in place. Delegates were beginning to arrive. Dorothy Furman, wearing an ankle-length black velvet skirt and a white ruffled blouse, stood like a conductor in the center. I wanted to talk with her, but this was no time to bother her.

Hector Furman, Sr., stood near the door, wearing just about what he had worn when I last saw him, except that in honor of the occasion he'd covered the sleeve garters with a nicely tailored jacket.

"Hi, Mr. Furman," I said.

"So it's little Cat. Have you finished your work?"

"People keep asking me that. I'm afraid I'm still working on it."

"It seems strange that it takes so long."

"I hear that from everybody. I figure this is the way I work. People can take it or leave it."

"Hmm. You may be short, but you're feisty."

"That's me. Speaking of feisty, I wanted to ask you something about Jack." Gorgeous segue, huh?

Mr. Furman didn't like it, either. He frowned. "The sooner we can forget about him—"

"I understand, but tell me this. You know Robert Layton Powers, right?"

"Sure. Lottery mouthpiece."

"Ever called him that?"

"Sure. Makes him spit nails."

"Did Jack have anything against him?"

Hector Furman cocked his head. His beautiful white hair reflected light as he did. "I never heard anything about it, if so. What is this?"

"Well, maybe nothing. I just got the impression."

"Hmmp. Beats me."

Hector Furman then personally got me the first glass from the first bottle of champagne. "Fizz for the feisty," he said.

"Fizz *from* the feisty, if you ask me."

I'd been keeping an eye on Dorothy, and when I saw her taking a break between one ceremonial duty and another, I said to Hector Furman, "Do you mind if I go catch Dorothy for a minute?"

"Of course I mind. You'll leave me with nothing but the Utah delegation to talk with." And there they were, in blue suits, white shirts, and ties. I may have looked contrite, because he said, "No, no. Go ahead. You may be a reporter, but you're sympathetic."

"Glad it's over?" I said to Dorothy.

"Glad it's almost over."

Tired of leading up to things subtly or unsubtly, I said, "Do you happen to know what Jack had against Robert Powers?"

"Against him?" She was startled.

"Yes. Some grudge? A natural antipathy?"

"I don't think so. I don't think they ever ran into each other much."

"Is Doris coming tonight?"

"Certainly. She ought to have been here by now." That frown that came so easily to Dorothy's forehead was back again. I supposed she thought Doris had stopped for a brandy or two.

Several delegates came into the hall from the direction of the elevators, which were out of sight around the corridor. No—several delegates and the little gray man. Dorothy said, "Excuse me," stepped away from me, touched a tallish man on the shoulder, and pointed to the little gray man. The tall man collected another gentleman, almost a carbon copy of himself, and together they strolled toward the little gray man. I heard one of them say, "—for the delegates only, sir."

There was a moment of protest, but they had adroitly turned him around and they walked, the three abreast, back down the corridor toward the elevators.

Dorothy was doing her bit to avoid unpleasantness.

I edged over to her again. While other delegates were coming in two by two, there were a couple of nondelegates, like me. I saw Seymour Dennisovitch enter, chatting with a beautiful woman, a delegate from Ohio. I turned to Dorothy and raised my eyebrows.

She was quick on the uptake, as usual. "Denny isn't a troublemaker. That little man always is. Eventually. He's quiet at first and then he starts nagging, and later he's shrieking."

"Oh. But Denny was a troublemaker on Monday."

"*Jack* was a troublemaker on Monday."

"Denny did his share. He really did hit Jack first. I was there."

"Okay. I didn't see the beginning of it. But I'll bet Jack egged him on. Jack used people."

"Maybe."

"And besides, we can't turn Denny out. He's a panelist, you know."

"I know. You didn't turn me out, either."

"Well, you're going to write something nice about us, aren't you?" Her smile was steely.

"I'm certainly not going to attack you. Really."

"Good."

One of the waiters pouring champagne slopped a drop on the hand of a delegate from Nebraska. Dorothy's head went up like a fox scenting a chicken. "Excuse me," she said again. I watched without hearing what she was saying, but the waiter's chin drew back into his neck and he nodded, short, sharp little "aye, aye, sir" nods.

While I was turned away from the entrance, Doris must have arrived. She was partway across the room now, and Hector Junior was shepherding her. Doris was walking straight, with no weaving or hesitation—so straight and so carefully I knew she'd had a couple of bracers on the way. She was making for the hard drinks bar, not the champagne table, and I moved out on an intercept course.

We met at the scotch and bourbon.

No matter how you looked at it, if Robert Layton Powers didn't kill Jack, Doris was next in line with motive. In fact, on the basis of motive alone, there was really no choosing between them. Powers would lose his income, job, reputation, and possibly his freedom. Doris would lose half her home, her net worth, and had already lost reputation and face, from her point of view, because of his womanizing. Who could choose?

Junior said, "I'd rather you didn't talk with Doris right now."

"Why?"

He tried to get between Doris and me. In fact, he picked up a bourbon and water that he had probably ordered for himself and handed it to me, putting his back to her, me facing him. "She's had a rough week."

"She's a grown-up. She's here at a cocktail party. Can't she talk to whoever she wants?" I could see the slight thickness of the gun under his coat. Aren't jackets usually tailored so well that you can't notice a gun easily? I wondered whether maybe Junior wanted it known that he carried it. Necessity? Or a macho thing? Maybe somebody who has been "Junior" all his life needs a macho enhancer.

"She doesn't want to talk to you."

"Yes, I do," Doris said, coming around to stand next to Junior.

"No, you don't."

"Yes, I do."

Junior glowered and then stomped away. He certainly did not have the grace of his father, which was odd, because in terms of dress and vocabulary, the elder Hector Furman was definitely a rough diamond and Junior was sleek as a ferret.

After a couple of seconds, I noticed that Doris hadn't said anything. I was in a peculiar position, wanting to talk with her, but wondering why she wanted to talk with me. I said, "Anything special you wanted to discuss?"

"Gawd, no. Just wanted to get ridda my shadow."

"Hector Junior?"

"Yeah. Hovers around me. Like I was gonna explode or something. Gawd!"

"I can see how that would be annoying."

"Annoying! Galls the hell outta me."

"Doesn't he have work to do?"

"Ha!"

"Mmmm. Doris, there was one thing I wanted to ask you about."

"Sure, dear. What did you say your name was?"

"Cat Marsala."

"Go right ahead, Cat."

"You know the lottery attorney, Robert Powers?"

"Yeah. Not well. Snooty type."

"That's the guy. Did Jack have anything against him, that you know of?"

Her face went blank. "Whattaya mean? Like a grudge?"

"Yes. Exactly."

"Gawd, no. Not that I ever heard about." She grabbed my arm with the hand that wasn't holding the brandy. And even though she leaned forward with great urgency, she didn't spill a drop. "You gotta remember, honey, he didn't *confide* in me a lot. Crappy bastard!"

She took a ladylike sip of her brandy and released my arm. People pushed past us to get to the bar. I gestured that maybe we should step farther back, but Doris ignored me.

Words like "residual takeout" and "retailer motivation package" swirled around us.

I was still holding the bourbon intended for Hector Junior, so I drank some. Doris was clearly not going to leave the bar, and I was tired of being jostled, so I nodded to her and walked away. She didn't show much sign of caring.

A waiter was circulating with canapés, tiny little pigs in blankets, not more than an inch long. I took two and wished it were four.

Mr. Scott, from the Utah delegation, was saying to a short, balding man from Kentucky, "—only five percent of the budget, anyway. Are you going to sell your soul for such a trifle?''

Near the drinks bar, another of the Kentucky delegation said, ''—with branch water. Then you take the mint and muddle it with sugar—''

''Call it Lucky Tuesday!'' said a woman from Arkansas.

''No, call it Bonanza!'' said the man with her, who was from Wyoming.

''The Money Tree!'' said another.

Seymour Dennisovitch was gloomy. He moaned to the beautiful woman from Ohio as I passed, ''Not one definite, voted commitment.''

''But they can't,'' she said. ''This is just a conference.''

''They could vote a resolution.''

''They don't have any power. That comes when the commission is set up.''

''They could have voted a sense of the meeting.''

They were talking, of course, about a set-aside of money for treating compulsive gamblers. I had almost dismissed Seymour Dennisovitch as a suspect in Jack's murder the first day I talked to him. But now I had a twinge of misgiving. He was so driven, so obsessed.

But, no. I didn't think so. And it didn't fit with Jack's plan to destroy Powers.

Speak the name, even mentally, and he appears. There was Robert Layton Powers himself, he of the expensive suits, passing me on his way to the bar.

''Miss Marsala,'' he said. ''How's the article going?''

''Almost done.'' Now, why did I say that? The man ticked me off, he was too sure of himself.

I didn't try to talk with him. Instead, I took another sip of the bourbon and made my way to a chair. I sat and took another sip of bourbon.

I don't drink much. It's not that I wouldn't like to, but when you work at night, it's a bad idea. The stuff puts you to sleep. Right now, though, it was making me pensive.

For the purposes of thinking this over, I decided to assume that Jack in fact didn't have any quarrel with Robert Powers. If that was true, was there *any* reason to drag him into the press and destroy his life?

Because he was a crook?

Well, that would be reason enough for the FBI or some state agency, maybe. It would be enough for many people. Me, I was pretty angry at Powers for taking the state for a ride and wasting my tax money. For a moral crusader, shooting Robert Layton Powers down would be a necessity.

But not for Jack.

He wasn't that kind of guy. He was pragmatic, selfish, and world-wise. No tilting at windmills for Jack Sligh. He had to have something to gain. What would he gain? The only thing that would happen is Powers would be made an example of in all the papers. An object lesson to the crooked.

Object lesson?

Example?

Oh-oh.

I put down my glass. Casually, I walked over to Dorothy and said as a sort of smoke screen, "May I check in at the banquet later and see if there's a spare ticket?"

"Certainly. Should be a couple."

"See you there." The banquet was at eight. It was now six forty-five. Ever so casually, I strolled toward the hall.

Down the hall, around the corner toward the elevators.

But I didn't enter the elevators. I deflected to the bank of three telephones against the flanking wall. Let McCoo be in his office. Ordinarily, he would be. But he was worried about Susanne and might have gone home early, early for him at least, to be with her.

He answered. I looked around to make sure nobody was listening.

"I know who killed Jack!" I said.

"Not Powers?"

"No."

"What's his name, then?"

"I don't know his name. Or hers, but—"

"You just said you did."

"I said I know who did it. Just listen a minute, will you?"

"Go ahead."

"It was one of the Furmans. My best guess would be Hector Junior."

"Why?"

"McCoo, why would Jack try to destroy Robert Powers?"

"Hated him?"

"Nobody thinks he did. In fact, all the Furmans deny Jack had anything against Powers. They're probably hoping I won't see any connection between them. Maybe some of them really don't know. But one of them certainly knows all about it and he or she isn't saying. No, Jack was going to shoot Powers down *as an example*. To show what would happen if they opposed him. To show he could do it."

"Opposed him in what?"

"The divorce settlement. There's serious money there. Doris keeps telling me he wanted more than his fair share. Doris is the loose lip in the group."

"So what did he want them to do?"

"Not contest his settlement offer. McCoo, we're talking *at least* several hundred thousand dollars here."

"Or else what?"

"Or else he would expose them like he had exposed Powers. I suppose he'd tell them a couple of days ahead of time what he'd done, how he'd collected the evidence and how he'd released the data. Naturally, he wouldn't want it attributed to him in print; he was a public employee. Then the Powers scandal would hit the papers and Powers would be a quivering bloody lump and nobody would have said 'Boo!' to anything Jack wanted. Poor old Powers himself didn't try to kill me or Jack, and he probably didn't even know this was coming. I say 'poor old' sarcastically,

McCoo. I think the man's somewhere lower than the green stuff you find underneath piers in the dead of summer."

"Just fine, Cat, but what did Jack have on the Furmans?"

"Exactly the same thing. That was the beauty of it. Exactly the same thing."

"Don't make me mad, here—"

"They're collecting money they're not earning. Fred Furman never goes to inspect the retailers he's supposed to. Doris doesn't do any work at all; the supervisor as much as told me so. Hector Junior just came back from Trinidad and is already getting ready to go to the Bahamas—or maybe it was the other way around. Hector Senior was a big help to the lottery once, but he's still being paid even though he's almost retired. This is pork barrel in the grand Chicago manner. Dorothy is the only one who's working, but they're drawing down five salaries, four of them management level. Between the lot of them, they're probably drawing down close to five hundred thousand dollars, and that's more than they could make if they'd rigged a win on the lottery!"

"Why hasn't somebody noticed this?"

"You told *me* why. Remember? The open secret? Of course, Jack probably collected some documentation you could start looking for. Like he did on Powers. I don't know why this didn't hit me sooner. I had every pointer in the world. When I saw Doris's desk, there was nothing on it. Hector Junior's was the same. From the very beginning, every time Dorothy sent me to interview somebody, it was never one of the family. I only ran into them by accident. She never even suggested I talk with her father, the grand old man of the lottery. I had to hear about him from you and John. When I asked about ads, she didn't even mention Jack. Mentioned Marks and Sales instead. She kept sending me to Gamblers Anonymous or Utah."

"Utah?"

"Not the state, the people. Never mind. Doris, too. She talked about retailers and never mentioned Dorothy's son

Fred. Even Hector Senior. You'd think he'd brag about his kids. He's very family oriented, very protective. But I don't think he would have introduced me to Doris if his back hadn't gone into a spasm.''

"That's nice, Cat. But you have to pin it on a particular person and you have to prove it. You can't go into court and say that somebody didn't introduce you to their sister."

"I know that. I'm working on it."

There was a moment's silence. Then McCoo said, "So who tried to burn down your apartment?"

"The Furmans hired it done. One of the Furmans. Whichever. I think Hector Junior."

"Why?"

"They thought Jack had told me about this. Or hinted it. I even—oh, Lord—I joked to Dorothy on Monday after I met Jack that I should do a story on the Furmans. The Lottery Family, I think I said."

There was another silence.

"Cat? Where are you right now?"

"City Hall."

"Where in City Hall?"

"The Lottery wing."

"Are you nuts! Why in God's name are you calling me from there, you idiot!''

"Don't call me an idiot. I'm the one who figured it out."

"Somebody might hear you, you idiot!''

"I've been watching. There's nobody in sight, you ingrate!''

"All right. All right! Just get out of there! *And leave the rest of this to us!*"

I said, "Yes, boss." He hung up.

The phone exploded!

God, no, the phone hadn't exploded. The mouthpiece blew up in my hand, a jagged chunk of the mouthpiece struck me in the cheek, and a fraction of a second later the sound of the shot hit my ears.

NINETEEN

I SPRINTED down the hall, away from whoever was shooting. I did *not* stand around looking for the shooter. I may not be athletic, but I know a crisis when I see one.

This was the Cook County Engineers section, which I wasn't really familiar with, and I raced along, taking first a right and then a left, not knowing where I would wind up. After the second turn, I stopped and listened. There were footsteps, far back.

Should I scream and hope help would come, or if I screamed would it only attract the killer?

All the offices here were dark, the glass panels gray in the failing daylight. I ran on again, through an open space that probably corresponded to the central pool in the Lottery hall. Here it was devoted to drafting boards in cubicles divided from each other by waist-high paneling. There was nowhere to hide for more than a few seconds. A person could walk between the cubicles and look into them easily.

If I had half a minute, I could dial 911. But I heard footfalls in the hall.

I ran out a side corridor, as fast as I could and still be as quiet as possible. Maybe, just maybe, the killer would stop and look in the cubicles, and then wouldn't know where I had gone.

The corridor was lighted, but the offices off it were all dark. There was a guard's stool at the bend, and just briefly, and foolishly, I thought of grabbing it up and throwing it at the killer. Sure. That would stop a bullet.

I rounded the bend. A dead end!

It can't be! The Lottery corridor didn't have any dead ends. What was beyond here? Some goddamn engineering computer room? Shit!

I was sweating. Even if he didn't know exactly where I'd gone, it wouldn't take him forever. I was trapped. Quietly, but desperately, I tried every door along the way, hoping somebody had forgotten to lock up this evening. But they hadn't.

I stood at the dead end, feeling like a trapped deer. I wished I could jump up into the air system and crawl away.

Wait! There was an end of the air duct here at the end of the corridor. With a grille covering the opening.

The duct itself was two feet wide and probably a foot and a half deep. Smaller ducts led off into the offices. If I could just get up to it—

I tiptoed back to the guard's stool and carried it to the dead end of the hall, where the grille was. I climbed on the stool, latched my fingers into the grid, and pulled. It didn't come off. I pried at it desperately with my pen.

Poor workmanship! City contracts! Bless them this time; the thing was held by two tiny set screws and it came off in my hand.

I pushed the grille into the duct ahead of me, then wormed my way in. I could bring up my knees, jackknife, and reach beyond my feet with the grille. My idea was to try to put it back into the opening. Then the killer would never know where I was.

I held the grille from the inside, angled it out of the opening and tried to snap it into place. It wouldn't sit right. I tried it again. It should fit into the same housing, even without the screws.

It fell out of my hands and clanged to the floor.

Frozen with fear, I listened. And I heard running feet.

I WORMED AROUND AGAIN, straightening out, my head away from the grille end of the duct, and then moved like a snake away from the opening. I'd seen pictures of army trainees making just this kind of motion as they crawled along on their bellies under barbed wire, using their knees and elbows like oars. The problem here was that I couldn't spread my knees far enough out to push along. The elbows, yes, but my legs were too cramped to be useful. I pushed with my toes, though, prying myself along with my feet to help the effort my elbows were making.

The duct made a sort of gentle bend, which was hard going, and for a moment I resented it. Then I realized that at least it would make it impossible for the killer to stand on the stool, look into the duct, and see me.

All I could think of was getting away from the opening as fast as I could, never mind what happened next. Never mind where I went. Get far enough away so that he couldn't guess where I was.

There were some advantages to being short and slight. Not many, but here was one for sure. Whoever was out there, he couldn't get in here with me. There was literally nobody I'd met on this assignment who was small enough to do that.

It was dark, but not totally dark. I had moved probably fifteen feet from the opening by now. There was very little light coming from it, and besides, my body was blocking most of whatever there was. But as my eyes got used to the darkness, I could see glimmers from the joints of the ductwork. Obviously, these things are not tightly sealed. And why should they be? They're not transporting water or anything that would make a mess if it leaked out.

Now that I was farther away from my attacker, I slowed down and crawled more quietly. Maybe when he got to the end of the hall he thought I went into some office and locked the door behind me. How would he know I didn't have a key? I might know somebody on the floor. Maybe he'd think I just knocked the grille off the duct in passing.

What about the stool? They were all over the building, so why would that one be suspicious?

Because it was right under the end of the duct, idiot, I said to myself. How could he miss it?

Okay, but he couldn't know how far I'd gone. I could be halfway to the other side of the building by now.

So it was time to settle down for a little while. Slow my pounding heart and consider options. Like, how long was I going to wait up here in the ductwork? Ten minutes? Not on my life would I come out that soon. The killer could be sitting on the stool, just waiting, for all I knew. He might wait there for hours.

Would McCoo come and rescue me? No. He had hung up before the shot and wouldn't know there was a problem.

All right—was I going to wait here all night? Should I wait until the Cook County Engineers came in sometime in the morning? That would be safe, at least.

Oh, *hell*!

Oh, damn! It was Friday!

If I knew anything about the enthusiasm of most public employees, there would probably be nobody in the office until Monday! Jeez! Not to panic—wouldn't there be cleaning people? Maintenance people? An occasional passing building guard? Security? But then, even if there were, how would I know he was there? I didn't have a view. How would I know he wasn't the killer?

Then I realized that I was being ungrateful. Five minutes before I was on the brink of being killed. Now at least I was up here and safe. If I had to starve awhile, if I had to chance slipping out sometime tomorrow, I should at least thank my stars that I was out of harm's way.

A hollow boom shook the air around me.

For a second I was completely disoriented. My flesh quivered from the adrenaline rush, and my skin prickled. I looked ahead of me. About twenty feet farther along the duct a ray of light was streaming in.

Through—as near as I could tell from here—a round hole.

He was shooting into the duct.

There was a fireworks burst of ideas in my head. The overriding one was that somebody would be sure to hear this. The second was *Duck!* But I couldn't duck; there was nowhere to go. The third was rage. After a moment, though, I doubted whether anybody really would hear. The noise of the shot ripping into the metal duct was loud from inside, but probably not so loud from outside. Probably from outside it was about the same as driving a nail into a metal wastebasket, a *chunk!*, not much more. And a silenced automatic made a *chunk*, too. It would sound like a workman doing minor repairs. And unless the person hearing it was right in this corridor, the twists and bends of the hallways would muffle it so that, around a bend or two, it would not be noticed at all.

Then he fired again, two or three feet closer to me.

The hole opened in the duct let in another little beam of light. What he was doing was obvious. He had gone to the end of the corridor farthest from where I had climbed into the duct in order to head me off before I got there. And now he was coming along the duct, shooting, methodically, until he got me. It was just a matter of time. In between shots he was waiting a few seconds to find out if anybody else heard.

Boomp-chunk!

Another hole, two feet closer.

I tried to guess how far away he was. In this square tunnel it wasn't easy to judge distances, even though the holes where the shots had come through were bright with light. Maybe eighteen feet? Twenty? Fifteen? How many shots before he'd get me? Five or six at most.

Wait. There was a way out. I'd get myself ready, poised to move, and when he fired the next to the last shot, the one that was just before the one that would hit me, I'd slither quickly past to where the previous shot had just been fired.

Chunk! The shot opened a hole, still closer. I got up on my elbows, ready to move. Hung there a few seconds.

Chunk! Twelve feet away, at most. I was shaking from fear and adrenaline. I splayed my hands out on the floor of the duct, palms flat for traction. I couldn't lift my back much because the duct was too shallow.

Chunk! Nine feet away. I could feel the duct vibrate with the hit.

Chunk! Six feet. I'd jump—or scramble—right after the next one. My face was hot and cold. This had to be done exactly right.

Chunk! I felt the air move as the shot passed through the metalwork and into the ceiling someplace above. I moved. I scrabbled toward the hole ahead like it was a beacon.

CHUNK! The shot hit just beyond my feet. I reached the hole ahead and froze there.

And the duct creaked!

Panicked, I figured I must be inside a part of the duct that was between the strap supports. And the joint had groaned. It wasn't made for bodies to crawl inside. Shit!

Still, it was possible he hadn't heard. I waited. Then I realized I was waiting too long. Too long without a shot. Longer than he had usually paused between firing.

He was listening.

I waited.

He waited, listening.

Then he fired at a spot just past my head.

My brains were scrambled by the concussion and terror. I didn't dare move. But I would be shot if I didn't.

Somewhere in my head I was thinking: He always shot into the middle of the duct. All the way down the line of bright holes I could see—he shot the center.

Slowly, as slowly it seemed as grass growing, I drew to the side of the duct. If the shifting of my weight made it creak,

I was dead. As quietly as snow falling, I twisted my body slowly against the side of the duct, trying to rotate up onto one hipbone and shoulder. It wouldn't quite work. My shoulders were a little wider than the depth of the duct. So were my hips. But I angled up as far away from the center as I could.

And still he waited and listened. In my mind's eye I could *see* him down there, just below me, standing, listening for the slightest creak of the metal, the faintest rustle of cloth.

Now I had to draw my legs straight against the side. I needed something to brace with, or I'd just roll back across the middle of the duct, but the thought of being shot in the leg, the bone shattered, was making me dizzy with fear, and I had to fight against pulling away from the middle fast.

I straightened them out. Now I was lying more or less on my right side, my legs against the side of the duct, my body not quite fully up against the duct side. I laid my left arm along my body, as close to it as possible. There was no room to put it on top, out of the way. I tried to retract my right arm, but if I did, my body started to roll to the center of the duct. So I propped myself by pulling my right elbow up against my stomach with my forearm at a ninety-degree angle, out into the middle of the duct, pressing down with my hand to hold the position.

And still he waited and listened.

Is it possible he'd gone away? Could some guard have come along the corridor? Somebody coming back to work at night? Or was the killer just reloading his gun? I waited, forcing myself to breathe, when my terror wanted me to hold my breath.

Crack! A shot came up next to my face. Not three inches from my nose, it burst up through the sheet metal in the center of the duct, up through the top of the duct and into the ceiling someplace. I was deafened.

Crack! Chunk! Crack! A series of shots blasted up at close intervals. *Crack! Crack!* Holes opened like a row of bright buttons, just a few inches apart, right down the ductwork.

I was so frozen, so impacted by the series of them, that it was a second before I realized I'd been hit. And still there was no pain. My right forearm was numb.

I couldn't see well enough to know what the damage was. But I held still. My friend McCoo, who had been shot once on duty, had told me that first you felt the impact, next you felt the pain. Be ready, I had just time to tell myself, and don't make a sound.

Then it hit. I pressed my lips together and squeezed my eyes shut. The wash of agony was like being hit by concrete—it was all I could think about. The world disappeared.

I don't know how long it was before I realized that it had stopped getting worse. Probably not more than half a minute, but it seemed forever. At least I could think again.

Despite the pain, I felt relief. The killer below me must have given up now. He'd have to conclude either that I'd been killed instantly or that I wasn't in this section of the duct at all. I just had to wait. Breathe carefully. And keep from screaming.

There was a little more light now, from the holes. I tried to see how bad the wound in my arm was. There seemed to be a ragged hole midway between the elbow and the wrist. The exit wound.

It hadn't hit an artery. Thank God. Blood was seeping out but not spurting. Just forming a little rivulet.

Running blood! Holy shit, it was running slowly toward one of the holes in the duct. The killer would only need to see that to know for sure where I was! Then another two shots bracketing it would finish me off.

I stared at the narrow river of blood. The shock of seeing it was worse than the pain. Quickly, I swiped at it with my left hand, trying not to shift so fast that the duct creaked again. I spread the blood around, slowing its creep toward the bullet hole, but the best this would do was to give me a little time.

I needed something to sop up the blood. But there wasn't anything available. I don't carry tissues or handkerchiefs. I wasn't wearing a scarf.

A sock? Maybe, if I could get my shoe off without making a sound.

My right arm shrieked with pain, but I had to lean harder on it to get my left hand down to my foot as I bent the knee to bring the foot closer. Grudgingly the shoe came off, and I set it softly on the floor of the duct. I stripped off the sock and patted it into the rivulet of blood. The blood started seeping into the edge of it, the little stream spreading out but slowing down. Excellent!

But the flow from the wound wasn't stopping, either. Even this would just buy time. What I needed was a tourniquet.

All right, damn it! Carefully, carefully, I took off the other shoe. This time, after stripping off the sock, I put the shoe back on, then the other shoe. Just in case I ever got out and needed to run. I should be so lucky! At least I was beginning to know which motions I could make without making the duct groan.

I brought the second sock up to my face. There was no way to tie the ends together around my arm; it was too short. The frustration brought tears to my eyes. For a moment it seemed like the best thing was to give up and die quickly.

But there was a hole in the end of the sock, probably made by my big toenail. My mother would have said I should have mended it when I first noticed it. A stitch in time saves nine. My mother was wrong.

With my teeth, I tore at the hole. My right hand was useless, but I held one side of the hole in the sock with my left hand and tore it larger with my teeth. Carefully.

When I got it just barely big enough to fit over my hand, I pulled it into my right arm, rolling it as it went up. The pain from the wound was excruciating. As the sock rolled, it got tighter, and finally, fighting, gagging from the pain, I got it to the middle of the forearm, and I rolled it into place over the gunshot wound. It wasn't tourniquet tight. But it was tight enough.

Blood started soaking into it, but very much more slowly.

I lay back, exhausted.

Again I forced myself to breathe, slowly and deeply. It was quieter than gasping, and also it forced oxygen into my lungs, where before I had been taking panting breaths that kept up with immediate demand but only barely. Now I thought in terms of replacing the deficit and getting oxygen to every twitching muscle cell of my body. Breathe slowly in, all the way down to the bottom of my lungs, hold, then slowly out, as deep a breath as I could take.

Gradually, I relaxed. In the dim light of the interior of the ductwork, I could see the pool of blood, stopped with my soggy sock as if by a little dam.

Breathe in. Breathe out. The makeshift bandage over the arm wound was soaked but not dripping. So far so good.

Now I pictured my assailant, down below me in the hall. He could be on his way to the elevator, thinking he'd killed me, or he could be standing just below me, which would put him not more than two or three feet away. I had been careful not to let any part of my body or clothes lie over those holes in the ductwork. If he saw fabric through the holes, he would know where to shoot.

So I listened, breathing steadily, so quiet that I could hear the slight soughing of the air moving past me through the air duct. I was fighting the pain from my arm, concentrating on listening. Hearing my heart beat. Listening, imagining the man, or woman, the gun in the unknown hand, its barrel pointing up at the duct.

That's when I heard him cough.

He was directly below me.

My body wanted to shrivel and stop breathing, but I forced myself to inhale. And I listened.

By angling my neck—carefully! carefully!—I was able to place my ear against the metal of the floor of the duct-work. This was somehow very frightening. Irrational as it was, it made me feel closer to the bullets, more vulnerable to getting shot. I could almost feel the bullet smashing into my ear. But this was silly. A shot could go through the ductwork, even layers of ductwork, and through air and through me, too.

So I forced myself to hold my ear to the metal and listen. After a minute or so, I thought I heard footfalls. They were going away! Getting fainter!

But I wasn't stupid enough to move yet. There was hope, but the secret was not to give in to it. It could be a ruse. Walk away so that I'd come out of the grille end of the duct, or at least start slithering toward it so that he'd hear me. I was too canny for that!

But wait a minute. If that was his intention, why didn't he walk more loudly? He had no way of knowing that I had my ear to the metal. Maybe he had really, *really* left. Maybe I was safe.

When I heard the first tap at the far end of the duct, I didn't know what it was. It was just a plain thump, not a shot, and I thought at first it was something like when heat pipes knock or the radiators bump in the winter as the heat comes on. Maybe the ductwork expanded and contracted as the air flowed through.

Then another tap. Then *tap. Tap.* I was puzzled. It was coming closer, though still down at the end near the grille opening. But definitely not shots. What was it?

Then sweat sprang out all over my skin. He was tapping the ductwork to see where I was. He was tapping it the way you tap a wall to find the stud.

And now I could hear that he was moving steadily along, tapping, working his way toward me. The ductwork gave off a hollow metallic bonging sound. When he reached the spot where I was, he would hear a thud. Then he would shoot me.

Quick. Think. How would it sound if I got my body up off the floor of the duct and supported myself on fingers and toes? I could straddle the center of the duct, maybe, toes on each far side near the walls of the duct, fingers the same at the other end. But could I do it with my damaged arm?

He was getting closer. There was no other choice. I couldn't head down one of the side ducts. They were too small and they might creak. He was too close for that.

I pushed my feet against the sides and got ready to rise onto my toes. My left hand would be okay, but what about my right? I put pressure on it and almost screamed. It was impossible. One of the two lower arm bones was broken. Had to be. It couldn't hurt like this otherwise.

I leaned on that elbow. He was almost here. I pushed up on the elbow, fighting the pain in my arm. Purple sunbursts broke in front of my eyes from the pain. But at least the elbow held its position. Then I pressed with the fingers of the other hand against the far wall of the duct, just three fingers on the floor of the duct where it joined the side. The ceiling of the duct was so low that it would take a lot of pressure just to keep my hand there. Then I pushed up with my toes.

It would be difficult to hold this position long. Why hadn't I started that health club course last winter? Why didn't I just do pushups and stuff at home to keep in shape?

Tap! Tap! I heard the hollow sound approaching. What was he tapping with? Probably the leg of the stool; it didn't sound like a metal gun barrel, and he might not be able to reach this high with the gun.

Tap! Tap! It was hollow as it came toward me. Tapping along, he came under where I was, spraddled out like a spider in the duct. *Tap! Tap!* I thought the sound changed a little. He passed under me, tapping along toward the far end.

But it had sounded different! Hadn't he heard? Just a little different.

Suddenly I was sure that, as it sank in, he would come back. And I couldn't hold this position any longer; I just *could* not. I sank back down, defeated. I was at the end of my rope. The tapping went on down the duct. Then I looked at the hole near my arm and saw that blood had sprung through my makeshift bandage while I was up on feet and hand and elbow. The blood had pooled near the hole and was dripping out.

It was hopeless.

One of the smaller ducts was nearby. At most, ten by fourteen inches, I couldn't go in there! I'd be stuck worse than a sitting duck. At least in this part, however confining, there was an illusion of some slight space. I'd get wedged in there and I wouldn't be able to breathe, and I'd die there.

I've always been a little bit claustrophobic anyway, and now I was on the verge of a screaming fit, just thinking about it. Then I heard the tapping coming back.

I angled into the side duct. My head would not fit in if I kept it in a vertical position. I turned it sideways, with my chin toward my shoulder. How would I get my arms in?

I backed out and put my hands in first, arms up above my head. Some years ago, I had done a story on stage magic, and without giving away how the illusions were done, I had at least said that people don't realize how small a space the human body can fit into. This was time to prove it.

With my arms above my head, head turned to the side, I pushed into the narrow opening. How could I move? I pushed as quietly as possible with my feet, and then felt my hips stick. Oh, God, no!

I squirmed, stuck, then realized that the hips would have slightly more room diagonal to the duct, so I went up slightly on the left side. Then I started pushing with my toes. My hands were almost useless, the right so painful that I couldn't use it, the left not much good, trying to pull me along as if it were a crab pulling a walrus.

But my feet worked.

Behind me, I still heard tapping. I pushed, cautiously. Better not even to move than to call attention now. Then I heard the tapping stop.

He had seen a drop of blood. I was as sure of it as if I were there, watching. But if he tapped the duct and didn't hear the thud in place of hollowness, he would know there was no body there. I pushed a little more with my toes. An inch forward. Another inch.

I waited again. The slightest squeak of a shoe would be fatal. I listened.

And he shot at the duct.

Shot at the hole where blood must be dripping, I was sure. Maybe he saw a drop fall from the duct. Shot right where I had been a few minutes before.

Now would he notice that the impact of his shot had a hollow ring, not as if a body were inside the duct?

There was utter silence. He was listening. Or thinking? Thinking was more dangerous to me than listening right now.

I inched forward again. Where was I? It didn't seem likely that I had covered more than one or two feet forward since getting into this small duct. And I was beginning to feel the signs of claustrophobia—the desire to take deep gasping breaths, a panicky need to move my arms to the sides, to stand up, to run.

I tried to picture the ductwork on the ceilings in this building. But who ever looks at it closely? In fact, who ever even looks up? The ductwork had large ducts that mostly ran down the middle of the corridors, didn't it, and then smaller ones, that branched out. And the smaller ducts went into offices, didn't they? I might get into a locked private office where the killer couldn't find me. But then again, some of the smaller ducts might feed air into the central secretarial pools, too.

I shoved with my feet. There was no sound behind me. I didn't know whether he was watching, quietly biding his time, or had gone away, or was creeping along under me, listening for the rustling sounds of my passage.

TWENTY

IT WAS DARKER HERE. With my arms out in front of me and my face buried in the upper part of my left arm, I couldn't see anything, anyway, but the darkness made it more claustrophobic. The tunnel was closing around me, not really narrowing, but feeling as if it were.

I pushed and pushed along with my toes. Wedging them against the place where the walls of the duct met the floor of the duct seemed to give me the most purchase, but there was terribly, painfully little progress with each shove. The balls of my feet ached from the unnatural pressure. I gained maybe another eighteen inches.

Eighteen inches to where? If the duct narrowed again up ahead, maybe to branch into two offices, I was sunk. I couldn't break out of this metal box. I could tap on the duct, but I would have to wait until hours and hours and hours had passed and I could be sure the killer had gone. By then it would be Saturday morning and there would be nobody around. Then Sunday. How long could a bleeding human body go without water?

If I died here, maybe nobody would know where I was until the corpse started to decompose.

This was not a happy thought. And the narrowness of the duct was not a good thought, either. Concentrate on not having been killed. Yet. Rest the feet, then push along another few inches.

Resting my feet for a couple of minutes turned out to be not a good idea, either. As often happens with unfamiliar muscle strain, it hurt more when I started again.

I couldn't see ahead. But with my fingers I was constantly patting the duct, walking the fingertips forward, fearful of coming to the end, a divider, maybe, where the tunnel branched into two smaller ducts. At the same time I was desperately hopeful of coming to an opening.

Another push with my aching feet, another scrape of my blindingly painful arm, and my fingers felt, neither an end, a divided section, a narrowing, or anything else I had anticipated. It was a curve, going down.

Down to what? What if it curved down to an electric circulator fan, or shot down to the basement, or—

My arms were so constrained that it was difficult to rotate them, but I managed to get the left hand against the side of the duct ahead, then felt the top. It curved down, too. The whole duct ahead did.

What choice did I have, really? I gave a push and inched along just a bit. My left hand pushed down into the curve. It felt a grille.

And now I thought I saw just a little bit of light.

I stopped, froze right there.

This was a problem. If I was lucky, the duct ended there, and with a giant push on the grille I might get out. Okay, that sounded fine. But suppose the killer was just sitting right there, gun ready, and when he saw the grille fall he fired?

The question really was this—was the end of the duct in the hall or in an office someplace? I tried to remember what the ceiling of the hall looked like. Really, I thought there was just one big duct down the center, and smaller ducts branching off into rooms. All right. What about this duct? I had crawled into it at a right angle from the main duct. So how far had I come in this direction? More than the width of the hall?

My best guess would be that, with all that effort and pushing and squeezing, I had come six or seven feet. That was more than the distance from the main duct to the wall of the hall.

I had to be in an office.

But what if I was in the secretarial pool area, or an adjoining hall? No, it couldn't be the Lottery secretarial pool area. That was too far away. But what about the Engineers' open space with the drafting boards? It was open to the killer. Still, the doors I had seen in this part of the hall appeared to lead to offices on both sides.

So was it safe to try to crawl down the bend?

Maybe. I hoped. Around and around in my head it went. What if the killer was waiting down there anyway? I wouldn't be able to see where I was going until my arms were fully out of the duct. What if the office door was open and he heard me or saw me? What if, what if—? Maybe I should wait until morning.

I never did decide to do it or not do it. Claustrophobia decided for me. While I was thinking or pretending to think, my lungs had started gasping for free air and my arms pushing at the sides of the duct. Then sweat broke out on my face and down my neck. I shoved desperately with my feet.

My arms wouldn't bend farther down the duct!

Now I was really panicky. I was crawling basically on my stomach, although canted up some on one hip because the duct was so tight. But my arms were out in front of me, and elbows don't bend down from that position. I struggled against the sides of the duct. Crying, pushing, gasping—it was the nearness of escape that triggered the terror. I started to whimper, but caught myself.

Now, wait. Freeze. I did, barely controlling myself.

If I squirmed around onto my back, my arms would bend down the duct.

But it was hard to do. For one thing, my hips wouldn't turn. The duct was just large enough to let my damn hips in sideways and they would not turn. They were wedged diagonally, and that was it. The other reason it was hard was emotional. Turning over on your back to fall or push blindly out into nowhere was too terrifying.

Forcing myself, I twisted my upper body until I got my elbows bent and pushed my hands down into the bend of the duct. The wounded forearm was useless from pain, but this was no time to think about it.

I felt a grille. My fingers went through the holes and I grasped and twisted. I knew from the earlier one that the set screws were pretty flimsy. I twisted and pushed, trying to hold it while I loosened it.

I had already learned the hard way about grilles, so I wound my fingers into the holes as I pushed. Suddenly it broke loose. But it didn't fall. Hooray for me.

I pushed with my feet. The distance from the bend to the opening was very short, just enough, I supposed, to make the grille horizontal facing down into the room.

My arms went through. I got my head out, not knowing where I was and half blinded by the increase of light. Even though there were no lights on in the office, and the sky was dark, the streetlights were brighter than the inside of the duct. I briefly distracted myself from terror by the thought of birth trauma. The room, as I started to perceive it, looked like an office. But no sooner were my head and one shoulder out than I slid forward, slipping in the slick trail of blood that my arm had left in the duct.

I fell out of the duct, onto my shoulder, holding the grille in my hand, on top of a desk.

There were flashing lights in my eyes from the pain in my arm, but at the same time I was thinking. How much noise did I just make? The distance from the duct to the top of the desk was no more than six feet. I hoped it was a soft landing, acoustically speaking, despite the fact that it hurt a lot. The office door was closed. So far, so good.

Apparently whoever used this office was some sort of bigwig. Private office, his own window, his own little coat tree, his own desk pen set, which I had missed skewering myself on by just about three inches. Wouldn't that have been fine? A bullet through my arm and a pen through my shoulder.

Which led me to think about the arm. I sat up on the desk and slowly, painfully, flexed the fingers. The arm hurt—in fact, it pulsed with the pain—but it didn't have the hit-by-a-truck feeling that I connect with a broken bone. Maybe I had been wrong about that. I rerolled the sock over the wound.

There was a nameplate on the desk that said JUSTIN TOLLER. Ah, thank you, Mr. Toller. The clock on the desk had been broken by some part of my body. But it had stopped at seven forty-two.

Got to remember to buy Mr. Toller a new clock.

Anyway, I was now safe. All I had to do was pick up the phone and call the cops. Where was the phone? No problem. I'd just knocked it aside. God, let's hope I didn't damage it.

I picked up the receiver and got a dial tone. I dialed 911. Nothing happened. Oh, of course, it went through a switchboard. I punched 9 and then dialed 911. Still nothing happened. A horrible, disgusting, nasty thought came over me. The switchboard had closed down for the night and I couldn't call out! Damn those civil service rules all to hell! Shit!

Think, Marsala! If it was roughly quarter of eight, people would be leaving the cocktail party to go to the banquet.

I folded my legs under me and tried to come up with a solution. Outside that door a killer with a gun could be waiting, not knowing exactly which office I was in, but knowing I was somewhere here. Waiting for me to step out into the hall and be blown away.

That was an argument for staying here.

On the other hand, people would probably still be in the Lottery central pool area. And around the elevators. Maybe even the caterers' people, who would still be cleaning up.

That was an argument for getting over there as fast as possible.

My arm wasn't bleeding quite so much, now that I had stopped using it. But it was still slowly oozing blood and it surely needed treatment. That was an argument for getting out of here.

Then, as I thought about it all, I heard a faint sound. The doorknob was slowly turning!

I watched as it turned, my breath caught in my throat. To come this far and be caught here! Then it stopped turning and held steady. I rubbed my forehead in relief. Thank you, Mr. Toller, for locking your door.

Faintly, I believed I heard the killer try the doorknob to the next office down the hall. Is it possible I could hear that faint a sound? Maybe it was imagination, but I really believed I could hear it. If so, he didn't know where I was.

That was an argument for staying right here.

He might not really know, for that matter, whether I was still up there in the duct somewhere, dead. Like the rat that dies in the wall and several days later people start to smell something unpleasant—

Stop that kind of thinking! It didn't happen.

I let my unsteady legs down off the side of Mr. Toller's desk. Wobbly, and making no sound, I tried to stand up. I could do it, but it was unwise. I folded up onto the floor and leaned my head back against the desk. Wait. Gather some strength and wait.

THERE NEVER was a sound of receding footsteps, but after an hour or maybe an hour and a half—I was guessing—it seemed safe to move. Not to leave the office yet, but at least to look round. I was horribly hungry, the effect of the adrenaline rush, which had now receded.

Mr. Toller's desk drawer, which pulled out without squeaking, thank God, yielded a Mounds bar and a Hershey's milk chocolate. Aha! Mr. Toller was a chocolate addict! Only the utmost willpower kept me from eating both at once. If I did, I knew I would be thirsty, and there was no water in here.

Vowing to buy Mr. Toller a box of Godiva chocolates, I ate the Mounds bar. Nothing in the entire world has ever tasted so good. There's something about thinking you are going to be dead and then getting a reprieve and then eating. But I wouldn't recommend it for an appetizer as a habit.

I was more and more desperate to get out of here. Surely the killer would have left by now. If a guard happened to walk through, and they must now and then, it would look very odd for a man to be hanging around the hall.

The only light was reflected from streetlights nine floors below. But the sky over Chicago is never really dark. I looked down at myself. My condition was not good.

Certainly I couldn't go out looking like this, a bloody sock around my arm, body streaked with blood along one side, and covered with grime from the ducts. Mr. Toller kept a mirror in his desk. Oh, excellent Mr. Toller! Bless Mr. Toller! I was able to wipe the dust off my face with my shirt and comb the dirt out of my hair with my pocket comb, one thing I didn't have to borrow from Toller, although he kept a comb in his desk drawer.

But my shirt was a thing of horror.

Mr. Toller kept some odds and ends of clothing on his coat tree. There was a thin gray zipper jacket, maybe for rain, and a white shirt. I hesitated over them, thinking that the shirt with the sleeves rolled up wouldn't be bad, but eventually recognizing that I'd be less conspicuous in this part of town in the jacket. I tried it on. It was much too big. That was okay.

Then to kill a little more time, I sat down and composed a note to wonderful Mr. Toller. I thanked him for the use of his office, gave him my address, promised to replace everything I'd used, thereby running myself into debt again.

As an afterthought, I added that, if I were never seen or heard from again, he could take this note to John Banks at Biller, Trueblood, and Banks for restitution of his belongings.

Now there wasn't much else to do but decide. Was it safe to step out in the hall? It had to be close to nine-thirty.

I SAT ON THE FLOOR and held my ear to the door for at least ten minutes. Nothing. I got down flat and tried to look under the door. There wasn't enough space to see, but I didn't hear anything, or smell somebody smoking, if he were stupid enough to do that.

All right. Give it a try? Or stay here all night? All weekend? No, I really had to get help for the arm. And impatience was taking over my mind.

This was it. I eased the knob around, listening for the click. But there wasn't any click. The spring lock worked well. Sometimes you win a few rounds.

I had Mr. Toller's ornate letter opener in my usable hand and a foot planted behind the door as I eased it open. Fat lot of good they'd do against a bullet. The crack between door and frame widened.

Hall light streamed in. The hall was empty. I opened it wider. No one. Stuck my head out. No one.

TWENTY-ONE

I PICKED MY WAY along the first corridor, but nobody lay in wait. The killer had put the stool down in the hall, carefully on its legs. Didn't want to call anybody's attention to a problem, I guess. The duct above was studded with holes. Just a guess, but I'd bet it would be days before anybody noticed. There were several small drops of blood on the dark industrial-grade carpeting. I'd bet nobody would notice them, either. Monday morning the workers would arrive in a Monday-morning stupor and trample the dried blood to powder.

Rather than go to the elevators, which would take me to the Lottery corridor, I followed an exit sign to the fire stairs. It was clearly marked, at the end of a short hall, a metal door with a panic bar. Which I pushed and nothing happened.

God damn it! The fire door was locked!

Shit! This had happened in another public building a few months back, and there had been a fire. Two people had died. I covered some of the ensuing scandal.

There was no choice but to go to the elevators. I peered around the first corner, exposing just one eye and the side of my head. But there was no one in the hall ahead. I walked softly out. When I came to the office area of the Cook County Engineers, I expected to see my assailant sitting in one of the chairs in one of the cubicles, gun cradled on his knee. But the place was empty of life.

I worked my way silently down the next hall and peered around the last corner, looking out toward the elevators that the engineers shared with the lottery. There was no sound of caterers cleaning up. They must have finished and left. They would hardly hang around any longer than they needed to. There was no sound of voices. There was no sound of footsteps.

Ahead of me were the elevators, beckoning, no, yelling *Safety! Let's get out of here!* But I paused and listened.

Good thing I did. Somewhere in the Lottery wing, out of sight, were voices. They weren't shouting or quarreling, but without being able to distinguish words, I could tell they were irritated, snapping at each other. Then they stopped.

After a couple of seconds, footsteps came down the hall.

If it was one of the caterers, I was going to jump out and go down in the elevator with him.

It was Hector Furman, Jr. I ducked back at the first glimpse of him. When his footsteps stopped at the elevators, I knew he hadn't seen me, and I drew a relieved breath. Then the elevator door clicked and hissed open. A couple of seconds went by. It closed. I let half a minute go by, during which there was no sound at all from the hall, then very, very gingerly eased my head around the corner. Hector Junior was gone.

However, he had been talking to somebody. Should I wait? No, no, no! I was running out of nerve; this was asking too much to wait here endlessly, in pain, for no reason. I was just starting toward the elevators when I heard another person coming. I ducked back again, and eased one eye around the wall.

Dorothy. So that's who he'd been talking to. Hector was the killer, I thought. Maybe Dorothy was all right. Maybe she knew nothing about this whole vicious thing. After all, she was the only one of the Furman bunch who was actually earning her money. Dorothy was solid. I almost started toward her.

Solid and sharp. She was the brains of the group, too. If anybody could have planned how to burn down my apartment, it was Dorothy. Plus, she should have been at the dinner. Why was she here if she wasn't watching for me?

I didn't move. The elevator door made its opening and closing noises. I waited a full minute, then looked. Nobody.

Still I listened. No sound. No voices, no footsteps, no people. I waited some more, waited until Dorothy would have to be getting out of the elevator in the lobby, waited some more until she would have had to have left the building. Then I edged around the corner.

The coast was clear. Swiftly and silently I walked to the elevators and pushed a button.

"Little Cat!" came a voice from the corridor.

Old Hector Furman. "Hi!" I said, as he came up to me. He looked old and frail except for his gorgeous white hair, but he was enthusiastic as always.

"What'cha doing here so late? You're missing the banquet," he said.

The elevator indicator had reached two on its way up.

"I guess I overwork."

He started to laugh, rearing back a little, showing gold molars, then said, "Yikes!" and put his hand to his bad back and doubled forward.

In the center of the top of his white hair was a single drop of red blood.

I hit him in the side of his wrinkled neck with my good left hand, a hard closed-fist blow, just as he was coming up with his gun. As he went sideways I kicked him in the neck with my foot.

He lay on the floor, twitching. I grabbed his gun out of his hand and backed away.

"You may be charming," I said, "but you're history."

TWENTY-TWO

MY ARM WAS not broken, even though I had been afraid it was. Nor was any artery cut; I had guessed that right, because the bleeding had never been profuse. However, they kept me at the hospital because a muscle they cheerfully called the *extensor digitorum communis* had been badly lacerated by the exiting bullet. The medics claimed that it would not heal properly left to itself, and if it didn't I would have trouble using my fingers normally. Fingers are extremely important to me. Therefore, I needed what they called "a little surgery." A little surgery is surgery performed on somebody else.

Saturday morning found me in the hospital, groggy from anesthesia. I used the time first to call Mike.

"I'm sorry I yelled at you, Mike. I apologize."

"You had every reason to yell."

"No. I wasn't being fair. You do have a problem, but it's your problem and not mine. You have to work on it. And I have to leave you alone to do it."

"Not even a movie next week?"

"Better not."

"*One Hundred and One Dalmatians* is being re-released."

"Well. No reason we can't do a movie."

John stopped by in the afternoon to tell me Disney had decided not to do a lottery television show. "Not in their image," he said. He carried under his arm a box of chocolate-frosted brownies. This is a man who knows the way to my heart. He didn't exactly refer to the fact that I had nearly managed to get myself killed. He said, "Your apartment is going to be livable in ten days. I suppose you want to move back?''

''My independence is very important to me.''

''What's so great about independence, anyway?''

''Well, gee.'' It seemed so obvious. ''Would you really respect me if I sat around all day and let somebody else clean my house while I ate bonbons, whatever they are, and went out shopping instead of having a decent job?''

I stopped abruptly, realizing that I had just tidily described his mother.

''But nobody is independent, Cat. We're all interdependent. You don't grow your own wheat. Or generate your own electricity.''

''No, I don't.''

''Although''—he smiled—''you generate *my* electricity.''

McCoo telephoned but didn't come. He was waiting out the weekend with Susanne. I told him to give her my love.

That evening I watched the Grand Lotto drawing on the hospital television. I had bought tickets to it way back when? Monday or Tuesday. The numbers on my two tickets were 26-03-19-47-35-48 and 04-36-27-17-38-51.

The Ping-Pong balls danced in the clear sphere. A gorgeous redheaded television personality I'd never heard of turned the balls to face the cameras.

02-18-21-22-36-53 in the first drawing. Well, I knew I never won stuff like that anyway.

Second drawing.

04. Omigod! I had that number! I leaned toward the television on both arms, not even noticing the pain in my stitches.

38! That's two I had right! If I won this—how much was it this week, seven million? I could write only what I wanted to write, instead of having to take assignments to keep eating. Get an apartment in a convenient location! Buy a car that always ran!

Another Ping-Pong ball came up.

27! I had that one, too! Three in a row. Millions of dollars waited for me.

09. Wait a minute. That wasn't one of my numbers. There must be some mistake. Well, never mind. If I had five, or even four, I'd win big.

49. Phooey. Well, there was still a chance for four. Let's just win that last one.

37. Oh, no. Damn. Off by one number. All it had to be was 36!

I sat back, disgusted. Suddenly my arm hurt worse than before. It took several minutes before I started to smile at myself. I could see how people got hooked. I had just felt the breath of the dragon.

The lottery frightened me a little. I didn't like it. Why?

I thought maybe I knew. I had learned something about myself. Reflecting on it, I decided that I really didn't like gambling. And the reason was that it forced me to be aware of the operation of chance in our lives.

Chance, actually, is a very scary thing. We are all, much more than we want to believe, a lot like the Ping-Pong balls. We really never know what's going to happen next, and only pretend we do. Underneath is an awareness that the only certainty is change. The lightning bolt can strike anybody. Thank goodness it's a rare thing. Much more likely is the unexpected heart attack, unexplainable infection, the failure of the car's steering. As we walk down the sidewalk, a car can careen out of control and hit any one of us. We all like to think that we're watching, maybe watching more closely than that person we heard about last week who was killed by an out-of-control taxicab. But it's not really so. We all daydream at times.

Have I a lung cell somewhere gradually mutating, cuddled up against the ragged fibers of an asbestos particle, breathed in with a million others from brake linings in years of walking the city's streets?

It seemed to me that the workings of total chance usually were unpleasant. Events that really come out of left field are not usually the unexpected inheritance or the hero on a white charger. They're the stick in the street that you trip over, or your uncle's stroke.

It seemed to me that the best things that happened were the result of effort expended, like cooking the special pasta, or building a relationship, or putting together a lot of neglected facts into a really good story.

Fortunately, I wasn't able to philosophize too long. Hal had showed up shortly after John left.

Being easily one of the most heroic persons in the entire history of the world, I was able to dictate to Hal a story on the Furmans using the lottery as their own private money fund. *Chicago Today* evening edition called it "Pork Barrel Chicago Style," which struck me as quite muckraking, but who am I to complain? We scooped everybody. There was a huge fuss about the lottery on the television late news broadcasts Saturday, with the usual blather of politicians who could hardly believe it could happen here. Here in Chicago? Corruption? Never!

Dorothy Furman may never be tied into the murder of Jack Sligh. I am morally certain she was the "finger man," as the mob used to call it, and I spent the last part of Saturday afternoon with McCoo's lieutenant, trying to convince him of the fact. He finally was convinced, for that matter. The problem was that there was no proof. And even suppose she admitted she told Hector Senior she had overheard part of my conversation with Jack Sligh. Suppose she claimed it was just gossip and her father did what he did entirely on his own.

Which, strictly speaking, was possible. It wasn't right, but it was logically possible. And I have enough belief in the value of presuming a person innocent until proven guilty that I am content that a person who cannot be *proven* guilty should walk.

Dorothy wouldn't entirely walk. In Dorothy's case, my high moral stand was made a whole lot easier to take by the fact that she would soon be out of the lottery on her ear, and her brother, sister, father, and son with her. Hector Senior was in the slammer on the twelfth floor at Eleventh and State.

Dorothy was also castigated in a number of other newspapers, papers that had not been swift enough to get the scoop. Hal says he'll let me write a fuller, in-depth story next week. That, plus the original lottery story, which will have to run later because it would seem so dull now compared to this scandal, will put some cash in my pocket. Enough to pay for the apartment renovations, plus a clock, candy, and a jacket for Mr. Toller, and quite a bit left over. But the most satisfying result is that Hal is going to do something very rare. He's going to let me make up the headline for my own article on the Furmans' scam, which will run with a photo of Dorothy and Hector Senior. I've already written the headline:

FAMILY HITS LOTTERY JACKPOT
WITHOUT EVER BUYING A TICKET

The Hour of the Knife
SHARON ZUKOWSKI

A BLAINE STEWART MYSTERY

REST, RELAXATION... AND MURDER

Blaine Stewart found work and self-pity moderately effective ways to cope with her husband's death. Tough, tenacious, burned-out, she was getting on everybody's nerves—including her own. A trip to the Carolina coast was going to give her the chance to tie up a case and then the time to catch some R and R.

But when her client—and friend—was found dead in the marsh, Blaine started asking questions.... Vacations had never agreed with Blaine, anyway, and this one wasn't about to change her mind...especially when it was highly likely it would be her last!

"The fast paced action, assortment of characters and the unsolved death will keep you reading far into the night."
—*Polish-American Journal*

A CHIEF INSPECTOR MORRISSEY MYSTERY

IN STO*h*Y PLACES

First Time in Paperback

KAY MITCHELL

LOVELY ENOUGH FOR A KILLER

Murder stalks the quiet English village of Malminster. There's no connection between the victims, except that they're all young and pretty.

The murders seem random, and the killer is very careful. All Chief Inspector Morrissey's got is a fattening file of paperwork and nothing to go on but the latest victim's diary. Worse, he can't get a feel for the mind of the killer he's hunting.

But the killer is watching him—aware that Morrissey is getting close. Perhaps it's time he introduced himself to Morrissey's eighteen-year-old daughter....

"Unpretentious, brisk, an engaging example of the village procedural."
—*Kirkus Reviews*

STONY

CHASING AWAY THE DEVIL

First Time in Paperback

THE DEVIL

A MILT KOVAK MYSTERY

SUSAN ROGERS COOPER

HEAVEN CAN WAIT

On Friday night, Sheriff Milt Kovak of Prophesy County, Oklahoma, proposed to his longtime ladylove, Glenda Sue. She turned him down. On Saturday morning, Glenda Sue is found brutally murdered.

Kovak begins a desperate search to find the killer, well aware he's a suspect himself. When he discovers a first-class, one-way ticket to Paris in Glenda Sue's belongings, it's pretty clear she had been keeping secrets—deadly secrets.

"Milt is a delightful narrator, both bemused and acerbic."
—*Publishers Weekly*

Available in October at your favorite retail stores.

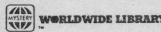

A Sheila Travis Mystery

MURDER

PATRICIA
HOUCK
SPRINKLE

on Peachtree Street

First
Time In
Paperback

NO MORE MR. NICE GUY

Prominent television personality Dean Anderson was as popular as he was respected, but he had incurred a good deal of animosity among family, friends and co-workers. Though the police are willing to rule his shooting death a suicide, his old friend Sheila Travis is not.

Because of meddling Aunt Mary, Sheila gets involved in finding Dean's killer. No easy task with a long list of suspects that includes a resentful ex-wife, an enraged daughter, a jealous co-worker, a spurned admirer, a mobster with a grudge. The truth goes deeper than either Mary or Sheila suspects. And it may prove equally fatal.

Available in November at your favorite retail stores.

WORLDWIDE LIBRARY ®
™

Corporate Bodies

SIMON BRETT

A
CHARLES
PARIS
MYSTERY

By the author of *Mrs. Pargeter's Package*

Surviving thirty years of an actor's fluctuating fortunes, Charles Paris had played many roles. But until now, a starring role as a forklift driver in a corporate video had yet to grace his résumé. Costumed in coveralls, he read his lines with finesse and his performance for Delmoleen foods was flawless. But the finale was murder.

A young woman is crushed to death with the forklift while the crew is at lunch. Industrial accident . . . or murder? Paris suspects a cover-up. The whole company atmosphere is troubling: the happy Delmoleen family seems riddled with mockery, jealousy, lust, envy. And secrets that may make this performance Charles's last.

"The most engaging new murder-solver in recent years has been Simon Brett's Charles Paris." —*Los Angeles Times*

Available in October at your favorite retail stores.

To reserve your copy for September shipping, please send your name, address, zip or postal code, along with a check or money order for $3.99 (please do not send cash), plus 75¢ postage and handling ($1.00 in Canada) for each book ordered, payable to Worldwide Mystery, to:

In the U.S.	In Canada
Worldwide Mystery	Worldwide Mystery
3010 Walden Avenue	P.O. Box 609
P.O. Box 1325	Fort Erie, Ontario
Buffalo, NY 14269-1325	L2A 5X3

Please specify book title with your order.
Canadian residents add applicable federal and provincial taxes.

BODIES

WORLDWIDE LIBRARY ®